UNNATURAL SELECTION

UNNATURAL SELECTION

by

Tony Stubits

ISBN: 0-75960-683-8

This book is printed on acid free paper.

1stBooks - rev. 2/22/01

Acknowledgements

As always, no man is an island. Therefore, I would like to thank the following people for their contributions to this book.

First, I would like to thank my longtime friends, Chuck Tomlinson, M.D., and Henry Rodeffer, M.D., for their input on the medical aspects of this book. Likewise, I would also thank my sister-in-law, Debbie Stubits, M.S.N., A.R.N.P., and Kathy Lowe, R.N., for reviewing the book from a nursing standpoint.

I would also like to thank the Amelia Island Museum of History for the use of their research library and George Clement for providing information about Cumberland Island where he works as a caretaker on one of the private properties.

Since I am nearly computer illiterate, I would like to thank my wife Donna for typing the original draft and I would like to thank Bob Land for his editing skills and computer ability in organizing my work. I would also like to thank Cheri Hooper, who works in my office, whose word processing skills were invaluable in sending my work to the publishers. I would also like to thank Don Shaw, owner of Books Plus, for his encouragement to go forward to publish this work. Also, I would be remiss if I didn't thank my parents whose love and support have been immeasurable over the years and who paid for my eight years of college tuition, bless their hearts.

Finally, and most importantly, I would like to thank my wife Donna, and children, Tracey and Troy, for sparing me the time away from their affections to write this book.

Chapter One

Hunter Davis was an idealistic young man. As he drove down the deserted beach road, Hunter's mind drifted back to all the long hours of study he had put in—first at undergraduate school at Mercer University in Macon, Georgia, then four more years at Mercer University Medical School, then another three years at Emory University Hospital in Atlanta for his residency in family practice.

Hunter's undergraduate years at Mercer had been wonderful. That time was full of all the things college is supposed to be about: ivy-covered buildings, fraternity parties, football games, intramural sports, co-eds, and expanding one's mind both academically and socially. Somehow, Hunter had managed to graduate magna cum laude with a B.S. in biology while also playing centerfield for the Mercer Bears baseball team during his freshman and sophomore years. By his junior year, Hunter had grown to his present size of six feet, two inches tall and 190 pounds. Hunter, however, had realized that although he was fast enough to run down almost any fly ball, he lacked the arm strength and the batting average to play beyond college, so he decided to concentrate on his medical career.

After studying hard his last two years in college, Hunter had sufficient grades and test scores to be accepted to medical school. After four years of medical school and three years of residency, Hunter was now ready for the real world. Hunter couldn't wait to put to practical use, with patients of his very own, all those years of training. The newly minted doctor would have liked opening up as a solo, independent practitioner, but two things prevented him. First, because of his parents' modest finances, Hunter had accumulated over $100,000 in student loans. Six figures worth of debt was not unusual for medical school graduates these days and was actually becoming the norm. Such significant debt made it difficult for new

1

practitioners to borrow the necessary funds to start a new practice. Second, given today's climate of practice acquisitions by hospitals, physician management groups, and HMOs, it seemed that completely independent, solo practitioners were going the way of the mom-and-pop grocery store and the neighborhood drugstore: toward extinction.

Hunter decided to work for Medi-Most, a large national health maintenance organization that had a network of doctors in Nassau County who referred their patients to a small, Medi-Most–owned hospital on Amelia Island, Florida.

Hunter's other reason for taking this job was that the island was his home. Hunter had grown up on Amelia Island and, after eleven years of being away at college and then residency, Hunter wanted to move back to his hometown and live there full-time.

Now, as the young doctor drove down the beach road, the top down on his new car, he breathed in the fresh ocean air that he had missed so much and glanced over the white-sand beach out to the open sea. Much had changed on Amelia Island in the eleven years since Hunter graduated high school and went to college. But change had always been a constant on this approximately thirteen-and-a-half-mile-long barrier island in the very northeast corner of Florida. Last night, dining out alone at the local seafood restaurant, Hunter had picked up an "Amelia Now" a local publication targeting tourists, that is freely distributed in local stores and restaraunts, and contains a brief history of the island.

Noticing all the new beach houses under construction as he drove down the beach road along with the white, wooden shrimp boats working the ocean in the background, Hunter couldn't help but think about Amelia Island's colorful history. Being the only U.S. location to have been under eight different flags or jurisdicitons, Amelia Island had experienced its ups and downs over the last four hundred years, but during the last few years had experienced a boom matched only once before in its history.

Reviewing, in his mind, the brief synopsis he had read the night before, Hunter mulled over how dramatically Amelia

Island had changed in the last four centuries. The Timucua Indians were the indiginous people when the French arrived in 1562. The Timucua were tall and olive skinned with tatoos covering most of their bodies. They were robust people, well-fed on a diet of fish, oysters, maize, beans, and squash.

France's Jean Ribault was the first European to visit the island, naming it Isle of May for its sweet scent and month sighting. The Spanish under Pedro Menendez defeated the French in the area before moving on to found St. Augustine in 1565. The Spanish then named the island Santa Maria after the mission they developed on the island. The mission was destroyed by the English under General Oglethorpe in 1702. Oglethorpe renamed the island Amelia (after the daughter of George II of England).

After the American Revolution, Britain ceded Florida back to Spain. With its deep natural harbor, the border town of Fernandina became a center of smuggling and piracy due to the Jefferson Embargo Act of 1807, which closed U.S. ports to foreign shipping. With the backing of the United States, the so-called Patriots of Amelia Island overthrew the Spanish and hoisted their own flag on March 17, 1812. The next day, the U.S. flag replaced the Patriot flag, but Spain demanded, and eventually received, the return of the island. To liberate Florida from Spanish control, Sir Gregor MacGregor seized the island in 1817, hoisting his own Green Cross standard. After MacGregor's withdrawal, the pirate Louis Aury gained control and raised the Mexican Rebel flag. Shortly thereafter, in December 1817, U.S. troops occupied the island and occupied it "in trust for Spain." Spain ceded Florida to the United States in 1821 and the U.S. flag has flown over the island ever since, except from April 1861 to March 1862, when the Confederate flag briefly flew.

Therefore, the eight flags that have flown over Amelia Island were in order: French, Spanish, British, Patriots of Amelia Island, Green Cross of Florida, Mexican, Confederate, and the United States. This led to the name "Isle of Eight Flags," which was a moniker sometimes applied to Amelia Island.

By 1868, the Union troops had left Fort Clinch to return to their homes in the north but the troops spread the word about the beautiful island with its warm climate, and soon a benign invasion of Yankee civilians was taking place. Back in the late 1800s, the so-called Golden Years of Amelia Island, vacationers from the northern states would arrive in Fernandina, the "Newport of the South," via train or steamship. Fernandina was blessed with a natural deepwater port, so even the largest ships could enter Cumberland Sound, then follow the Amelia River south until they reached the port of Fernandina on the westward, leeward side of Amelia Island. After arriving in Fernandina, the tourists would stay in one of two elegant hotels in the downtown area and then take a trolley the mile and one-half to the beach on the Atlantic side of the island. There the tourists would enjoy swimming, fishing, croquet, skeet shooting, bicycling, horse or trotting races, and walking the pristine beaches during the day and then later, at night, dining and gambling at the grand pavilion on the beach.

Then around the turn of the century, two events occurred that would set Fernandina's tourism economy back for decades. First, the railroad was extended down the east coast of Florida. At that point, St. Augustine, and then Palm Beach, became the winter playgrounds of the wealthy. Second, a hurricane destroyed the pavilion at the beach.

The downturn in tourism caused several metamorphoses in Fernandina's economy. First, in the 1920s several people in the Fernandina area developed techniques that led to the modernization of the shrimping industry, and Fernandina became the shrimping capital of the East Coast. After awhile, however, as the waters around Fernandina became overfished, the shrimpers left for more fertile waters off of Key West, Galveston, and even South America.

Then, in the 1940s, two paper mills were built on the island to take advantage of river access and railroad availability. The paper mills remained the major employers and dominant force on the island until tourism started to make a resurgence with the development in the 1970s of Amelia Island Plantation, a major resort and residential complex on the south end of the island, and in the late 1980s with the building of the Ritz-Carlton Hotel. The same temperate weather and pristine beaches that brought tourists in the 1890s was bringing them back a century later. Fortunately, Fernandina's downtown area had retained many historic structures and a quaint Victorian atmosphere that was, at the end of the twentieth century, again in vogue. Ironically, the lack of progress in mid-century made possible the caught-in-a-time-warp, Victorian-village-by-the-sea image that the tourism council was promoting in their advertisements.

Now, as Hunter drove down the beach road, the signs of progress were everywhere. Old wooden beach cottages were being torn down to be replaced by condominiums or large private beach homes. It seemed to Hunter that when the Ritz-Carlton opened, it was like a seal of approval that this island was a pretty good place to visit or live. Now people from all over the country were moving to Amelia Island. There were even some people migrating northward from south Florida to escape the overcrowding and the blandness of seasons that occurs there.

Hunter felt ambivalence to the changes going on. As a native, Hunter fondly remembered growing up in an ideal, almost sheltered environment where everybody knew everybody. Hunter thought about the fact that their family never locked the doors to their house at night when he was growing up. When Hunter went to Mercer it took him several weeks to become accustomed to locking the doors to his car, something he never did in Fernandina. Hunter also remembered being able to ride his bike anywhere about town or hitchhiking to the beach without any concerns about safety. As Hunter grew into his high school years, he appreciated the fact that Fernandina was small enough to know the policemen by name so that if you got caught speeding or throwing eggs on Halloween or even drinking, you were often let off with a warning or an escort home, instead of a trip to jail.

But the sheltered environment can become boring or even suffocating as one grows to young adulthood. Hunter eagerly left for college after graduating high school. Hunter flourished socially while at college and medical school, learning to savor the finer things in life like a good dinner or a fine wine. So Hunter could appreciate the fact that the drive-in-movie theater, which, unbelievably, was the only place on the island to watch a movie during his teenage years, had been replaced by a seven-screen multiplex theater, and that the fried seafood shacks of previous year had been supplemented by the five-star dining at the Ritz and Amelia Island Plantation, not to mention several other fine restaurants that had sprouted up with progress and the increase in tourism.

Hunter also realized that the growth of the island had been responsible for his employment. Medi-Most had recently built a small private hospital to compete against the old county-owned hospital, Nassau General. Hunter figured he would work for the HMO for about three years or so, pay off some of his student loan debt, then open up his own practice.

These thoughts rushed through Hunter's mind as he drove through the early morning fog that enshrouded the beach road. The cool air swirled around him in his new BMW Z-3 convertible. The car was a present to himself, a reward for all the years of studying. Hunter had bought the car the day before with the last of his student loan money and a copy of his employment agreement verifying his income. So as Hunter drove toward his first day of work at Medi-Most Hospital, he felt feelings of both accomplishment and anticipation. Unfortunately, Hunter's enthusiasm and daydreaming led him to exceed the speed limit as he drove down the beach road. The excited, young doctor did not notice the police cruiser behind him until the policeman driving the patrol car hit its lights and siren.

"Damn," said Hunter, hitting the steering wheel with the palm of his hand as his reverie was interrupted by the reality in his rear-view mirror. Hunter edged his new car over to the side of the road and stopped. As the policeman stepped out of the patrol car, the young doctor began to look through the glove box for his registration. Hunter removed his wallet from his back pocket and located his driver's license as the patrolman approached the side of Hunter's car.

"May I see your driver's license and registration, please?" the officer began as he stood just behind the driver's door of the car.

Aggravated at himself, Hunter stuck the documents out the window for the officer to take. The patrolman was wearing a hat and the requisite mirrored sunglasses, but Hunter realized there was something vaguely familiar about the police officer. As the patrolman began to ask Hunter if he had a reason to be driving fifty miles an hour in a thirty-five-mile-an-hour speed zone, Hunter spotted the officer's name tag.

"Billy?" Hunter asked hopefully, then added, "It's me, Hunter Davis."

"Hunter?" asked the patrolman in disbelief as he stared at the person in the car. The patrolman, now known as Officer Bill Reilly, hadn't seen Hunter since Hunter left for college eleven years ago. The two men had been friends growing up together, going to school together, and even playing on the same baseball teams together over the years.

"Hunter!" Billy shouted in recognition. "I haven't seen you in a 'coon's age," followed Billy, using a local colloquialism referring to a raccoon's life span.

"Not a very nice welcome for a local boy returning back to town," said Hunter solicitously.

"Well, I thought you were one of those rich tourists that are invading our island," Billy said apologetically.

"No, I've come back to practice medicine," offered Hunter.

"Well, I remember you talking about that in high school, and look at you now," said Billy, admiring Hunter's car.

"Yes, it's good to be back," responded Hunter, hopeful that Billy would let him off with warning.

"I guess we can't treat our returning heroes badly, so I'm going to let you off this time," said Billy smiling. Then Billy added, "Give me a call now that you are back in town. It would be fun to go fishing again."

"I'll do that," Hunter promised as he eased his car back on the beach road and headed for the hospital.

Chapter Two

Hunter turned off the beach road onto Sadler Road and drove the two blocks to Medi-Most Hospital. Hunter's interview and hiring had taken place in Atlanta at Emory University Hospital during the last week of his residency. Since Medi-Most Hospital was built while Hunter was away at school, Hunter was unfamiliar with its layout. Hunter knew from his interview that his office would be in a temporary building outside the hospital, but Hunter's first order of business was to meet with Dr. Barry Hockman, chief of staff, in his office at seven-thirty in the morning.

Hunter pulled into the parking lot designated for doctors and employees. The parking lot was also used for the entrance to the emergency room. Hunter noticed that some of the parking spaces were reserved with doctor's names, but not seeing his name, he pulled into an unmarked space. Hunter put the top up, locked the car, and walked toward the emergency room entrance.

As soon as Hunter went through the automatic doors, he went from the still and quiet of early morning into an area of bustling activity. Since it was just after seven o'clock in the morning, the day shift was replacing the night shift and there was twice the usual number of people in the small reception area behind the desk. The night staff was wearily going over the charts with the day staff, filling them in on every patient's status. The waiting room was also unusually full for a Monday morning.

Hunter approached the counter, and his early-morning grogginess suddenly disappeared. Behind the counter, talking to a gray-haired older nurse, was the prettiest woman he had ever seen. The younger nurse stood about five feet, eight inches, had shoulder-length blond hair, and a trim, athletic figure that made even her white nurse's dress look sexy.

As Hunter walked up to the counter, neither nurse looked up as both were occupied with the details of changing shifts. After listening to their conversation for about a minute and without either one of them acknowledging his presence, Hunter decided to interrupt.

"Excuse me," Hunter began.

Without looking up the younger nurse said, "We'll be with you in a minute."

Hunter started to speak again, but not wanting to get off to a bad start with this lovely woman, he held his tongue, turned around, and leaned against the counter.

The doctor's gaze fell upon one of the patients who appeared to be sleeping in the waiting room. An obese man approximately sixty years of age was sitting in a chair next to a wall with his head and shoulder leaning against the wall and his mouth halfway open. The man's loud breathing, which could be heard even where Hunter was standing, indicated a blissful, deep sleep, except for one thing. Hunter noticed the man had several beads of sweat on his forehead and above his upper lip. Hunter walked over to the man as the nurses obliviously continued their conversation. Hunter reached down and touched the man's forearm. When the man did not awake, Hunter quickly took the man's pulse, which was dangerously low. The doctor reached up and felt the man's forehead, which was cold and clammy to the touch. Hunter then reached down with his thumb and gently lifted the man's eyelid. The morning light elicited a barely noticeable sluggish reaction of the man's pupil.

Hunter turned around and walked back to the counter where the two nurses were still in an animated conversation. This time Hunter said emphatically, "Excuse me, please!" Both women looked up at Hunter simultaneously. Hunter found himself staring into the greenest eyes he had ever seen, and the aggravation he had felt at the nurses' nonchalance melted away. Hunter glanced down at the younger woman's name tag: Savannah Jones, R.N.

Savannah also had felt perturbed at the intrusiveness of this man. She was at the end of a ten-hour shift where she had helped treat a heart attack victim, a stroke victim, two fight participants—one of whom was left with a blow-out fracture of his orbit—and various other minor emergencies. Savannah just wanted to go home and go to sleep, and she was in no mood to deal with one last pushy patient. But as Savannah looked up she realized the tall young man with piercing blue eyes and blond, slightly disheveled hair was not a patient. The man before Savannah on the other side of the counter was wearing a neatly pressed blue and white dress shirt, a silk tie, a gold tie clasp, and a straight-from-the-cleaners white lab coat with the name "Hunter Davis, M.D." embroidered above the breast pocket.

Hunter finally spoke, "I'm Hunter Davis, the new family practitioner. Could you please direct me to Dr. Hockman's office?"

The older nurse intervened. "Just go through those doors there, it's the third office on the left," the older nurse said.

"Thank you," said Hunter smiling.

Hunter returned his gaze to Savannah, then spoke, "By the way, see that man leaning against the wall that appears to be sleeping?" Before Savannah had a chance to say anything, Hunter continued, "He is apparently falling into a hypoglycemic coma."

With that remark Hunter turned and went through the doors, as both nurses jumped from their respective chairs to rush to the aid of the sleeping man, who was actually in the early stages of insulin shock.

Hunter walked down the hall feeling triumphant and also glad the man was going to get the proper care he desperately needed. As he came to the door marked Barry Hockman, M.D., Hunter was not sure if he had made a good impression or a bad impression on the pretty nurse, but he felt sure he had left an impression. Hunter thought to himself that he would make sure their paths would cross again soon.

Hunter knocked on the door and heard a man's voice from inside.

"Come in," said the voice.

As Hunter walked into the office, Dr. Hockman rose from his chair behind the desk. Hunter guessed Dr. Hockman was about fifty-five years old. His brown curly hair seemed to be styled in a permanent, like many men his age wore. Dr. Hockman gripped Hunter's hand in a firm handshake and said, "Dr. Davis, I'm Barry Hockman. We've been expecting you." Then the older man motioned for Hunter to sit in the chair opposite the desk. As Dr. Hockman returned to his seat, Hunter noticed a slight bald spot on the back of the older doctor's head.

"Dr. Davis," Hockman began, "we're very glad to have you here. Did you get settled all right?"

Without waiting for Hunter to respond, Hockman continued, "Ever since Dr. Baker had his heart attack and died, we've been undermanned. Dave Schiller, our other family practitioner, has been swamped and unable to keep up with his practice load. You'll be working out of Dr. Baker's old office, building two. We've already got your patients lined up, starting this afternoon. Take the morning to familiarize yourself with your office and meet with your staff. You'll start seeing patients at one o'clock."

Dr. Hockman seemed to Hunter to be a very blunt man with a bit of an ego.

"I'm sure you discussed your salary with Mr. Cobb during your interview in Atlanta," continued Dr. Hockman. You should be aware, however, that as a member doctor in Medi-Most's HMO network you will also be eligible for the year-end bonus pool."

Hunter had agreed with Daniel Cobb, the hospital administrator, on a salary of seventy-five thousand dollars a year for three years. Hunter vaguely remembered Mr. Cobb mentioning something about a bonus, but Hunter, being naïve in the ways of managed care and being distracted by his newfound raise of 500 percent over his fifteen-thousand-dollar-per-year residency stipend, had not listened carefully.

Unexpectantly, Hunter asked, "Dr. Hockman, just how does the bonus work?"

Dr. Hockman stared at Hunter for a few seconds as if he was perturbed, then said, "They don't teach you guys much about the real world in school, do they? Let me make this simple for you. Medi-Most is an HMO, a health maintenance organization. HMOs were developed years ago by some large employers as a way of containing medical costs. Originally, the idea was to have a single clinic owned by the HMO with all the doctors on staff paid by salary. All of the patients had to come to this one facility. Every patient would be assigned to a family practitioner, or general practitioner, as they used to be called. The family practitioner would be responsible for doing all the easy stuff, the primary care. If the patient needed something beyond the scope of what the family practitioner could do, the patient was referred within the clinic to specialists, who came in part-time on a negotiated basis, for the secondary care. If the patient needed tertiary care, as in surgery, the patient would be sent to a hospital that had contracted to accept that HMO's rates."

Hunter knew all of this, but wanting to make a good impression he didn't interrupt.

Dr. Hockman continued, "The original idea was that if the patient could be encouraged to come in for regular, no-cost checkups, and preventive medicine could be practiced, the patient's health would be maintained and the patient would need less secondary and tertiary care, which is more expensive. The single-facility HMO concept never caught on with the public because it was too restrictive. While it may have been convenient for the worker since the HMO facility was usually located near a large employer, his wife and kids may have to drive for miles to visit the clinic. Also, HMOs had trouble finding and keeping competent doctors who wanted to work on a salary and see a large number of patients. Therefore, care was rationed due to time, resulting in long waits for appointments, disrupting the theory of preventive care. So HMOs mainly existed around large employers in the northeast part of the country, and in California as a way of taking care of their employees.

13

"However, in the nineties we have seen a rebirth and proliferation of HMOs. This has occurred for a couple of reasons. First of all, in the early nineties Bill and Hillary Clinton put the spotlight on medical reform. As lawyers, you would think they would have tackled reform of our judicial system, which they may have been more qualified to amend. Instead, they wanted to socialize medicine, a field they knew nothing about. Their attempt at national reform failed, as you know, but emphasis on reform did propel many states to examine ways of reducing medical costs. States loosened regulations governing HMOs and set an environment for for-profit HMOs to proliferate."

In asking a simple, routine question that would be expected from any physician coming on staff, Hunter had clearly touched a nerve in Dr. Hockman, who stood up from behind his desk and started pacing the room.

"Consumers," Dr. Hockman continued, "scared by the media about rising health costs and also dissatisfied with traditional medical plans containing large deductibles and only eighty percent coverage, started joining HMOs. For-profit HMOs, realizing that the single facility was too restrictive for the majority of people, started signing up a network of doctors to give patients some freedom of where to go. Doctors, who did not want to lose market share or who were trying to build a practice, started joining the panel of HMOs accepting lower reimbursements in hopes of increased volume.

"Are you with me still?" Dr. Hockman asked. Hunter nodded his head in agreement.

"Therefore," Dr. Hockman went on, "HMOs have grown like wildfire in the last few years. HMOs have done a pretty good job of slowing down rising medical costs. Unfortunately, this has come at the loss of patient freedom and doctors' incomes.

"I hate to tell you this, being a recent graduate, but do you know that doctors' income on a national level went down four percent last year, while medical costs continued to climb at twelve percent for the year? If it was just doctors charging too much, don't you think the overall medical costs would have gone down?

"Of course you would," Dr. Hockman continued without waiting for an answer. "But they haven't. The insurance companies have won the war of medicine. They control both the patients and the doctors, telling each what they can do. The patients give up choices by joining the HMO—choice of doctors, choice of hospitals, and even choice of which tests can be run or whether they can see a specialist—all for a lower premium. HMOs offer a lower premium to gain market share, but as soon as they sign up enough people, like most insurance companies, they will raise their premiums yearly to the maximum amount they think the market will bear. Pretty soon they are back at the premium level of traditional plans with a lower level of service and without the costs to the HMO of a traditional plan. Plus, after the HMOs have signed up enough people, they can use their power to get doctors to accept reimbursement levels that are sometimes even below the doctor's profit levels.

"This is the world of medicine you now enter, Dr. Davis," said Dr. Hockman. He then returned his lecture to its starting point.

"Now, to get back to your original question about the bonus: Medi-Most has a network of doctors that refer to the hospital. Some doctors like yourself and Dr. Schiller are on salary. Others are independent doctors that take several HMO plans beside Medi-Most. I am chief of staff of the hospital and also medical director in charge of the network of doctors. Medi-Most knows how many patients they have on their plan in this area. Medi-Most knows on the average how much it should cost to provide care for each patient. Medi-Most then has to provide care for each patient. Medi-Most adds in their appropriate profit margin over the average cost to come up with the premium they charge the patients. Our bonus is a percentage of what our patients' actual costs are compared to the average cost that Medi-Most projected for the year. If the network doctors as a group can keep the actual costs under the projected costs, then each doctor receives a share of the bonus pool money in relation to whatever percent he was able to keep his patients' care under the projected costs. If a doctor's patient-care costs exceed the projected costs, not only does he not receive any bonus money, the other members' bonus money is at risk because the group as a whole must come in under their projected cost before there is any bonus money to be divided."

Dr. Hockman walked behind the desk and sat back down, his dark brown eyes staring at Hunter from across the desk. "As medical director of the group, my bonus comes off the top, based on how the group does as a whole. Therefore, I have a vested interest in how you practice medicine, and you can believe I will be watching you. There will be forms to fill out and your clients will be reviewed per your contract agreement with the HMO. Specialty tests you want performed on patients will have to be pre-authorized by our HMO panel. The 1980s' method of medicine that was probably taught in school—using whatever means available regardless of cost—has changed in the 1990s. A cost-benefit analysis is performed for every procedure. An HMO may deem it too costly to perform an MRI or CT scan on everybody with a headache to catch that rare patient with a tumor or aneurysm. Therefore, an HMO may place stringent guidelines about when an MRI or CT scan can be performed on such a patient, which may delay treatment in those not meeting the guidelines.

"And you know what really stinks about that?" asked Dr. Hockman.

"What?" said Hunter instantly, eager to at least interject a syllable into this tirade.

"Not only may you lose a patient because of a disallowed or delayed treatment, you will probably get yourself sued by the patient's family. While there has been medical reform of a sort, there has been no tort reform. According to the courts, every test should have been performed, no stone unturned, regardless of costs. As you see," Dr. Hockman continued, "it puts us doctors

16

in a very tenuous position. Now if you will excuse me, I have work to do. Have a nice day," Dr. Hockman added with intentional irony.

Hunter sat flabbergasted. He had not expected a lecture this early in the morning, particularly not one so detailed and cynical. Nevertheless, Hunter gathered himself, thanked Dr. Hockman shaking his hand again, and left the office to begin the first day of his career.

Hunter's office was adjacent to the hospital. A group of four small doctors' buildings clustered around its own parking lot. The temporary buildings were erected when the hospital first opened, with the anticipation of replacing them later with a permanent doctors' complex. The buildings were prefabricated, similar to modified double-wide trailers, with wood siding to make them look more like permanent offices.

Even Hockman's diatribe couldn't dampen Hunter's enthusiasm for his new job. Hunter bounded up the steps, eager to meet the staff and get settled into his new office. Hunter opened the door and saw his staff ready to greet him. There were three women, lined up together, all dressed alike in matching nurse's uniforms. They were Dr. Baker's old staff, who had been laid off temporarily after the doctor's sudden death and reinstated last week in anticipation of Dr. Davis' arrival, so they were as eager as the young doctor to get started.

Hunter first shook the hand of a professional-looking woman with dark, straight hair who appeared to be in her mid-forties.

"Hi, I'm Rosa Martin, the office manager," the woman said.

Hunter shook her hand and said, "I'm Dr. Davis, glad to meet you."

Then he turned to meet the next staff person. An energetic young woman with blond curly hair and an open smile said, "Hi, I'm Bonnie Evans, your receptionist."

Hunter took her hand and said, "Hi, Bonnie, its nice to meet you."

Hunter took a step to meet the last staff person. Hunter guessed the auburn-haired young woman was in her late twenties.

"Hello, I'm Sheila Jones, your doctor's assistant," the woman said.

Hunter shook Sheila's hand warmly and politely said, glancing back at the others, "I'm looking forward to working with all of you. Now, let's get started. Sheila, please show me the examination rooms."

Hunter spent the first part of the morning familiarizing himself with the examination rooms. The three identically equipped rooms, which were lined up in a row down a hallway, were designed so that a doctor could move efficiently from room to room, seeing as many patients as possible. All the equipment Hunter would need was in each room, in identical places, so he could find things easily. Hunter was satisfied with the layout, so he spent the second part of the morning talking with Rosa about how the paperwork and the computer worked in the front office.

By noon Hunter felt confident enough with his new environment to take a break for lunch. The office staff had already left to eat their lunch outside. Hunter had brought his lunch in a paper bag, and he went to a small room in the back of the office that served as an employee lounge. Hunter put his lunch on the table beside some billing sheets he wanted to study and sat down to eat.

In a few minutes, Hunter would be seeing his first patient outside of his residency. He was excited but found it difficult to concentrate on the billing sheets as his mind kept drifting back to the pretty blond emergency room nurse with the beautiful green eyes. Hunter made a promise to himself that he was going to follow up with the nurse at the first opportunity, but for the meantime he had a practice to start.

Chapter Three

Two weeks had passed since Savannah's rather abrupt run-in with the new doctor. Savannah had thought about the young physician occasionally and even endeavored to find out about him—was he married? where had he come from?—but she consciously tried to dismiss any thoughts of getting together with him. There were two reasons behind Savannah's reluctance.

First of all, there was Savannah's last boyfriend, Thorn Bailey. Savannah and Thorn met when they both were going to Georgia Southern University. Savannah was studying nursing and was also a cheerleader for the football team. Thorn was a pre-med student and a reserve strong safety for the football team. Savannah and Thorn seemed to be the perfect couple, and at first Savannah was deeply in love. Thorn, however, had a violent side, particularly when drinking. At first, Thorn exhibited this trait just in general rowdiness with his friends when they were partying. Then one night toward the end of their senior year, Thorn picked up Savannah after a day of drinking with his buddies. Savannah took exception to Thorn's being late and drunk. An argument broke out between them and Thorn punched Savannah, giving her a black eye. Savannah immediately left Thorn, never to associate with him again. Savannah did not go to the police as many of her sorority sisters wanted her to do, but neither did she go back to him—as many women do—despite his phone calls, flowers, and letters of apology pleading to get back together. Soon graduation came and Savannah, after passing her board exam to become a registered nurse, moved to Jacksonville, Florida, to begin her nursing career at Baptist Hospital. Savannah had heard Thorn had gone on to medical school and had severely cut back on his drinking, but Savannah had lost faith in him and written him off completely.

The second reason for her lack of desire to pursue the new doctor was that, while in Jacksonville, Savannah had dated several physicians who invariably ended up being egotistical and self-centered. Savannah concluded there was something about medical school that gave young doctors an elitist attitude. Because of these experiences, Savannah was distrustful of men in general and doctors in particular. Therefore, after two years of working the E.R. in Jacksonville, Savannah decided to concentrate on her career and take a job at the newly built Medi-Most Hospital on Amelia Island as nursing coordinator for the emergency room. Still, despite her past history and the awkwardness and brevity of their first meeting, Savannah felt a curious pull towards the new Dr. Davis.

"Are you going to the hospital's Fourth of July picnic, Savannah?" Betty Williams said, breaking Savannah's train of thought. Betty was the gray-haired nurse that had been with Savannah the day of Hunter's entrance in the emergency room. Betty was about sixty years old and loved getting involved in Savannah's personal life in a benevolent way. Savannah knew instantly what Betty was insidiously trying to get across. Betty sensed an electricity generated by the brief encounter between Hunter and Savannah across the counter in the emergency room, and ever since then Betty had been making comments to Savannah about how attractive the new doctor was and what great compliments his patients had for him.

Savannah, for her part, had at first been irritated by her brief encounter with the illustrious Dr. Davis. The way the brash, young doctor had interrupted Savannah's conversation with Betty and then embarrassed them by pointing out their inattentiveness made Savannah think that Hunter Davis, M.D., was just another young doctor who thought his time was more important and his knowledge superior to everybody else's. So far, Savannah had been very cold to the overtures about Dr. Davis when Betty had brought him up in conversation, and the young E.R. nurse was prepared to nip this attempt in the bud.

"I already have plans for the Fourth of July," said Savannah.

"What plans?" asked Betty. "Are you going to read a book, walk your dog on the beach, or go camping by yourself like you did on Memorial Day weekend?"

Before Savannah could answer, Betty continued, "When I was your age I was always around men. I had dozens of suitors. A beautiful girl like you should be going out every night, not spending them at home with a book and a dog for company."

"I go out," responded Savannah. "I just don't always tell you."

"Sure," said Betty sarcastically, "and I'm dating Kevin Costner, I just haven't told anyone yet. Well, if you're interested," continued Betty, "I hear from Rosa Martin that Dr. Davis may be going to the picnic. It might be a good plan for you to bump into him."

"Thank you," Savannah said in a business-like fashion. "I'll take that under consideration," Savannah said as she turned her attention back to her work, but she thought that maybe, for once, she might follow Betty's advice.

Chapter Four

Hunter's first two weeks of practicing medicine had been hectic but satisfying. There had been quite a backlog of patients due to Dr. Baker's sudden death after his heart attack. Dr. Baker had trained Rosa, Bonnie, and Sheila well in their respective roles, and Hunter found them particularly helpful during the first few busy days while he familiarized himself with his new working environment. Hunter realized that some things were being done in old-fashioned or inefficient ways, but he didn't want to step on any toes too soon. He contented himself with making mental notes of what he would change after he had gained the confidence of the staff.

Hunter found his patients to be mostly working-class people and their children. He also inherited a large contingency of geriatric patients. All of this latter group had switched off of traditional Medicare coverage to Medi-Most's new Medicare HMO coverage for senior citizens. Although Hunter was fresh out of his residency he understood the changes going on with Medicare and the elderly.

Under traditional Medicare, the government would take approximately $140 out of all eligible Medicare recipients' monthly Social Security payments. Then the government, under its Medicare guidelines, is responsible for 80 percent of all allowable charges for that patient's medical care. The patient, however, must first meet a $100 deductible for doctor visits before the government starts paying their 80 percent. The deductible and 20 percent participation by the patient was supposed to keep people from overusing the system. This system worked satisfactorily in the early years of Medicare because health-care costs were low; as health-care costs rose and the deductibles were increased, many Medicare recipients found that they needed to buy supplemental insurance to cover the ever-increasing 20 percent plus deductibles.

The original Medicare coverage was good for patients: they could go to just about any doctor at any time and have any tests performed that they desired and be covered by the combination of their Medicare and supplemental insurance benefits. However, with no control on utilization, rapidly increasing health-care costs for the elderly over time resulted in higher Medicare and supplemental premiums. The rising premiums squeezed people living only on Social Security checks and others on a fixed retirement income as more of their dollars went to health care and less was available for spending.

Then the Medicare HMOs entered the market. At first Medicare HMOs seemed to be a good thing for both the government and the consumers. If a patient enrolls in a Medicare HMO the approximately $140 monthly premium that the government takes out of the patient's monthly Social Security check, along with an additional government subsidy of $160 to $260 depending on the area of the country, goes to the HMO. The government now had a known and fixed cost for enrolled beneficiaries. The HMO is then to cover all of the member's health-care costs. As a result, the government has limited its liability. For seniors, the Medicare HMO concept was less expensive than traditional Medicare, and it covered a limited amount of prescription drugs as well.

Medicare HMOs have steadily increased their enrollees due to the lack of a deductible to be met and no need for supplemental insurance. A person on a fixed income could join an HMO and pay less for their health care. However, like most things in life, cheaper health-care costs for the patient came with trade-offs, such as a loss of freedom. The HMO now has to control both the patients and the doctors to maintain costs. The patients' choice of doctors would be limited to those doctors on salary to the HMO or private doctors that have decided to join a panel of doctors and accept a diminished reimbursement for their work. The patients' choice of hospitals would be limited to those hospitals that had contracted with the HMOs. Doctors could only refer to other doctors on the panel. Tests that needed to be performed would require pre-authorization in order for the doctors to be reimbursed. Patients with money, who didn't want to give up control of their medical care, could stay on traditional Medicare.

Since Hunter was on salary to the HMO, the only patients over sixty-five years old he saw had signed up with Medi-Most's Senior Care program. One such patient was Ben Johnson. Ben had been a pulpwooder for most of his sixty-seven years. Ben was from Chester, a small unincorporated community near the Bell River. Unlike Amelia Island, which was on the east side of the county next to the Atlantic Ocean and becoming loaded with wealthy retirees living in their oceanfront condominiums, the west side of the county was rural. The main industry in the western stretches of Nassau County was timber related, mainly harvesting the large tracts of pine trees in the area and hauling the pine trees to the paper mills for conversion into pulp and then eventually to paper products. People who helped harvest the trees and who drove the trucks loaded with wood were called pulpwooders. Pulpwooding was tough, hard work. The trees had to be harvested from land that was many times swampy and loaded with sharp, thick palmetto bushes, as well as snakes and alligators.

Ben was a crusty old guy with a tough-as-leather, weather-beaten face. After Sheila had performed some preliminary tests on Ben, Hunter examined him. Ben told Hunter that he was not one to complain and, in fact, this was the first time he had ever voluntarily been to a doctor in his life despite many on-the-job injuries. But Ben reported he had been dizzy at times lately and sometimes the vision in his right eye would gray out. These symptoms had scared the tough old man.

The new doctor was very concerned by Ben's symptoms. Hunter immediately suspected a carotid artery problem. Hunter took out his stethoscope and listened to the right side of Ben's neck over his carotid artery. The large carotid arteries, one on each side of the neck, are the main conduits that transport blood through the neck area from the heart to the brain.

As Hunter suspected, he heard a carotid bruit—a swooshing sound of blood as it flowed through the narrowed artery with each heartbeat. This blockage was caused by hardening of the arteries and buildup of plaque along the interior arteriole wall. Hunter guessed from the sound that Ben had about an eighty percent blockage of his right carotid artery. Hunter moved the stethoscope to Ben's left carotid artery and listened again. The sound was better on this side, but Hunter guessed there was approximately a forty to fifty percent blockage on this side.

"I'm going to be alright, ain't I, Doc?" Ben asked with concern.

"Sure you are," replied Hunter. Then he added, "You're just having a little trouble getting blood to your brain."

"Well, this ain't the first time I've been accused of that," joked Ben. Hunter knew that Ben was at an extreme risk for a stroke with his carotid arteries in this shape, so Hunter had Ben admitted to the hospital to keep an eye on him. Hunter also put Ben on Coumadin, a blood thinner that would reduce his risk of stroke.

Now Hunter had to concern himself with the protocol of the HMO. During his residency at Emory University Hospital, Hunter would have simply referred the patient over to the vascular surgery department, where the patient would have had an arteriogram to confirm the diagnosis. Then the patient would have had surgery to unclog or clean out his carotid artery that same day. Here, at this small hospital on Amelia Island, there was no full-time vascular surgeon. Medi-Most did have a vascular surgeon based at their main hospital in Jacksonville, and Hunter wanted to refer Ben there for immediate evaluation. However, the physician learned that the vascular surgeon went over to Medi-Most's hospital in Lake City on Tuesdays.

Hunter had to be content with a phone conference with Dr. Hockman about Medi-Most's protocol for this situation. Dr. Hockman told Hunter to first discharge Ben from the hospital— to keep costs down—and to have Ben come back on Friday when the vascular surgeon made his monthly visit to Medi-

Most's Amelia Island hospital. Dr. Hockman also told Hunter it would be a month or more before the vascular surgeon could perform the surgery because the one vascular surgeon available served five Medi-Most hospitals in the Jacksonville area. Hunter was aghast at this fact and wondered privately if Ben could last that long without something happening. Being new and not wanting to start badly with Dr. Hockman, Hunter decided not to pursue the issue any further. Hunter did decide, however, that he would mark some time off his schedule around Ben's appointment with the vascular surgeon on Friday to meet the surgeon and perhaps lobby for an earlier surgery date. Hunter found out that Ben's four o'clock appointment was the surgeon's last for the day, so the doctor told Rosa to not book any patients for himself after three-thirty that day.

On that Friday, July third, around four-thirty, Hunter had finished up with his patients and hurried over to the office the vascular surgeon used on his monthly visits. As Hunter was approaching the door of the office, Ben Johnson came out through the door.

"Hey, Doc," said Ben pleasantly, "What are you doing here?"

"I was coming to make sure they took good care of you," answered Hunter smiling.

"Well, Dr. Snead took pretty good care of me. Not as good as you did, mind you, but he said the same things you did and they set my surgery for August eleventh," said Ben proudly, obviously glad to have the issue decided and a course of action set.

Hunter tried to hide his disappointment at the announcement that it would be five weeks until Ben's surgery. "That's great, Ben," Hunter said flatly. "I'm going to go meet with Dr. Snead. Good luck."

Hunter shook hands with Ben warmly then spun around and entered the office. After introducing himself to the receptionist and about a five-minute delay, Hunter was led into John Snead's private office. Dr. Snead, who had been busily dictating the day's patient directives into a small recorder, stood up from behind his desk and greeted Hunter with a weary smile.

"Dr. Snead," Hunter began as he reached out to shake hands, "I'm Hunter Davis, the new family practitioner."

"Well, it's nice to meet you," said Dr. Snead. "Please have a seat," Dr. Snead continued, pointing to the chair across his desk.

As Hunter sat down, he observed that Dr. Snead was a neat, trim man, probably in his early fifties with very short gray hair that gave him an ex-military look. After both men sat down, Hunter began, "Dr. Snead, I just wanted to come over and meet you because, hopefully, I'll be referring patients to you for quite some time. In fact, I made my first referral to you today, Ben Johnson. I believe he was your last patient."

"Ah, Mr. Johnson," replied Dr. Snead. "Your diagnosis was correct, that man definitely needs surgery."

"Yes," said Hunter, "I saw Mr. Johnson on his way out and he said the surgery is set for August eleventh."

"That's right," said Dr. Snead.

"Well, excuse my saying so, Dr. Snead, but isn't that a little too long to wait to do this procedure for a man in Mr. Johnson's condition?" Hunter asked.

The weary smile that Dr. Snead had been wearing faded away. "Where did you do your residency, Dr. Davis?" asked the older doctor.

"Emory University Hospital," replied Hunter.

"Ah, Emory," nodded Dr. Snead. "A teaching hospital. A teaching hospital where every specialist is at your command and no expense is spared for the patient. Well, welcome to the real world. Yes, you are correct. Under the best-case scenario I would operate on your Mr. Johnson as soon as possible, but I am only one vascular surgeon covering for five hospitals. My caseload is such that August eleventh is the first time we had available. I've have been trying to get Medi-Most to hire another vascular surgeon for over a year, but they say it's not necessary. I guess since I was an army surgeon for twenty years, they think I'm used to being overworked and underpaid. When I got out of the army, I thought I wouldn't have to deal with rationed medicine and constrictive bureaucracy, but I went straight from the army to this HMO and I don't know which one is worse. Now, if you will excuse me, I must finish my dictation if I'm going to get home in time to go out with my wife."

Hunter stood up, shook hands, and walked dejectedly back to his office to finish his paperwork. Rosa was just beginning to lock the front door when Hunter arrived. "That's all right, Rosa, I'll lock up," said Hunter.

"Oh, Dr. Davis, I didn't think you were coming back," said Rosa.

"I still have some paperwork to fill out," said Hunter glumly.

"No, you don't," said Rosa cheerfully. "While you were gone I finished the charts for you. All you need to do is to sign at the bottom," Rosa added.

"Thanks," said Hunter. "What would I do without you?" Hunter added smiling.

"You know," Rosa began, "you've been working real hard the last couple of weeks. You need to take a break and have some fun. Tomorrow is the Fourth of July, and the hospital has its annual picnic out at Ten Acres. You should come."

"Oh, I don't think so, Rosa," said Hunter. "I think I'll just lay in the pool on a raft with a beer in my hand."

"I hear a lot of nurses will be coming to the picnic," countered Rosa.

"I'll take that into consideration," responded Hunter smiling. Then he added, "Have a good weekend, Rosa."

"Well, the picnic starts at noon if you change your mind," said Rosa.

Hunter turned and let himself through the front door and went into his office, where he sat down wearily behind his desk and began signing papers. As Hunter signed the papers, his mind wandered off about Ben Johnson. Hunter hoped the old man would be fortunate enough to last until August eleventh.

Then Hunter realized it was Friday night and he should be thinking about more pleasant things. He wondered if the pretty nurse from the ER would be attending the picnic. It might be worth going if she did. Hunter thought to himself for a minute, struggling to remember her name, his mind befuddled from all the activity of the past two weeks. Hunter remembered it was a slightly unusual name that had something to do with a town.

The young doctor thought back to the moment they met, when he stared into those luminous green eyes and glanced down to read from the gold name tag placed halfway between her shoulder and the perfectly shaped breast contained in the white nurse's uniform.

"Savannah!" Hunter thought to himself. "Yeah, that was her name."

Chapter Five

Hunter woke up at nine the next morning, which was late for him as he was accustomed to waking up at six. Hunter was surprised that he was able to sleep that late because his biological clock usually woke him up early, even on the weekends when he could sleep in. The doctor guessed he must have been more exhausted than he realized.

Now, after sleeping ten hours, Hunter felt great. He rolled over to the side of the bed next to the window and lifted the blinds slightly to peer out of his beachfront cottage. Hunter had rented the bottom floor of a small, old, wooden two-story house on a six-month basis back in May after he signed his contract with Medi-Most. Hunter had been looking to find a place near the beach to use during the summer months. Even though the location was on the north end of the beach where the old wooden houses were crammed together and dated back many years to when Fernandina Beach was a south Georgia vacation spot, the rent during the summer was always high; if there were any units available on a long-term basis at all. Most of the homeowners lived elsewhere and rented their cottages out during the summer on a weekly basis.

So even though the cottages were old, some even without air conditioning, they were still in high demand from families in south Georgia. Some of the families had been coming for three generations, using the same location for a cheap vacation spot at the beach. The landlords could get anywhere from two hundred to three hundred dollars per week during the summer months, and the vacationers could get a relatively cheap seven-day stay at the beach. Hunter had been lucky that Mrs. Sparrows, who lived above him and owned the house, had grown tired of renting on a weekly basis and wanted someone quiet and stable that could rent on a more long-term basis. Hunter had come along at just the right time, and Mrs. Sparrows enjoyed having the young man around as protection since she was getting older and her husband had died four years earlier. Hunter wasn't sure he would stay in this apartment past the six months because the wind at the beach in north Florida gets surprisingly cold during the winter months, also the lack of a garage combined with the salt air would quickly begin to cause his new car to rust. But Hunter missed the ocean during his many years at school and wanted to spend his first few months back on Amelia Island at the beach area.

Now as Hunter peered through the crack in the blinds, he was enjoying a perfect view of this Fourth of July morning. Thanks to constant erosion, which had taken down the dune line, Hunter's bedroom window had an unobstructed view of the ocean. The mid-morning sun was shimmering off the nearly flat sea. Hunter knew the sun, cloudless sky, and lack of breeze would soon send the temperatures into the upper nineties. This would eventually cause the land to heat up, and the hot air would rise, forming clouds over the land. The circular motion of the hot air—rising over the land then falling over the cooler ocean only to be sucked back up by the hot air rising over the land—would cause the sea breeze to kick in around one or two o'clock in the afternoon. The cooling sea breeze would relieve the stifling heat at the beach and delight the Hobie Cat sailors and sailboarders that would be waiting for its arrival. The clouds would build up over the inland areas as far away as Gainesville. Then as the hot air rose, it would condense into cumulonimbus clouds capable of horrendous thunderstorms. These clouds would then move eastward toward the ocean until they met the sea breeze. Sometimes the clouds would overpower the sea breeze and roll across Amelia Island; sometimes the sea breeze would halt the thunderstorms' advancement and it would only rain on the west side of the county across the river. Anyhow, this weather pattern was so predictable in the summer months in the north Florida area that the weatherman's summertime mantra has become "Clear skies in the morning giving way to partly cloudy skies in the afternoon, with a fifty percent chance of afternoon thunderstorms, highs in the nineties."

Hunter decided to go for a run, so he put on his jogging shorts, tank top, and running shoes and headed out the door. Hunter immediately noticed how muggy it was since there was virtually no breeze and the humidity was probably ninety percent. Hunter stretched for a minute then walked across the pothole-ridden, one-lane beach road that separated his cottage from the beach. Hunter walked down to the hard-packed sand by the water line and began a leisurely jog northward along the edge of the sea. Hunter had spent three summers during his college years working as a lifeguard at Amelia Island Plantation. Every other day during those summers, as part of the job, the lifeguards had to run six miles in the morning under these conditions. Hunter remembered that, at that time, he could run twenty minutes in the heat of the morning before he even began to sweat. Now Hunter noticed he was sweating profusely after only two minutes of running and he promised himself he would get in shape before the summer was over. Hunter laughed to himself as he passed a round, red-faced man in his early forties running barefoot on the beach in the other direction. Hunter surmised that the tourist was probably on his summer vacation and by the look of his physique hadn't run since his last summer vacation. Hunter also laughed because the tourist would soon realize what Hunter learned the hard way; that running on the beach barefoot was equivalent to rubbing sandpaper on the bottom of your toes and the soles of your feet, leading to painful abrasions. Hunter imagined that the pain radiating from the bottom of the man's feet would probably matched the pain from the sunburn the man was going to acquire by the end of the day.

As Hunter was running he started to think about what he was going to do for the rest of the day. Last night, Hunter was exhausted, so he went to bed early, slept soundly, and woke up feeling completely refreshed. Last night, Hunter had been completely against going to the hospital picnic, but this morning after waking up feeling so good, Hunter began to rethink his position.

Since there was just a skeleton crew at the hospital today, there was a good chance that Savannah would be at the picnic. But Hunter wasn't sure Savannah would be there and he didn't want to waste his time there if she wasn't going to be there. In the end, Hunter convinced himself it would be worth the chance and he decided he'd try the picnic. Hunter turned around and ran the two miles back to his cottage, showered, and changed clothes. The young doctor then ate some cereal and relaxed until it was time to go.

Around noon Hunter stepped into his car and drove south along State Road A1A. A1A starts in Callahan on the west side of the county, comes east to Fernandina Beach, and then follows the beach southward along the east coast of Florida all the way to Key West. Hunter only drove south along the beach a couple of miles before he turned westward on Simmons Road. When Simmons Road intersected with fourteenth Street, Hunter turned left on fourteenth Street and went a few hundred yards until it dead-ended on Amelia Island Parkway. Hunter took a left on Amelia Island Parkway, which curved around the airport, and headed towards Ten Acres.

After Hunter drove past the airport, he encountered an area of the road that used to be called "Dead Man's Curve." Before the road had been re-routed and straightened, the road had previously taken a nearly ninety-degree turn. After many fatal one-car accidents, where people couldn't make the curve, it was modified. The road now goes into a straightaway that enters a hollow. A small creek at the bottom of the hollow runs transverse to the road. On either side of the road, in close proximity, are the massive trunks of many old oak trees. Because the dense foliage of the oak trees always made this section of the road dark and gloomy—and because of the gauntlet effect one experienced when driving through this section of road with the huge trees lined up on either side bearing scars on their trunks where unfortunate cars or trucks had veered slightly off the road—this area of the road had always reminded Hunter of the scene in *The Wizard of Oz* where the characters are attacked in the forest by the flying monkeys. Hunter laughed at the thought as he left that area and started up a small rise to turn into Ten Acres. Ten Acres was a rare piece of property on the west side of the island overlooking the marsh. It was purchased by one of the paper mills many years ago and since that time has been used as a retreat for company picnics and meetings and rented out for private parties.

Hunter turned on the dirt road past the sign that said Ten Acres and drove through the open gate. Hunter chuckled to himself and wondered who the genius was that named the property "Ten Acres" in honor of the ten acres of property it encompassed. The doctor continued down the dirt road, past the large indoor meeting facility, and drove to where all the cars were parked at the outdoor picnic area. The outdoor picnic area consisted of a large, tin-roofed, open-sided building under which there were about forty picnic tables. Outside the structure were several large barbecue pits for cooking. In front of the structure was a recreational area for children, including swings and playground equipment. Behind the building toward the marsh were horseshoe pits and a large grassy field for games and activities. Hunter found a parking place in the shade of a tree so his car would not get too hot from the blazing sun.

Most of the Medi-Most employees were already in attendance, more than Hunter expected. Except for the skeleton crew working the hospital, almost everyone had come and brought their families. Also, as Hunter learned later, the other area Medi-Most hospitals had also been invited, so the number of people swelled by a couple of hundred people.

Hunter meandered through the crowd looking for a familiar face. Eventually, Hunter spotted Rosa. Rosa was working her way through the crowd handing out pieces of paper.

"Oh, I see you made it," said Rosa.

"How could I ignore your most kind invitation?" responded Hunter, smiling.

"There," said Rosa, thrusting a piece of paper into Hunter's hand. Hunter looked down at the piece of paper, which had the number eleven on it.

"What's this?" asked Hunter.

"This number matches you up with your partner for the three-legged sack race," responded Rosa.

"Oh, I don't think I want to participate in that, Rosa," said Hunter quickly.

"Oh, yes, you do," countered Rosa with a wink. Then Rosa turned quickly and disappeared into the crowd before Hunter could discuss the issue any further.

Hunter spotted Bonnie across the crowd, motioning him to come over. Hunter made his way through the people until he arrived in front of Bonnie. Bonnie had her arm around a man who she introduced as her husband, Bob, and Hunter talked with them for awhile. Dr. Hockman then found Hunter and took Hunter around to meet several specialists he would be working with. Dr. Hockman also introduced Hunter to some of his superiors in the Medi-Most hierarchy. Hunter was beginning to think it was a mistake to come to the picnic as it had been all business so far, when he heard a man with a megaphone call for everyone's attention.

"Could I have everyone's attention, please?" the man began. "We are getting ready to start the Medi-Most Olympics. Please look at the number on the ticket you were given and locate your partner and report to the field behind the picnic area." Hunter looked down at his number eleven. Hunter looked around and saw everyone holding their ticket aloft and shouting out their number. Hunter thought this was lame and unorganized but he decided to join in and waded through the crowd, calling out his number. Hunter was beginning to think this process was hopeless as he made his way through the maze of people simultaneously calling their numbers when the crowd seemed to part slightly and Hunter spotted Savannah about twenty feet away holding the number eleven. Savannah smiled as Hunter approached. Hunter noticed how white and straight her teeth were.

"Looks like we're going to be partners," Hunter said as he approached.

"Funny coincidence, huh?" Savannah responded, still smiling.

"Oh, something tells me it was more than mere fate that brought us together. Look," said Hunter, pointing. Savannah turned around and there was Betty Williams and Rosa standing together about twenty yards away. When Betty and Rosa saw Savannah turn to look towards them, they both turned their faces away from Savannah and Hunter and tried to act nonchalant.

"Oh, Betty is always trying to meddle in my business," said Savannah in mock anger.

"Yeah, now I know why Rosa twisted my arm so much to come today," said Hunter laughing, but secretly pleased. "Well, I guess we better go see what's in store for us, shall we?" Hunter gestured toward the field behind the picnic tables.

Savannah led the way through the maze of tables toward the field. Hunter fell into step behind Savannah, watching her every move. Savannah was wearing a short-sleeved white cotton shirt that was tied in a knot, revealing a darkly tanned, bare midriff. Over Savannah's slim hips were a pair of tight-fitting khaki shorts. Hunter's gaze continued down Savannah's long, lean legs all the way to her white canvas tennis shoes, which she wore without socks. Hunter shook his head in amazement as he followed Savannah onto the field.

After the crowd had gathered, the man with the megaphone began to speak.

"Welcome to the Medi-Most Olympics," the man began. "Does everyone have a partner?" the man queried.

"Yes!" responded the crowd.

Savannah cast a glance over at Hunter, who smiled back appreciatively. Savannah's first impression of Hunter in his starched, white doctor's coat and starched dress shirt had been of stuffy arrogance. But now the young doctor, with his open smile and piercing blue eyes, who was wearing an Atlanta Braves hat and a Hard Rock Cafe T-shirt and who walked with the gait of an accomplished athlete, did not seem stuffy at all.

"Good!" said the man, then continued, "The Medi-Most Olympics consists of three games: the egg toss, the water balloon relay, and the three-legged sack race. Whichever teams have the best combined results in all three events will take home the first, second, or third place trophies; one trophy for each partner. So let the games begin!"

The first event was the egg toss, in which the participants lined up shoulder to shoulder in a long line across the field, facing their partners in a similar line ten yards in front of them. A participant on one side would then toss an egg over to the partner in the opposite line facing them. Whichever teams' egg broke would be out, and the remaining teams would back up ten more yards and continue until only one team remained.

Hunter was a veteran of the egg toss since it was a main event of the Greek Games, which was a yearly contest the fraternities held at Mercer University. So as the fifty or so couples squared off in their lines and the crowd lined up to watch, Hunter motioned to Savannah, who was in the line facing him. Hunter showed Savannah not to stand directly under the egg as it came down and to not stop it suddenly with her hands, as it was sure to break and splatter all over her. Hunter motioned to Savannah to stand to the side of the egg as it was coming down and catch it in a sweeping motion to cushion its fall. Savannah nodded her head in affirmation as the man with the megaphone readied Hunter's line to toss the egg.

At the man's command, Hunter's line simultaneously tossed their eggs underhand toward their partner. Fifty eggs tossed through the air gave way to mass confusion on the receiving end as fifty people went forward, backward or sideways to try and catch their respective eggs. About half the eggs broke due to poor tosses, catches, or technique. Hunter's toss and Savannah's catch were flawless. Other people were not as fortunate and they were asked to step aside, some with egg dripping from their hair or clothes.

37

The man with the megaphone asked the remaining people to move back ten yards so the lines were now twenty yards apart. When everyone was set, the man yelled to toss the eggs. Savannah's toss was low but Hunter made a diving catch a foot from the ground rolling on his back holding the unbroken egg aloft. Hunter gazed over to Savannah, who mouthed the word "Sorry" as she held her hands to her face.

Now the lines were set thirty yards apart and Hunter did not think they would survive this round. There were only ten couples left as Hunter tossed the egg toward Savannah. Savannah got in perfect position to catch the egg, but as she was making her sweeping motion, the egg fell from her grasp and tumbled along the ground. Miraculously, it did not break due to the soft grass and Savannah's slowing of its momentum. Savannah scooped up the egg and showed it to Hunter and everyone else. Hunter laughed and clapped as Savannah jumped up and down in a victorious, girlish manner.

Now, the contest was down to three sets of partners, including Hunter and Savannah. The contestants now backed up so they were forty yards apart. This seemed like an impossible distance, and Hunter wasn't sure Savannah would be able to throw the egg underhand this far. At the man's command, Savannah wound up and threw with all her strength. Unfortunately Savannah held onto the egg a little too long and the egg went straight up. Hunter ran as fast as he could, dove and caught the egg right before it hit the ground, but the force with which Hunter hit the ground jarred the egg out of his hands and it hit him in the forehead and broke. The sight of Hunter laying prone on his stomach with egg dripping from his face made Savannah break out in hysterical laughter. Hunter sat up and glowered at Savannah.

"Sorry . . . sorry," Savannah said between laughs, then added, "You literally got egg on your face."

"Very funny," responded Hunter. Then Hunter added sarcastically, "Nice throw."

"Hang on," said Savannah, "I'll fetch some paper towels."

Hunter looked over to the other contestants and saw that one couple's egg had broken and one had not, so Hunter and Savannah had tied for second.

After Hunter had wiped his face clean, the participants readied themselves for the next event. In the water-balloon relay the contestants had to place a water balloon under their chin and run to their partner lined up twenty-five yards away. Then, without using their hands, the participants had to pass the water balloon to their partners, who then run back to the starting line with the water balloons under their chins. The first team to relay three balloons without bursting a balloon wins. Hunter and Savannah took their places across from each other. Hunter hoped for Savannah's sake that none of the water balloons would break while Savannah was running with them under her chin because he feared the white cotton blouse she was wearing would be rendered nearly invisible if wet.

The race began and Hunter raced toward Savannah with the water balloon tucked under his chin. Hunter made it without incident and stooped to pass the balloon from under his chin to under Savannah's chin. Hunter noticed how lovely and slender Savannah's neck looked, and the sweet smell of her hair gave Hunter pause even during the frantic atmosphere of the race. Savannah, for her part, noticed how tall Hunter was as she had to stand on her tip toes to receive the balloon. Hunter and Savannah successfully passed the three balloons without incident and they were the first to finish.

"We make a great team," said Savannah smiling.

"Yes, we do," said Hunter with a laugh.

Now it was time for the last event: the three-legged sack race. Burlap sacks were passed out to each couple. Hunter fondly remembered that burlap sacks in this area were called croaker sacks because the old timers would catch fish called croakers and put them in the wet burlap sacks so they would stay fresh until the fisherman could take them home to eat or to the fish camp to sell. Hunter and Savannah each put a leg into the sack. Hunter placed his arm around Savannah's slender waist and they practiced for the race. After several awkward attempts with Hunter having to physically restrain Savannah from falling, they started to get their rhythm down and run in unison. Before long, it was time for the race to begin and Hunter and Savannah lined up with the other couples.

"Bang!" went the starter's pistol, and Hunter and Savannah took off. After a slight stumble at the beginning of the race, Hunter and Savannah got their rhythm going and were among the leaders. Hunter had his arm around Savannah's waist and was whisking her along. After making the turn successfully, the two of them had a slight lead and then expanded their lead to cross the finish line first. The happy couple fell to the ground in exhaustion and exhilaration in a semi-embrace.

"Good job," said Hunter, gasping for air.

"What do you mean?" said Savannah, laughing uncontrollably. "You practically carried me the whole way."

Just then, Hunter's beeper went off. "Damn, not now," said Hunter, hoping he had just bumped the beeper to set it off accidentally. Hunter checked the beeper and its digital read-out told him to call the hospital.

"Looks like I have to go. It's the hospital," said Hunter, standing up and brushing himself off. "What are you doing next Saturday?" asked Hunter.

"I have no plans, as far as I know," responded Savannah smiling.

"How about a picnic at Fort Clinch?" Hunter asked.

"Sounds good to me!" Savannah said happily.

"I'll pick you up at elven-thirty Saturday morning," said Hunter as he walked away, then added, "Give Rosa directions to your house." Hunter turned and walked to his car.

Once in his car, Hunter dialed the hospital from his car phone. Hunter learned from the emergency room nurse on duty that Ben Johnson had been delivered to the hospital by ambulance following a major stroke. The emergency room doctor had stabilized Ben and he wanted Hunter to come in and admit Ben into the hospital and assume Ben's care. Hunter told the nurse he would be there shortly, then slammed down the phone in disgust. Hunter cursed the rules under which he had to work now. Hunter blamed himself for not doing more, but what else could he have done? Hunter had talked to both Dr. Hockman and Dr. Snead on Ben's behalf. There wasn't much else Hunter could have done. He had been right that Ben should have had surgery sooner, but that was little solace to Hunter as he drove hastily to the hospital to see what kind of condition old Ben was in. Hunter promised himself he would visit Dr. Hockman the first chance he had, to give him a piece of his mind.

Chapter Six

Hunter was sitting outside of Dr. Hockman's office waiting for his turn to go inside. Hunter glanced at his watch impatiently, his right leg nervously bouncing up and down. Hunter had a slow spot in his schedule on this Monday morning, so he had rushed over to see if he could talk to Dr. Hockman for a minute before returning to his patients. Dr. Hockman's receptionist had told Hunter that Dr. Hockman was with somebody in his office, but Hunter was welcome to wait. Hunter had been waiting about ten minutes and was contemplating leaving when the door to Dr. Hockman's office opened. Hunter overheard Dr. Hockman saying good-bye to a strange-looking man in a hospital orderly's uniform. The man was very tall and thin with sunken eyes and a very pale, almost translucent complexion. Hunter stood up and walked past the man toward Dr. Hockman's door. Hunter and the man exchanged sideways glances as they passed each other. The man reminded the young doctor of Lurch from *The Addams Family* television show. Hunter knocked on the door, which was still askew.

"Dr. Hockman?" Hunter inquired.

"Come on in, Dr. Davis. What can I do for you, son?" Dr. Hockman inquired as he motioned Hunter to have a seat.

"Well, I wanted to talk to you about Ben Johnson," said Hunter.

"Yes," replied Dr. Hockman, as they both sat down. "A very unfortunate circumstance."

"An unfortunate circumstance that could have been prevented," said Hunter sternly.

"You don't know that for sure," replied Dr. Hockman, then added, "As you know, Mr. Johnson could have experienced a stroke at any time, even during the surgery, as occurs in a significant number of cases. One of the things you are going to learn throughout your years of practicing is that you can't save everyone," continued Dr. Hockman. "You are going to win some and you are going to lose some," he added.

"I just think this was a winnable case," interrupted Hunter. "If it wasn't for the restrictions placed on us by the HMO, I think we could have prevented Ben from being in the state he's in."

"Exactly what is Mr. Johnson's prognosis, Dr. Davis?" asked Dr. Hockman.

"Not very good, I'm afraid. There appears to be severe neurological damage, and the patient is still unconscious," responded Hunter.

"Ben Johnson was an accident waiting to happen," retorted Dr. Hockman. "Ben's arteries were probably so clogged up, this was bound to happen sometime," Hockman added.

"Well, I would have preferred it had occurred some other time than waiting for HMO protocol to run its course," said Hunter.

"Nobody forced you to come work with us, Dr. Davis," responded Dr. Hockman sternly. Then he added, "When you signed your contract you agreed to adhere to our protocol. I know you're straight out of residency where things may have been done differently, but the days of doing what's best for the patient regardless of cost has died a recent death, and you have graduated into a medical landscape that has changed. These days, quality medical care is still most important, but cost-effective medical care is running a close second."

"Be that as it may, Dr. Hockman, I still think exceptions should be made in some circumstances for the benefit of the patient," said Hunter.

"Exceptions are made, if necessary," responded Dr. Hockman, "but the protocol is established by what is appropriate in most cases. Nobody has a crystal ball to know what is appropriate to do in every case. For example, consider a patient who comes into your office with a headache. The best thing to do medically regardless of cost would be to do an MRI on every single headache patient to possibly catch a brain tumor. The cost of this, however, would be astronomical. There has to be a protocol for ruling out more innocuous causes, with an MRI or brain scan used as a last resort. Do you see my point?"

"Yes, I guess so," responded Hunter hesitantly.

"Good," said Dr. Hockman. "I'm sure you must have patients waiting for you."

Hunter glanced at his watch and realized he should have been back at his office fifteen minutes ago. Hunter rose from his seat as did Dr. Hockman.

"Hunter," began Dr. Hockman, "you are going to be a fine physician. Just try not to take things so personally. It will eat you up inside. I know. I was once idealistic like you, and now I'm just a cynical old cuss.

"By the way, I'm playing golf Friday afternoon with Jack Wheeler, the regional head of Medi-Most HMO for this area, and his assistant, and we need another person to complete our foursome. Why don't you mark off your schedule after one o'clock and come play with us? You can talk to Mr. Wheeler yourself about your complaints," suggested Dr. Hockman.

Hunter hadn't played golf in awhile but realized this would be a good opportunity to lobby his case. "I'll see if I can juggle my schedule around. Thank you, Dr. Hockman," Hunter replied.

Dr. Hockman extended his hand. Hunter shook hands with the older physician and then left the room. The smile faded from Dr. Hockman's face as soon as Hunter turned to walk toward the door. During the interview when Hunter was hired, Dr. Hockman had thought Hunter was naïve—which would make Hunter easy to manage—but Dr. Hockman realized that assumption may have been wrong.

For his part, Hunter hoped he never became cold and cynical as Dr. Hockman had joked about becoming. As Hunter arrived back at his office and saw the full waiting room, thoughts of Ben Johnson and HMO protocol vanished from his mind. Hunter immersed himself in caring for his new patients.

Chapter Seven

Hunter pulled onto the short road that led to the Ritz-Carlton, which also served as the entrance to the Golf Club of Amelia Island. The entranceway leading to the Ritz-Carlton was visually very impressive. It was a divided two-lane road with trees in between the two roads. The Ritz-Carlton sat slightly uphill at the end of the road, set on the old dune structure. There was a circular drive in front of the Ritz-Carlton surrounding a large fountain. The large, horseshoe-shaped hotel sat at the top of the hill, its two prongs facing the ocean with a large grass courtyard in between the two prongs.

Hunter had never been able to afford to stay at the hotel, but when he first moved back to the island, he did have a drink in the lobby and walked around the grounds.

The Golf Club of Amelia Island's clubhouse was a compact, stucco-and-mirrored-glass structure on the left about halfway up the road that served as the entranceway to the Ritz. There was a small circular drive in front of the clubhouse that serves as a bag drop area. Hunter pulled his convertible up to the area where there was a wooden bag rack. Since it was a nice, clear day, Hunter had put his top down, and his golf bag was sitting upright in the passenger's seat. A bag attendant came running out dutifully from in front of the clubhouse to retrieve Hunter's bag. The attendant asked Hunter who he would be playing with that day. Hunter informed the attendant he would be playing with Dr. Hockman and tipped the attendant as he grabbed Hunter's bag. Hunter asked the attendant where he should park, and the attendant pointed toward the two-story parking lot that served both the Ritz-Carlton and the golf clubhouse and told Hunter the code on the gate to gain entrance.

After Hunter had parked his car on the bottom floor of the parking lot so it would be in the shade, he walked back across the road to the clubhouse. Hunter made his way across the road and up the steps and through the large double doors with

45

mirrored glass. Hunter entered a small lobby area filled with flowers, a sitting area with leather couches, and straight ahead was a large reception desk with a female attendant behind the desk.

"May I help you?" asked the woman behind the desk pleasantly with a practiced smile.

"I'm looking for the pro shop," Hunter responded inquiringly.

"It's that way, sir," the woman said agreeably.

Hunter walked to the left in the direction the woman had pointed, noticing there was a restaurant off to the right in the other direction. As Hunter walked down the hallway toward the pro shop, he spotted a dark walnut door that had a gold plaque on it that said Men's Locker Room. Hunter decided to step in through the doorway so he could find a place to relieve himself before the match since Hunter felt slightly nervous playing with these people for the first time.

Hunter stepped into the nicest locker room he had ever been fortunate enough to enter. The plush carpet led to a dressing area with row upon row of dark walnut lockers with individual names on each locker. Past the locker area was a marble-lined men's room. Hunter found a urinal and relieved himself, then washed his hands at the gold-leaf sink. As Hunter was leaving the locker room he noticed an etched glass door that said Members Only that led to a private card-playing area. After going out the door that led back to the hallway for the pro shop, Hunter spotted another etched glass door that said Members Only that led to a private bar and dining area for members that had an expansive view of the eighteenth green. Hunter admired the carved wooden bar and the patrons laughing and drinking beer and vowed one day he would make enough money to be a member here.

After walking down the hallway and up to the counter in the pro shop, Hunter identified himself to the young golf professional working behind the counter.

"Ah, yes, Dr. Davis, the rest of your party has already checked in and are waiting for you on the practice tee," said the young pro pleasantly. Hunter started to reach for his wallet, but was stopped by the young man.

"Everything has been taken care of for you, just show this slip to the starter, and the practice balls are already at the range," the young man added smiling.

"Thank you," Hunter said appreciatively.

Hunter walked out the side door and down the steps leading to where his clubs were already waiting on a golf cart. After being pointed in the direction of the driving range by the cart attendant, Hunter headed across the road and drove until he came to the driving range.

After Hunter pulled the cart up to the driving range, he spotted Dr. Hockman at the far end of the range with two other men he did not know. Hunter pulled a few clubs out of his bag to warm up with and walked over to join his group.

"No fair getting in extra practice time," Hunter jested as he approached the men, causing Dr. Hockman and the other two men to look up from hitting their practice balls.

"When you get as old as we are, you need the extra time on the range just to limber up the old muscles," responded Dr. Hockman jovially.

Dr. Hockman and the other two men stopped hitting balls and came over to meet Hunter.

"Hunter," Dr. Hockman began, "I want you to meet Jack Wheeler and Bill Simpkins."

Hunter turned to meet the first man, a large, overweight man that Hunter guessed to be about fifty-five years old. Hunter shook the man's hand as Dr. Hockman gave a more formal introduction.

"Mr. Wheeler is the area manager for Medi-Most HMO and Bill is his right-hand man," explained Dr. Hockman.

Hunter turned to shake the other man's hand. Bill Simpkins appeared to Hunter to be about forty years old, thin, and wore thick spectacles that made him look like an accountant.

"Nice to meet you," said Hunter politely to each man.

47

"These men are our bosses, more or less, since they run Medi-Most and we are employed by Medi-Most," added Dr. Hockman.

"Well, I guess I better not shoot the lowest today," Hunter joked, knowing that he had only played twice in the last year and would be in no danger of doing that since these guys probably played regularly.

"Well, you guys are the doctors. You make the real decisions. We are just the administrators that try to set the protocol to make your decisions easier," Wheeler inserted with false modesty.

Hunter wanted to blurt out that their protocol had just administered Ben Johnson into an early stroke, but Hunter held his tongue, planning on diplomatically broaching the subject later in the round.

All four men hit some more range balls, loosening up for the round until it neared their tee time. Wheeler told Hunter to put his bag on his cart and the men headed to the first tee. Once on the first tee, the four men waited for the group in front of them to clear the fairway so they could hit their first drive. While the four of them were waiting, Wheeler decided to make the bet.

"Well, what's it going to be, boys?" Wheeler began to open negotiations for the bet. Then, before anybody could say anything, Wheeler followed with a suggestion of his own.

"How about a ten-dollar Nassau with automatic two-down presses, doctors against the administrators?" Wheeler offered.

Hunter looked over at Dr. Hockman who would know better than he, since Hunter had never played with these guys before, if this was a fair bet. Dr. Hockman gave Hunter a reluctant nod and said that would be fine.

The fairway had cleared and Wheeler went to hit first. Wheeler took an awkward swing and the ball dribbled off the front of the tee. Wheeler quickly threw down a mulligan and swung with the same ingrained, awkward swing, the second ball only slightly improving on the first. Simpkins hit next and Hunter saw why Dr. Hockman had been reluctant to agree to the bet. Simpkins was a thin but wiry man and had a perfect, smooth golf swing. Simpkins needed only one attempt to place his drive perfectly in the middle of the fairway two hundred and fifty yards away.

Dr. Hockman safely placed his drive two hundred and forty yards down the right side of the fairway with a practiced fade, starting the ball down the left side of the fairway and ending up on the right side on the fairway. Now it was Hunter's turn. Although Hunter had not played much golf recently, like a lot of ex-ball players he had a natural affinity for golf and could crush the ball. The only problem was he did not always know which direction it was going.

Hunter misfired on his first drive—a massive drive that hooked out of bounds to the left.

"That would have been three hundred yards long if you had straightened it out," Wheeler said in amazement.

Hunter placed another ball on the tee and, swinging easier, managed to keep one in the fairway just beyond Simpkins' ball.

"Looks like we have us a player," Wheeler commented, following Hunter's ball with his eyes as it landed in the fairway.

"Sometimes I get lucky and find the fairway," Hunter responded.

As the match progressed over the first nine holes, it became apparent that Wheeler was no help at all to Simpkins. Fortunately for Wheeler, Simpkins was a steady near-par player on his own ball, and it was basically Dr. Hockman and Hunter playing against Simpkins. Dr. Hockman made a good partner for Hunter because, while not spectacular, he was steady, and when Hunter's drives missed the fairway, Dr. Hockman was able to keep his team even with Simpkins. When Hunter's ball did find the fairway he was able to make par and he even had a birdie on the fourth hole.

The match on the front side had been a close one with neither team getting more than one down to enact the two-down press. Going into the ninth hole, with the front-nine bet riding on its outcome, the match was dead even.

Hunter and Dr. Hockman had the honors since they had won the seventh hole to even the match, and both teams tied the eighth hole. Dr. Hockman hit first on the par-three ninth hole and hit safely on the green about thirty feet away. Hunter followed with a shot that ended up on the fringe of the green about thirty-five feet from the hole.

The usually reliable Simpkins hit next and hit a pretty draw, but it was a little long and left and hit the downslope on the back left of the green and rolled down the hill and out of bounds. Wheeler was not pleased, his face turning red as he glowered at his partner, the same partner he had been riding the entire front side. Simpkins had finally made a mistake and this was Wheeler's first realistic chance to help the team. Instead of coming through in the clutch, Wheeler hit his ugliest shot of the day, a fat iron shot that left a foot-long divot and sent the clod of dirt almost as far as the ball traveled, which was barely past the ladies' tee.

Hunter had to refrain from laughing at the awkward, almost comical, shot while Wheeler cussed up a storm walking down the front of the tee to hit the ball with the same club. Wheeler sculled his next shot over the green out into the woods, effectively giving Hunter and Dr. Hockman the hole, particularly after each of them two-putted for par.

Hunter realized Wheeler took winning and losing seriously as Wheeler sat in stony silence as they drove in the cart across the road to the tenth tee. Hunter was afraid he may have missed his chance to bring up Ben Johnson's case and changing Medi-Most's protocol regarding vascular surgery. But a couple of holes later, both of which were won by Simpkins who had been properly motivated by the icy stare of his boss, Wheeler started a conversation of his own. As the golf cart rambled down the twelfth fairway, Wheeler spoke to Hunter.

"Are you a religious man, Dr. Davis?" Wheeler inquired of Hunter.

Hunter, somewhat surprised by the tack of the conversation, responded, "I don't always go to church regularly, but I do consider myself religious, or at least spiritual."

"As a man of science, what do you think happens to people when they die?" continued Wheeler as they made their way to their balls in the fairway.

"Do you mean is there a heaven or a hell?" Hunter asked of Wheeler in response to Wheeler's question.

Wheeler nodded affirmatively.

"Well, I guess we will all find out for ourselves one day," responded Hunter.

"Do you believe in the circle of life, that some animals must perish for the survival of others?" Wheeler continued in a line of questioning that puzzled Hunter.

"Well, I guess so," Hunter responded. Then Hunter quickly added, "If not, God would have made all animals, including humans, vegetarians, wouldn't he?"

Wheeler laughed at Hunter's quip, as he ambled out of the cart to his shot. After Wheeler had hit his usual horrific shot, he plopped back down into the golf cart.

"Do you believe in medical euthanasia?" Wheeler asked of Hunter nonchalantly.

"Well, part of the Hippocratic Oath that doctors take upon graduation states, 'Above all else, do no harm.' So with that in mind, I do not believe in euthanasia except in extreme circumstances," responded Hunter.

"What if a patient is completely brain-dead and only breathing with the help of a ventilator? Wouldn't it be better to spend the health-care dollars on somebody, for example, that needs a liver transplant, rather than keeping this shell of a human being alive?" queried Wheeler, looking over at Hunter as the cart arrived at Hunter's ball.

Hunter continued the conversation as he got out of the cart to hit his ball.

"Well, if the patient didn't have any brain response and couldn't breathe on his own, and the family was in agreement, then I would allow the patient to be disconnected from the ventilator, causing his demise," Hunter answered.

Hunter hit his shot, which hooked into the sand trap just to the left of the green.

"Darn," said Hunter, wondering if Wheeler was trying to distract him from his game in order the win the bet.

Hunter got back into the cart to travel to Wheeler's third shot on the par-four, in which he still had one hundred yards to the green.

"But what if the patient is a widower with two sons, and one son wants him to be disconnected from the ventilator and the other son does not. What do you do then?" asked Wheeler.

"Well, if you adhere to the Hippocratic Oath, you would err on the conservative side and abide by the wishes of the son who did not want his father to be disconnected from the ventilator," answered Hunter.

"But what if the HMO had a protocol for handling such cases? Wouldn't that make it easier for the doctors to relieve them of that burden?" Wheeler asked as he chunked another shot well short of the green.

"I'm not sure I'm ready to abdicate those kinds of decisions to the HMO," responded Hunter.

Wheeler looked over at Hunter as he sat back down in the cart and said, "You already did. You did that when you signed up to work for us."

Hunter, feeling kind of sheepish now, decided to take a different tack.

"But what if the protocol is wrong? Don't the doctors have some input?" asked Hunter as they finally reached the green.

"Yes, they do have some input, but the protocol is mainly determined by the medical director in conjunction with the HMO officers."

Hunter let the conversation die momentarily while he blasted out of the sand trap to about four feet and then eventually making the putt for a par to tie Simpkins on the hole. Wheeler meanwhile, already lying four at the front of the green, picked up his ball and put it in his pocket, saying to put him down for a five on the score card.

Playing golf with someone can determine a lot about that person's character, and Hunter came to the conclusion that Wheeler was definitely someone who liked to bend the rules to his own advantage. On the way to the tee on the next hole, Hunter continued the conversation.

"I have a patient, Ben Johnson, that's in the hospital with a stroke because of Medi-Most protocol," reported Hunter.

"How so?" inquired Wheeler.

"Ben had carotid artery stenosis and had a five-week delay on his surgery because Dr. Snead's schedule was so backed up since he has to do all the vascular surgery for all the hospitals," replied Hunter. "Ben then had a stroke before he made it to his scheduled surgery," Hunter added. "Wouldn't it have been cheaper to treat the underlying problem in a more timely manner than to incur the expensive hospital stay that will now occur?" continued Hunter, trying to make his point.

"You are quite correct but hindsight is 20/20, and we are aware that Dr. Snead is slightly overworked. But we haven't found it in our budget to hire another vascular surgeon. And besides, we would rather have one vascular surgeon working at one hundred and ten percent capacity than two vascular surgeons working at fifty-five percent capacity," responded Wheeler.

"But we are talking about people's lives here," replied Hunter incredulously.

"Yes, of course, but if we try to save everyone, the costs are tremendous. Somebody has to decide when trying to save that small percent of the population becomes too expensive. Doctors, as is their nature, want to save everyone. Every patient is a personal challenge. Doctors hate to lose even one battle. Therefore, it is up to the HMO to make those decisions based on what is the best allocation of the contributed health-care dollars for their population of patients. Besides, if the HMO has a rigid protocol, it relieves the doctor of making those tough decisions, making his job easier, don't you think?" Wheeler asked, concluding his argument.

Hunter thought to himself that Wheeler would make a good debate team member because he knew how to manipulate the conversation to his advantage. Hunter wanted to respond that the protocol did not make his job easier but instead felt like shackles on his decision making. Hunter, however, did not want to rile his purported boss and had always felt that more could be accomplished by friendly persuasion than confrontation. Hunter, therefore, replied meekly, "I guess so."

The men turned their attention back to golf. After losing the first two holes on the back side to go two down and evoking the automatic two-down press, Hunter and Hockman had tied Simpkins on the rest of the holes, until Hunter won the seventeenth hole with a birdie. Wheeler, as usual, had been a non-factor.

Now, as the men stood on the eighteenth tee, Hunter and Hockman were one up on the press and one down on the original back-nine bet. All four men hit safely into the fairway on their drives, even Wheeler's ball finding the fairway for a change. Wheeler hit his second shot first on the par-four finishing hole since he still had two hundred yards to transverse and the other three golfers were fifty yards ahead of him. Somehow, Wheeler made solid contact with his three-wood and the ball made it on the green about twenty feet from the hole. The other three men, including Hunter, missed the green with their iron shots. Simpkins hooked his into the tall grass just left of the green. Hunter's ball went over the green into a small swell just behind the green. Hockman's ball ended up on the tall mound just to the right of the green.

Hockman was the first to try to chip to the green. Hockman's ball had nestled down in the long grass on the mound, and Hockman also had an uncomfortable downhill stance hitting to a green that ran away from him. Hockman took a swipe at the ball, went under it, and only moved the ball about four feet. Cussing, Dr. Hockman moved around and took a powerful jab at the ball sending the ball scurrying over the green. Simpkins hit next, doing a good job of getting his ball out of the tall grass to about eight feet from the hole. Hunter was in the short grass in a low swell behind the green and had a relatively easy chip back to the hole. Hunter made the shot and the ball come to a stop only three feet from the hole.

Hockman, still muttering, walked over to his ball and picked it up and put it in his pocket, knowing that Hunter's chip rendered him out of the bet for the hole.

Wheeler was the first to putt of the three men who were left in the match. Wheeler's putt from twenty feet away rolled to within six inches from the hole and Wheeler jubilantly waltzed up and tapped the ball into the hole. Wheeler proudly picked up his ball from out of the hole and looked over at Simpkins' eight-footer left for par.

"That's good," Wheeler told Simpkins, referring to Simpkins' eight-foot par putt that was now irrelevant thanks to Wheeler's only par of the day. Simpkins grudgingly picked up his ball, not appreciating Wheeler's smugness after carrying him all day long.

Now, it was Hunter's turn to putt. If he made his putt for par, tying the hole, Hunter and Hockman would still lose the back-side bet but win the press bet to go along with their win on the front-side bet, making them overall winners for the day. If Hunter missed the putt, Hunter and Hockman would tie the press bet and lose the back-side bet, making everybody even because Hunter and Hockman had won the front-side bet.

Hunter carefully lined up the putt and rolled the ball on its way. The ball just missed the right side of the cup and slid past the hole.

"I knew he couldn't take the pressure," Wheeler crowed, smiling broadly. You would have thought Wheeler had won the Masters single-handedly, instead of winning one hole of an insignificant ten-dollar Nassau bet.

Hunter walked over to congratulate Wheeler and shake hands with him. Wheeler shook hands and pounded Hunter on the back, telling him not to feel too bad about losing the last hole. Hunter also shook hands with Hockman and thanked him for inviting him to play as they walked back to their carts. As Wheeler shook hands with Simpkins on the green—loudly reporting that he had saved Simpkins' butt by winning the last hole, conveniently forgetting that Simpson had carried the first seventeen holes for the team—Hockman asked Hunter a question in a low voice.

"You missed that last putt on purpose, didn't you, kid?" asked Hockman.

Hunter didn't respond verbally, but gave Hockman a little wink and a grin.

Hockman let out a laugh and said, "You're learning how the game is played now, aren't you, boy?"

Hunter didn't say anything, but Hockman was obviously pleased and slapped Hunter on the back and invited him to come in to the members-only bar and have a drink. As much as Hunter wanted to go into the plush bar and feel like a bigwig, he didn't think he could stand the company of these men any longer. He also wanted to get a good night's rest before his date with Savannah the next day, so Hunter politely declined, even after Wheeler joined in with a plea of his own. Hunter left the course feeling despondent that he hadn't been able to accomplish more on Ben Johnson's behalf. But at least Hunter knew who his bosses were now and they knew him. And maybe he would be able to lobby them harder for changes on subsequent meetings down the road.

Chapter Eight

Hunter's convertible pulled up at Savannah's apartment exactly at eleven-thirty Saturday morning. With the directions Hunter had received from Rosa, he had no trouble finding Savannah's apartment. Savannah lived in one half of a duplex on First Avenue, which was one block away from the beach. There was no garage, so Hunter recognized Savannah's car in front of the duplex and pulled in behind her car.

Hunter was a little nervous as he walked to the front door. Due to Hunter's hectic week he hadn't bothered to call Savannah to confirm their date. He had just assumed they had firmly set everything up at the picnic last week. Hunter was berating himself for not calling during the week at all when the door flung open and Savannah came out with a gorgeous smile on her face. Hunter caught just a glimpse of a young man sitting on the couch in Savannah's living room before the door closed again.

"Hi, Hunter," said Savannah giving him a little peck on the cheek, "I've been looking forward to this all week."

"So have I," said Hunter, only now realizing how true his statement was as they turned to walk toward his car.

"Nice car," said Savannah, admiring Hunter's new Z3 as they walked past her old Pontiac Sunbird.

"A graduation present to myself," said Hunter, reading Savannah's mind, as he opened the door for her. Savannah slid her lithe body into the front seat.

"Let's stir up a breeze," said Hunter as he cranked the ignition, bringing the BMW to life. The summer sun had already raised the temperature to the mid-nineties and since the sea breeze had not yet started up, the hot, humid air made sitting still uncomfortable.

"Good idea," responded Savannah, smiling at Hunter.

Hunter threw the gear shift into reverse and backed out of the driveway. Soon the BMW had reached the beach road. Hunter turned left and headed north, back towards his house. As the car made its way up the beach road Hunter asked, "Who was that guy in your house?"

"Oh, that was my brother, Darrell," said Savannah. "Darrell has been having a hard time lately so I'm letting him stay with me," explained Savannah. "Darrell is nineteen and he has been going to the community college while working part-time at the Ritz-Carlton, doing valet parking. Darrell hasn't been doing well in school, however, because he has been making good money at the Ritz and then going out at night with his friends, drinking and partying. My parents got fed up with his poor grades and his coming home in the early morning hours and kicked him out of the house. So Darrell has been staying with me temporarily until he can find a place of his own. I have been talking to Darrell about how important an education is to his future and that he will not want to park cars all his life. But Darrell's young and has money in his pocket, and it's amazing how much he makes in tips at the Ritz-Carlton. So far, it's been like talking to a brick wall. Darrell just doesn't listen. Hey, maybe when we get back you can talk to him since you've had so much education."

"Oh, no, we're five minutes into our first date and you're trying to get me to help you with a family problem," responded Hunter, laughing. "I don't know about this!" Hunter added with a smile.

Savannah smiled at Hunter seductively and Hunter realized that this was a woman used to getting her way and that he would probably comply with her wishes. Savannah's brother was probably the only man on this island immune to her charms. Hunter admired the fact that Savannah had taken in her brother and was trying to play mother to him. The thought crossed Hunter's mind that these attributes might make Savannah a good wife and mother to her own children one day, and Hunter was shocked at himself for thinking this way about a woman he barely knew.

Hunter reached the red light at Atlantic Avenue and then turned left onto Atlantic and went about one-quarter of a mile until he reached the entrance to the park. Then Hunter pulled up to the park ranger station, paid the $3.25 admission, and drove forward into the park. The road from the park entrance to Fort Clinch is a unique road. First, the road is very serpentine as it winds its way through the overgrown dune structures. In Florida, most roads are fairly straight due to the flatness of the terrain, but during the road's course of several miles, there are only a couple of straight-aways where one car could pass another. Secondly, the trees have grown over the road to form a canopy that gave the effect of driving through a tunnel formed by foliage. The Spanish moss, an epiphyte or air plant that forms long, gray festoons that hang from limbs of the giant oak trees, contributes to the romantic mood of the drive. Neither a moss nor Spanish in origin, this air plant belongs to the pineapple family and thrives in areas of high humidity and rain, such as the swamps and coasts along the lower Atlantic and Gulf of Mexico, and was once used as stuffing for mattresses and furniture. It is a very scenic and shady drive, and Hunter and Savannah were enjoying the respite from the sun and the wind on their hair. The secondary dune system would occasionally give way to a view of the primary sand dunes to the right or to a view of the marshy creek to the left as they drove slowly down the road, keeping under the twenty-five-mile-an-hour speed limit.

As Hunter and Savannah drove down the meandering road, Hunter regaled Savannah with stories of how when he was a boy he and his friends would ride their bikes into the back entrance to the park via the Fourteenth Street bridge. This access was blocked to vehicular traffic but it was no problem for a boy on his bike to sneak in the park. The only problem was if the park rangers caught you in the park without a sticker on your bike proving admission to the park, they would escort you out of the park. This cat-and-mouse game with the park rangers just heightened the adventure for Hunter and his friends, and they would routinely sneak into the park. Once inside the park, there were several options available to the boys. The youngsters could go to the campground area on the Amelia River, which offered great climbing trees, tall sand dunes to run up and down, and fishing opportunities. The boys could also go to the Willow Pond area, which was a swampy algae-covered pond complete with alligators and the occasional otter.

Sometimes the boys would go to Egan's Creek, near their neighborhood, catch some fiddler crabs, and then ride their bikes into the park and head for the jetties to go fishing. The jetties were large boulders or jettisons that were brought in to line the north and south end of the entrance to Cumberland Sound. The Cumberland Sound is the body of water that separates Amelia Island on the south with Cumberland Island on the north and connects the Atlantic Ocean to the Amelia River. The big rocks started at the south tip of Cumberland Island and the north tip of Amelia Island and extended in a line due eastward into the Atlantic Ocean for about half a mile to keep the shifting sand out of the channel.

An adventuresome boy could climb out unto the barnacle-and-oyster-encrusted rocks with a cane pole in hand and, using the fiddler crabs for bait, catch sheepshead, a variety of fish that hangs around the rocks. The boys had to pay attention to the tides, however, fishing mostly around the low tides when the rocks were best exposed. Due to the seven-foot tide variance between low and high tide, if the boys didn't head back to shore soon enough to beat the incoming tide they could find themselves stranded on the high rocks with the lower spots submerged. Swimming back to shore was out of the question due to the treacherous currents and waves pounding the sharp rocks, so if you were stranded you had a long wait until the tide went out again. The boys also had to wear tennis shoes to protect their feet from the barnacles and oyster shells, so even if the tide didn't catch them, one slip on the algae-covered rocks could lead to a painful gash on the sharp crustaceans and a long, painful bike ride home.

The boys' favorite option, however, was to ride straight to the five-sided, Civil War-era fort that overlooks Cumberland Sound. The fort, located at the extreme north end of Amelia Island and surrounded by the 1,121-acre state park, is composed entirely of brick and came complete with a moat, a draw bridge, rifle ports, cannons and a two-story bastion on the end of each of the five points. The boys would divide up into two teams and play a form of hide-and-seek in which one team would try to capture the other. If you were tagged by the seeking team then you had to go and sit in the old jail, which was a four-cell jail complete with bars. A player could be released from jail by a tag from one of his teammates if that teammate could get in and out of the jail without being tagged himself. There were hundreds of hiding places in the fort, and the game would sometimes last hours. There were long chases along the top of the brick walls, up and down stairs, and through the numerous hallways and tunnels. The boys would be almost too exhausted by the end of the day to ride their bikes home.

Savannah had been almost mesmerized by Hunter's stories and the sunlight filtering through the tree canopy. As Hunter's story came to a close, their car burst out into the bright sunlight as they came out of the tree-lined road and entered the wide-open space of the fort's parking lot. After Hunter's story, Savannah was teeming with anticipation, for although her family had moved to Fernandina from Waycross, Georgia when Savannah was in high school, she never before had visited the fort. Even though it was a gloriously sunny day, there were only four cars in the parking lot, probably due to the heat. Hunter knew the sea breeze would kick in soon, so he suggested they have their picnic first, in the shaded picnic area on the other side of the parking area away from the fort.

Hunter parked his car near the picnic area and they unloaded their picnic items. The picnic area was a short walk through the woods into a hollow surrounded by wooded secondary dunes with large oak trees. The picnic area consisted of several tables and a couple of swing sets in the flat area at the bottom of a natural amphitheater formed by the overgrown dunes. A tree canopy provided complete shade from the grueling summer sun. There was no one there, and Hunter and Savannah chose a table and began to spread the tablecloth.

"Looks like we have the place to ourselves," said Hunter. Then Hunter added, "I brought a little something to quench our thirst."

Hunter reached into the bottom of the small cooler he had brought and pulled out a bottle of wine, knowing it was against park rules to have alcohol on the premises.

"Still hiding from the park rangers, are you?" responded Savannah, as they both laughed.

After Hunter had poured them a cup of wine, Savannah offered a mock toast, "To the rangers."

"To the rangers!" responded Hunter.

Savannah and Hunter had a leisurely lunch, sipping wine and laughing. No park rangers or other picnickers arrived to disturb their privacy. After lunch, Hunter showed Savannah a huge oak tree with large horizontal branches that was perfect for climbing that Hunter had discovered as a young boy during picnics with his parents.

With her long legs and fueled by the wine, Savannah scrambled up the tree. Hunter stood initially admiring Savannah as she climbed the tree, then he followed her example. Soon they each had settled into a comfortable nook in the tree and rested after their big meal. Hunter remarked that they looked like leopards, hanging out in trees to take advantage of the cool breeze after a big meal. At this higher altitude, Hunter noticed that the sea breeze was starting to kick in.

After a brief but beneficial rest, Hunter and Savannah gathered up the picnic items, tossed them into the trunk of the car and headed for the fort. Savannah found that the fort was all that Hunter said it was. Hunter showed Savannah the old jail, the barracks, and the old-fashioned kitchen. Hunter then took Savannah on a guided tour of the rest of fort, pointing out all of the old hiding places. After awhile Hunter said, "Come on, Savannah, I want to show you the best view on Amelia Island."

Savannah followed Hunter from the flat, grassy field in the center of the fort through a tunnel in the earthen berm that lines the interior walls of the fort and on top of which sits the cannon.

At the end of the tunnel they came to the northwest bastion. A bastion was a two-story, five-sided extension at each of the points of the five-sided fort. On the bottom floor were four small cannons on wooden carriages with rollers facing sideways out of the bastion. At the most outward point of the bastion was a windowless, triangular-shaped powder room used for storing the powder to fire the cannons. A brick spiral staircase connected the bottom floor to the open-air top floor. The top floor had been designed to hold one large cannon and also to give riflemen an angle on attackers trying to scale the walls between each bastion. It was the view from the top of the bastion that Hunter wanted Savannah to see, so they climbed the spiral staircase. Hunter let Savannah go first so she would get the first, unobstructed view as they reached the top of the spiral staircase. At the top, Savannah ran toward the point to get the full effect of the view. Savannah jumped up to the flat, elevated position at the point of the bastion. The wind was really blowing now as the sea breeze had picked up to its usual fifteen to twenty knots. Savannah stood there, like at the bow of a boat, looking in every direction.

Hunter stood admiring the view of Savannah admiring the view of the surroundings. The sun glistened off Savannah's blond hair as she portrayed the wonderment of a child on Christmas morning seeing the presents under the tree.

After awhile, Hunter stepped up beside Savannah and began pointing out the sights. To the right was the Atlantic Ocean and the jetties lining the entrance into Cumberland Sound. Straight ahead was Cumberland Sound with its endless parade of shrimp boats and pleasure boats headed to and from the ocean. On the far side of Cumberland Sound was the south end of Cumberland Island. Hunter pointed out the wild horses that usually are present, grazing on the vegetation near the beach. To the left the Cumberland Sound splits into the Amelia River to the south, St. Mary's River to the west, and the Cumberland River to the north. Behind Hunter and Savannah to the south was a view of treetops and sand dunes of the state park.

"Oh, thank you, Hunter for dragging me out here," explained Savannah. "I've lived here for six years and have never been out here," Savannah added. Savannah turned to Hunter and kissed him. The kiss was just a peck on the cheek, but Hunter had put his arm around Savannah and did not immediately let her go. Hunter gazed into Savannah's eyes for a second or two, then they really kissed. It may have been the wine or salt air, but their kiss was a prolonged, passionate kiss for all the world to see.

Hunter released his embrace and said sheepishly, "I'm sorry if that was too forward."

"No, I quite enjoyed it, Dr. Davis," said Savannah coyly. Then Savannah added, "I look forward to further collaborations in the future."

Hunter felt quite reassured by this last statement for he was beginning to feel quite smitten by Savannah and it was nice to hear the feelings were probably mutual.

"Come on, Savannah, I've got one last thing to show you," said Hunter mysteriously. Hunter and Savannah descended the spiral staircase down to the bottom floor of the bastion. Hunter led Savannah over to a cannon port that overlooked the land.

"Legend has it," Hunter began as he placed Savannah in front of him so she could peer out of the port, "that the pirate, Luis Aury, buried some treasure on Amelia Island at the base of a large oak tree shaped like a cross. If you look carefully out of this cannon port you should be able to see an oak tree shaped like a cross," informed Hunter. Savannah studied the numerous trees visible through the port, but none of them resembled a cross to her.

"I don't see any trees shaped like a cross," said Savannah in exasperation as she turned to Hunter, but Hunter was nowhere to be seen.

Savannah whirled around to try and locate Hunter, but it was as if he disappeared. Savannah peered down the tunnel leading back to the center of the fort, but it was too long for Hunter to have traversed in so short a time. Also, if Hunter had gone up the spiral staircase Savannah would have heard him. That left only one other option. Savannah walked toward the doorway of the powder room. It was doorless, and there was a step up at the bottom of the doorway. Savannah stepped up and peered into the room but since it was windowless, it was like peering into a black hole. Savannah took one step inside to let her eyes adjust to the light. After about ten or fifteen seconds her eyes were beginning to adjust, but the room still appeared to be featureless. All of a sudden a form sprung toward her from off a ledge, growling. Savannah screamed and jumped in the air.

Hunter started laughing as he tried to comfort Savannah. Savannah pushed him away and said, "You scared me!"

"I'm sorry," said Hunter. Then Hunter explained that as boys they would hide on the ledge and wait for some unsuspecting tourist to poke their head into the dark room. Then the boys would jump off the ledge growling. The tourists would always jump, scream, and run, usually in that order. It was amazing that the boys' actions never caused a heart attack. It was even more amazing that none of the men they scared ever came back and beat them up. But since it was so dark, none of the people were sure of what or who was exactly in there, so they ran away and did not return.

Suddenly, Hunter's pager went off. Hunter was startled by the sound and jumped noticeably. Savannah laughed at Hunter for the small payback he received after startling her.

"Damn, not again," said Hunter as he pulled a small cell phone from his back pocket and dialed the number displayed by the pager as he walked toward the center of the room. After a brief conversation with a nurse at the hospital, Hunter ended the conversation by pressing the "end" button on his cell phone.

"It's the hospital," Hunter informed Savannah with a blank look on his face. "It's about Ben Johnson. He's dead."

"What happened?" asked Savannah.

"They don't know," responded Hunter. "The head nurse said Ben was still unconscious but everything was stable, then he went into cardiac arrest."

"Who was on duty?" asked Savannah.

"Vickie and Kay," said Hunter.

"They're good," said Savannah, shaking her head over the tragedy.

"Yes, Vickie assured me they worked on him vigorously, but to no avail," responded Hunter dejectedly.

Savannah and Hunter were standing near each other just inside the doorway of powder room where there was enough light to see each other faces. Savannah turned to Hunter and reached out to him to comfort him. Savannah and Hunter embraced, their bodies fitting together like two pieces of a puzzle. Hunter, who only seconds before had been totally dejected over Ben Johnson's passing, now felt a wonderful warm feeling overcome him. The young couple embraced for a long time, then they loosened their hold on each other and stood face to face. Hunter's temporary warm feeling was now slowly being replaced by anger over his belief that Ben's tragedy could have been prevented.

"I need to go to the hospital," said Hunter blankly.

"I understand," said Savannah.

Chapter Nine

Fifteen minutes after dropping Savannah off at her house, Hunter strode purposefully toward the automatic doors that the ambulance uses to bring patients into the emergency room. Hunter found that this was the quickest entranceway from his parking space into the hospital. The emergency room personnel didn't like him using the entranceway because the swoosh of the automatic doors opening always startled them, thinking it was an emergency. Hunter was walking so fast that he had to pause to give the doors a chance to open, then he walked briskly through the doorway into the side entrance of the emergency room. The emergency room personnel looked up apprehensively. Relieved that it wasn't an emergency, but annoyed at the interruption, the nurses and attendants returned to their work.

Hunter quickly walked through the emergency room area, down the hall, past the X-ray area, toward the nurses' station. At the nurses' station, Hunter saw several nurses working. Hunter spotted Vickie Jackson and approached her.

"Hi, Vickie," said Hunter to the perky young nurse with her curly hair pulled back into a ponytail. Hunter did not know Vickie that well, but knew she had a reputation as a competent nurse.

"Oh, Dr. Davis," responded Vickie, "I am so sorry about Mr. Johnson. I don't know what happened," said Vickie with a baffled look on her face. "Mr. Johnson was stable and everything was fine and then his monitor alarm went off. When we got there he was flat-lined. We called Dr. Braziz and tried defibrillation but there was no response. We did all we could, but maybe he had a massive coronary."

"Well, I'm sure you did everything possible," said Hunter. Then Hunter asked, "Where's Mr. Johnson's chart?"

"It's right over here," said Vickie helpfully.

Hunter took the chart, sat down in a nearby chair, and started flipping through the pages. Hunter arrived at the progress notes of what had transpired earlier. Hunter studied them carefully and came to the same conclusion Vickie had earlier. The same atherosclerotic disease that caused Ben's first stroke must have affected one of his coronary arteries inducing a massive heart attack and there was no chance to revive him. An autopsy might reveal some answers but Hunter would have to convince the family it was necessary. Hunter came to the conclusion it probably wasn't worth putting the family through that just to satisfy his own curiosity.

"Where is Ben's body?" Hunter asked Vickie.

"The funeral home people have already retrieved it," answered Vickie. Well, that settles it, Hunter thought to himself. Hunter also reluctantly came to the conclusion that it may have been a blessing that Ben had the heart attack and died because there was no guarantee his neurological state was going to improve after the stroke, and Hunter knew an independent man like Ben Johnson wouldn't want to live in a dependent, severely handicapped state. Satisfied that everything possible had been done, Hunter thanked Vickie and walked back down the hall toward the parking lot.

Hunter glanced at his watch and saw that it was getting too late to resume his date with Savannah. Hunter decided he would call her when he got home and apologize again for the interruption and ask her out for the next weekend. The smell of Savannah's hair and the feel of her embrace came drifting over Hunter's consciousness like a warm cloud. Hunter quickened his step as he went down the hallway because he couldn't wait to call Savannah and hear her voice.

Just then Hunter heard a voice, but it wasn't Savannah's sweet tones. Instead, it was the gruff voice of a stranger.

"You're Dr. Davis, ain't ya?" said a weathered old geezer who was mopping one side of the hallway.

"Yes, I am," said Hunter, slowing down in his gait but still impatient to get to his car.

"I was sorry to hear about Ben Johnson," continued the old man as Hunter stopped beside him. "You know, old Ben and me used to work the turpentine together when we was young men. Ben worked hard, but he liked to party hard also. I guess Ben will have to play in heaven now, or hell, or wherever he ended up."

Hunter nodded at the old man and muttered as he turned to leave, "I guess so."

The old man spoke again, "You know, it ain't none of my business, but there seems to be an awful lot of old folks that come here to this hospital only to leave by way of the funeral home," said the old man. Hunter didn't know what the man was getting at with that last statement nor did he care as he was impatient to leave.

"I'm sorry about your friend. I'm just as disappointed as you are. Now if you will excuse me, I'll be on my way," said Hunter with a tired tone in his voice.

Now Hunter was really depressed and he couldn't wait to hear Savannah's sweet voice.

Chapter Ten

The next week went quickly for Hunter. In order to make up for the previous weekend's disappointment of having to end their date unexpectedly, Hunter promised Savannah a trip to Cumberland Island by private boat during the day, followed by dinner back on Amelia Island that night. Hunter had been busy this week not only with his patients, but also making preparations for the weekend. First, to prevent any interruptions, Hunter arranged for one of the other doctors on staff to take his emergency calls. Second, Hunter had called on an old high school friend of his, Dan Taylor. Dan was a local real-estate agent who had done well for himself and among his many possessions was a twenty-two-foot Boston Whaler boat. Dan magnanimously agreed to lend Hunter his boat with the only stipulations being that Hunter would clean it up afterwards and refill the gas tank so the boat would be ready for Dan's next spur-of-the-moment boat outing.

Hunter picked up the boat Friday night so he would be ready to go Saturday morning. Dan let Hunter use his sports utility vehicle to pull the boat, and Hunter lent Dan his convertible. Hunter had momentary second thoughts as Dan roared out of the parking lot of his real-estate office, where the two men had exchanged vehicles. Those thoughts passed quickly, however, and Hunter pulled the boat to a gas station to top off the gas tanks and then transported the boat to his house. Hunter went next to the grocery store to make sure he had all the provisions necessary for the next day.

Saturday morning dawned bright and clear. Hunter was up early making last-minute preparations. He had told Savannah to meet him at the municipal docks at nine o'clock in the morning. Hunter wanted to get an early start for two reasons: Cumberland was a big island to explore, and he also wanted to beat the afternoon thunderstorms that were prevalent this time of year.

Hunter arrived at the municipal docks and boat ramp at eight-thirty in the morning. The boat ramp was empty as most of the fishermen had already launched their boats earlier in the morning, so Hunter positioned the boat and trailer at the top of the ramp to prepare for launching. Hunter released the safety latch that held the boat to the trailer and made sure there was a bow line handy for when he launched the boat to make sure the boat did not float away. Hunter also checked to make sure the drainplug was in place at the rear part of the boat. Not replacing the drainplug before launching was a major faux pas in the boating community and a major source of embarrassment to the novice or hurried boater. Hunter transferred all of the provisions from the back of the sport utility vehicle into the boat and then bought some ice from the bait shop next to the boat ramp and put it into the cooler inside the boat in front of the center console. Hunter then got into the SUV and backed the boat and trailer down the ramp and into the water. Hunter pulled the boat over to a side dock, secured it, then drove Dan's vehicle and the empty trailer over to the designated parking lot. Hunter walked back to the boat, cranked the engine and waited for Savannah's arrival.

Savannah arrived at ten minutes to nine. Hunter smiled to himself when he spotted Savannah's car. Being on time or even early was a trait Hunter valued dearly, so Savannah's timely arrival endeared her to him even more. Savannah herself soon appeared, bouncing down the dock eager with anticipation.

"Ahoy, captain," Savannah said as she approached the boat.

"Ahoy, matey," answered Hunter.

"Request permission to board your vessel," inquired Savannah coyly.

"Permission granted," responded Hunter, following Savannah's cue with fake formality.

Hunter extended his hand to Savannah to assist her aboard. Hunter noticed Savannah was wearing a white mesh cover-up over a red bikini top and a pair of short cut-off jeans. Savannah also had on a pair of plain white tennis shoes, sunglasses and an old baseball cap with her hair in a ponytail out of the back of the cap. She was carrying a large beach bag. Savannah took Hunter's hand, put one foot on the boat's rail and jumped into the boat right beside Hunter. Savannah leaned forward, gave Hunter a peck on the cheek and said, "Captain, I'm at your command."

"Good," responded Hunter matter-of-factly, trying to play his part. "Then stow you gear forward in the cubby cabin so it won't get wet and I'll get the lines."

Savannah put away her gear as Hunter unsecured the lines holding the boat to the dock. Savannah stole a glance over at Hunter as he knelt over the stern of the boat unsecuring the line from the cleat. Hunter was wearing only a baggy bathing suit, boat shoes, a cap, and sunglasses. Savannah admired his strong, muscular back as Hunter struggled to get the line from around the cleat. After stowing away the gear and untying the lines, Hunter and Savannah both sat side by side in the swivel seats behind the center console of the boat. Hunter put the transmission in reverse and backed carefully away from the dock. Once clear of the dock and pointed in the right direction, Hunter put the transmission in forward and they idled out of the marina.

"It's a shame the marina has filled in like it has," said Hunter, pointing to the many boat slips that are unusable because silt and mud has rendered them worthless. Hunter went on to explain how the city had built a beautiful new marina several years ago complete with concrete floating docks and a long breakwater to replace the dilapidated, old wooden dock that had preceded the present docks. The only problem was, however, that the location and configuration of the new docks did not allow a free-flowing current and over the next several years mud and silt built up in the marina, leaving about half of the slips useless at low tide. The city had taken back control of the docks from the private management firm it had originally leased it to, but even the city was having trouble obtaining the necessary permits from the appropriate state and federal regulators to resolve the problem, so the marina sat in silt-filled limbo. Fortunately, the boat ramp and path out of the marina always had enough water due to its constant use.

Savannah and Hunter exited the marina and turned north toward Cumberland Island. Hunter continued to idle north through the no-wake zone past the breakwater as Hunter and Savannah admired the large yachts docked there. Unlike the interior of the marina, the outside of the breakwater had plenty of depth due to the swift current that ran along the outside of it. This marina, with its long, outside breakwater, was a popular stop for boats traveling north or south along the intracoastal waters.

North of the marina were the shrimpboat docks, and several of the handsome white fishing boats were usually tied up there depending on the weather and the season. Further north from there was the port of Fernandina. Two large cranes were loading a container ship bound for Bermuda. The container ship seemed huge as Savannah and Hunter idled past its side in their small boat. Past the port was the paper mill with its accompanying odor. Savannah wrinkled her nose up at the smell.

Hunter laughed at Savannah and said over the noise of the engine, "My father used to work there. Whenever the wind would blow the wrong way and the smell would engulf our house, and we'd start complaining, my father would just breath deeply and say, 'It smells like money.'"

Past the paper mill was the entrance to Egan's Creek. On the other side of Egan's Creek was the dilapidated pogey plant. In its heyday, the pogey plant would send out boats with long nets to catch pogey fish. Pogey fish, or Menenhaden, as they are more correctly termed, are a particularly oily fish. The fish would then be brought back to the plant to be ground up and their by-products used in oils, perfume, and fertilizer.

"If you think the smell from the paper mill is bad, you should have smelled the pogey plant before it shut down," Hunter told Savannah over the engine noise. Savannah smiled and nodded her head knowingly since she had already heard from locals about the particularly rancid smell.

Past the pogey plant was the western border of Fort Clinch State Park and the northern end of Amelia Island. Hunter told

73

Savannah to hold on as he pushed the throttle forward. The boat accelerated across Cumberland Sound as Hunter pointed the bow of the boat toward the back side of Cumberland Island. Hunter asked Savannah if she had ever been to Cumberland Island, and she replied that she had not ever had the opportunity since it was only accessible by boat. Hunter reported to Savannah that he had spent the summer after his first year of medical school working as a first mate on a forty-four-foot charter sailboat, and that one of the favorite things to do with the passengers was to visit Cumberland Island, so Hunter was quite familiar with the island.

Hunter explained to Savannah that Cumberland was a big island, bigger than Amelia Island. Most of the island was a National Park now, and—except for the approximately three hundred people brought over for the day by the park service's ferry—was inhabited only by turkey, deer, and wild horses. In the 1800s, most of Cumberland Island was owned by several well-known industrialist families, including the Rockefellers and the Carnegies. Over the years, the Carnegies and their descendants built three large mansions on the island. Two of the mansions, Greyfield and Plum Orchard, were still standing today, explained Hunter, but the third mansion, the Dungeness, was mostly destroyed in the 1950s by a fire. As local legend has it, the fire was set in retribution because the caretaker shot and wounded a local who was poaching deer off the island.

Hunter wanted to show Savannah all three mansions since she had never been to the island before. The Dungeness ruins were the southernmost, Hunter explained, and they would visit there first. Hunter pointed the bow of the boat toward the National Park Service's dock, which was up the river on the back side of the island. The National Park Service would let you tie up at their dock for free, as long as you didn't block where the ferry docks. Hunter found an appropriate spot, and after wrapping the boat's lines securely around the dock's cleats, Hunter and Savannah disembarked for the one-half mile walk through the forest to the Dungeness ruins.

After about a twenty-minute walk, Hunter and Savannah arrived at the Dungeness. The large mansion had been built of coquina, a mixture of mud and coquina shells, which are prevalent on the beach. Therefore, although the roof and interior had burned, the walls were left mostly standing, leaving a monument to the former mansion. A large grassy field separated the mansion from the forest. Hunter and Savannah walked up the path that led from the forest to the front of the old mansion. The young couple scaled a low wall for a better look. The large grassy field was surrounded by woods on three sides, but to the south was a marsh, with a view toward Amelia Island.

"This is beautiful," Savannah remarked as she took in the view.

"It's quite a setting," answered Hunter. "Come on, let me show you the pool house," Hunter said excitedly.

Beside the mansion was a large, wooden structure that had not burned in the fire but was slowly falling down on its own accord due to neglect. Hunter and Savannah carefully peered through a small window into the interior of the building. Although the roof was partially caved in, Hunter and Savannah could see the large indoor swimming pool that was located inside the building. The completely tile-lined swimming pool was devoid of water, except for the rainwater that had collected at the bottom. Savannah marveled at the grandeur of what this place must have been in its time in this remote location.

Savannah and Hunter explored the grounds. The young couple visited a small cemetery near the marsh. Hunter pointed out that one of the inhabitants was "Lighthorse" Harry Lee of Revolutionary War fame. Then Hunter and Savannah walked over to another graveyard of sorts. Underneath some large oak trees were the rusting hulks of old cars. Ten or so automobiles from the twenties, thirties and forties lay in their final resting spots. After thoroughly canvassing the area, Hunter and Savannah headed back to the boat.

Next Hunter wanted to show Savannah the Greyfield Inn, but from a distance, because Greyfield Inn was still privately owned by the descendents of the Carnegie family and run as an inn. Greyfield was built in 1901 as a home for Lucy and Thomas Carnegie's daughter, Margaret Ricketson. In the 1960s, Greyfield was opened as an inn by Margaret's daughter, Lucy Ferguson, and her family. Hunter had been to Greyfield several times back when he helped charter the sailboat. The charter captains would arrange with Greyfield Inn for a private lunch or dinner. Hunter and his captain would bring the passengers over on the sailboat to the large, white mansion.

Walking up the path from the private dock, their visitors would encounter a majestic mansion complete with porches and horses' hitching posts. Entering the mansion was like entering a time capsule with everything as it was almost one hundred years ago. All of the furnishings, down to even the books in the library, date back to the turn of the century. The guests would be served mimosas and allowed to wander through the mansion with wonder. After being called to dinner, the guests would sit down to a provincial meal of heart-of-palm salad, wild rice, quail, fish, and cornbread. It was a unique experience that Hunter and the captain of the charter boat liked to share and would invariably lead to happy and fulfilled passengers on the boat ride home. Hunter regretted that he no longer knew anyone that worked there so he and Savannah could have lunched at the mansion. Hunter promised himself that after he saved some money and got to know Savannah better, he and Savannah would come over and stay at Greyfield some day.

After cruising by Greyfield slowly in the boat, Hunter and Savannah took the five- or six-mile trip north up the river to see Plum Orchard. This mansion was accessible only by boat or by a hard overland trip down a one-lane, oyster shell road from Greyfield Inn. There are no paved roads on the island.

Plum Orchard seems to appear like a mirage out of the jungle after miles of nothing but trees. It is a large, stately mansion with a huge front yard now used by the wild horses as a pasture. The scene is more reminiscent of Virginia or Kentucky and seems out of place on this barrier island, but it is a reminder of the tremendous wealth the industrialist families had to build such an elegant mansion in such a remote spot. Hunter hoped Savannah would view it with the same awe Hunter did as a ten-year-old boy when his family visited the Greyfield Inn for the first time and was given a jeep excursion around the island. On that day, after miles of riding in the jeep under the shaded tree canopy, the mansion appeared at the end of the oyster-shell road, illuminated like a dream by the brilliant sunlight, a horse grazing peacefully in the front yard. The large white stucco mansion was now owned by the Park Service and they were doing their best to restore the mansion to its original glory. The outside of the mansion had been restored at great expense, and now the Park Service was working on the interior although it was not yet open to the public.

Hunter and Savannah's day went as Hunter had hoped, with the young couple enjoying the sights and timelessness of Cumberland Island. Hunter and Savannah also were enjoying each other's company. A comfortable and playful conversation had been ongoing all day, and after Hunter had shown Savannah the Dungeness, Greyfield Inn, and Plum Orchard, Hunter turned the boat south and headed for the southern end of the island to have a picnic on the unspoiled beach. Once there, Hunter pulled the boat up on the deserted beach, and they unloaded the picnic basket and cooler onto the beach. Savannah stepped on the shore while Hunter backed the boat back to deeper water and anchored. Hunter then jumped over the side and waded to shore to join Savannah. The beach was deserted except for a family of wild horses grazing on the marsh grass down the beach. Hunter spread a blanket and he and Savannah enjoyed a wonderful picnic lunch, their appetites fueled by their explorations.

After Hunter and Savannah had sated their appetites and consumed a bottle of wine with lunch, the young couple laid side by side on the picnic blanket soaking up the sun. Hunter felt very content, his belly was full, and the wine was giving him that warm, relaxed feeling. Hunter rolled over on his side to gaze at Savannah, who was laying beside him with her eyes closed in a blissful state. Hunter allowed his eyes to wander from Savannah's feet, past her slender ankles, up the long, evenly tanned legs, past the small red triangle of her bikini bottom, over the deeply tanned stomach to those perfect breasts, rising gently with every breath, and finally to Savannah's face. Savannah's eyes were closed and her chin was raised slightly toward the sun. Hunter gazed at Savannah's sweet face, then encouraged by the wine he slowly bent over and kissed her on the lips. Savannah, startled out of her splendored state by the contact, bolted upright.

"Oh, you think you can just steal kisses, do you?" Savannah said in mock anger. "Well, you will have to catch me first," Savannah added as she took off running down the beach. Hunter jumped up quickly and gave chase. Savannah had a head start but Hunter closed the gap quickly. Savannah ran along the edge of the water weaving back and forth. When Hunter finally caught up to her, Savannah made one last desperate attempt to elude Hunter by running into deeper water. As the water became about thigh-deep, Hunter tackled Savannah and they landed softly in the water with a big splash.

Hunter pulled Savannah toward him and said, "I caught you, now you owe me a kiss."

"So I do," replied Savannah as she leaned forward.

Savannah and Hunter embraced in a long, sensuous kiss, their bodies pressed together in the warm water. Their passion might have overwhelmed them, had not a speed boat filled with young men passed by in the channel and blown its horn, startling the young couple. The men in the boat laughed and gave the thumbs-up sign. Hunter and Savannah released their embrace and Savannah, who was shaking slightly, said, "Let's go for a walk along the beach."

Savannah stood up and took Hunter's hand to assist him up. Savannah glanced down at the well-muscled man at her feet. Hunter's years of working out had given him a chiseled, well-defined form almost like that of a male model. Hunter brushed his wet hair back from his face and with a dazzling smile accepted Savannah's hand in his and pulled himself to his feet.

Hunter and Savannah spent the next hour or so exploring the beach, hand in hand, looking for shells and other artifacts that had washed up along the shore. After a while Savannah said to Hunter, "It's been a great day."

"Yes, it has," Hunter responded, his arm around Savannah's waist. "But I'm afraid I've had all the sun I need, and I don't like the way those clouds are building up to the west. I think we better head back. But if you think the day has been great, wait until you see what I've got planned for tonight."

"What makes you think that I don't already have other plans for tonight?" asked Savannah in mock indignation.

"Well, if you do have other plans, cancel them. You're my girl now," responded Hunter with feigned self-assuredness.

"Oh, is that so?" said Savannah turning to Hunter and looking into his eyes.

"Yes," said Hunter as they embraced for another kiss standing on the deserted beach.

After they released, Hunter and Savannah loaded up their picnic gear and made the short run back to city marina. It was a good thing Hunter and Savannah left when they did, because by the time they unloaded the boat and pulled the boat out of the water, the afternoon thundershowers were threatening. Hunter said good-bye to Savannah, promising to pick her up at seven o'clock, and watched her as she drove away.

Then Hunter turned his attention to cleaning up the boat. Dan liked to keep his boat spotless and Hunter wanted to return it that way. After cleaning the boat thoroughly, Hunter pulled the boat to Dan's parking lot, then drove to Dan's house to trade Dan's vehicle for his own. Hunter then hustled home to shower and shave and ready himself for his date with Savannah that night. Hunter was tired, but as he took his shower, visions of Savannah in her red bikini kept wafting through his mind, keeping him motivated and looking forward to the night ahead.

Chapter Eleven

Hunter arrived at Savannah's townhouse at precisely seven o'clock. The afternoon thunderstorm had blown through and it was beginning to clear up again. When Hunter knocked on Savannah's door, he was expecting Savannah to answer all dressed and looking beautiful, but instead Darrell opened the door, hair disheveled and a two-day stubble on his face.

"Come in," Darrell mumbled almost inaudibly, then added, "Savannah will be down after awhile."

Darrell plopped back down on the couch to continue watching television. Savannah's brother stretched out on the couch, remote clutched to his hand, so Hunter settled into a wooden chair beside the couch. Savannah's dog Snickers, a brown-and-cream-colored peek-a-poo, came out of an adjacent room and jumped into Hunter's lap. Hunter petted the dog and tried to calm the animal down as it tried to lick Hunter's face. After calming the dog down, Hunter thought briefly about the talk on responsibility that Savannah had asked Hunter to give to Darrell, but Darrell was so completely engrossed in professional wrestling that Hunter didn't think a lecture from a stranger would be a good start. Noticing a particular wrestler on the television, Hunter decided to take a different tack.

"You know, I met Goldberg one time," Hunter said, breaking the silence.

"No way, man," Darrell responded. "Goldberg is my hero."

"Yes, it was several years ago," Hunter said. "Goldberg was playing football for the University of Georgia. I was dating a cheerleader from the University of Georgia and we went to a fraternity party. Goldberg was there with some of the other players having a good time."

"What was he like?" Darrell asked, now watching Hunter with newfound interest.

"Well," said Hunter, struggling to come up with something interesting, "I remember he was huge." Knowing this would not satisfy the young man, Hunter added, "and he had hair back then."

Darrell's face broke into a smile, then said, "No kidding? I can't imagine Goldberg with hair." Then Darrell turned around, consumed by the television again.

Hunter was relieved, then awed at the sight of Savannah coming down the stairs. Savannah wore a tight-fitting yellow sun dress. Her sun-bleached hair and bronze tan made her appear nearly radiant.

"Are you boys getting along?" asked Savannah as she descended the steps.

"Uh-huh," grunted Darrell, his eyes never leaving the television screen. Then Darrell added, pointing in Hunter's direction, "He knows Goldberg."

"Oh, is that so?" said Savannah, not having the vaguest idea who or what Goldberg was, as she walked up to Hunter smiling. Hunter stood up and clasped Savannah's hands.

"You look great," said Hunter appreciatively. Savannah gave Hunter a little kiss on the cheek, then turned to Darrell.

"What are you doing tonight?" Savannah asked Darrell. But before Darrell could answer, she continued, "I bet you are going to meet up with your buddies, get some beer and ride around."

"You got it," answered Darrell smugly.

"Well, try to get home before dawn," Savannah responded sarcastically.

"Your wish is my command," said Darrell, his eyes still glued to the television.

"Come on, let's go," Savannah said to Hunter. "Bye, Snickers, I know you'll be good," said Savannah lovingly as she patted the dog on top of its head and then turned to Hunter.

Hunter put his arm around Savannah and led her outside to his car. Hunter could tell Savannah was upset about her brother's behavior as she plopped herself silently into the car. Hunter closed Savannah's car door gently, went around to the other side of the car, and stepped inside. As Hunter turned on the car's ignition, he said to Savannah, "Darrell will be alright. He's just

81

going through his wild stage, like a lot of people do at his age. Hopefully he'll grow out of it soon."

"If he lives through it," said Savannah sadly.

"Well, I had some pretty scary moments when I was young, drinking and driving, and look how I turned out," said Hunter with mock egotism.

"Well, if Darrell turns out half as good as you have, I'll be happy," said Savannah, suddenly smiling seductively. Then Savannah put one arm on Hunter's shoulder and a hand on his thigh. Hunter thought he was going to jam the accelerator to the floor when Savannah touched his thigh, but he collected himself and said, "I thought we would go to the restaurant at the Inn at Amelia Island Plantation. They have a beautiful ocean view."

"That would be wonderful. I've never been there," Savannah shouted over the wind and engine noise.

Hunter drove towards the restaurant, which was inside the resort of Amelia Island Plantation on the south end of the island. Once through the security gate, Hunter drove along the winding roads toward the Inn. Amelia Island Plantation was a beautiful resort built on a great natural setting. The resort encompassed nearly fourteen hundred acres on the south end of the island, its borders being the sea-oat-covered sand dunes and glorious beaches to the east, the Nassau Sound to the south, and the marshes of the Amelia Island River to the west.

Having a very strict, self-imposed environmental code, the Plantation was planned so that all of the condominiums and residences seemed to blend in with their natural surroundings. Even the stop signs on the streets are green instead of red in order to not be obtrusive. In spite of all the environmental concerns, the resort had managed to squeeze in fifty-four holes of golf and a tennis center that is home to a major women's tennis tournament.

Hunter was very familiar with the resort. For three summers while he was going to Mercer, Hunter had worked as a lifeguard on the beaches of the resort. Those were wonderful, carefree times for Hunter. The pay wasn't great, but the fringe benefits were wonderful. Hunter spent his days soaking up the rays on the beach and his nights chasing girls. Hunter became friendly with the other employees and soon had the run of the place, whether it was free golf, tennis, food, or drinks, which were great perks for a poor college student.

Hunter wanted to take Savannah somewhere special, and he knew the restaurant at the Inn had a panoramic view of the beach. The restaurant sat high on a secondary dune overlooking the sixth hole of the Oceanside links golf course, which ran right along the beach. The restaurant's view took in the golf hole, the beach, and the ocean.

Hunter had reserved a table for two near the window for the best view. Hunter and Savannah then proceeded to have a long, leisurely, and sumptuous meal. The sight of Savannah in the candlelight across the table from him, along with the rising moon above the ocean, enthralled Hunter. Savannah was equally enchanted by her companion. The serious and hard-working young doctor was fun and exciting away from work. The young couple laughed and joked, ate and drank. A couple of hours later after a five-course meal and a couple of bottles of wine, the couple was fully sated.

Hunter leaned back in his chair and said with a relaxed sigh, "I guess we are going to have to work off all this food."

"Oh? What did you have in mind?" Savannah asked suggestively, as she leaned forward with her eyebrow arched.

"I thought we would go dancing at the Beach Club, then take a midnight walk on the beach," Hunter responded, not knowing whether Savannah's forwardness was feigned or serious.

"That sounds fun," said Savannah merrily, the wine starting to make her a little giddy. Hunter paid the bill and they made the short walk to the beach club, arm in arm. The beach club was packed and the place was hopping. There was a resort band with a female lead singer and many people were dancing. Hunter and Savannah found a table in the back, ordered some drinks, and soon found their way to the dance floor. The young couple danced, had some drinks, and danced some more. The night went quickly, and after the band played one last set of fast songs the lead singer announced that this was the last dance. It was a slow song and Hunter and Savannah wrapped their arms around each other and swayed to the music, their bodies pressed together. Soon the dance was over and Hunter and Savannah walked back to their table to finish their drinks.

Savannah sat close to Hunter. She leaned over and whispered in his ear, "I had a wonderful time today and tonight." She brushed her leg against his underneath the table. Hunter nearly melted at the touch of Savannah's leg against his own.

"Well, the night's not over yet," Hunter managed to say. "The band is quitting. Let's go for a walk on the beach. I have something to show you."

"Oh? What might that be?" asked Savannah.

"Well," Hunter said, "you'll have to see for yourself."

The couple finished their drinks and walked out of the bar. The warm, gentle sea breeze and the sweet smell of the ocean engulfed Hunter and Savannah. The ocean swells crashing on the beach could be heard over the ringing in the couple's ears from the loud music they had just left. Hunter held Savannah's hand as she walked along the edge of the pool on their way to the boardwalk that led over the sand dunes to the beach. The young couple then walked with their arms around each other down the boardwalk to the beach. There was a full moon rising over the ocean, giving the couple just enough light to see what they were doing. The ocean was calm except for the swell hitting the beach, the moonlight reflecting off the ocean in a straight line.

"What is it that you wanted to show me?" Savannah asked as they arrived at the beach.

"Oh, it's a special spot. It's just down the beach aways. Come on," said Hunter.

The young couple set off down the beach, arms around each other, slightly staggering, partly because of the uneven ground due to the many footprints in the sand and partly from the drinks they had consumed. After a couple of hundred yards or so, Hunter pointed out a small boardwalk that led back over the dunes. The boardwalk went over the dune and down to a foot path that went across one of the links-style golf holes, which rested between the primary dune and the secondary dune, below the Amelia Inn where Hunter and Savannah had dined earlier.

The golf hole, number six of the Oceanside nine, was a par-three. The ladies' tee and the regular men's tee were at the same level as the green. The men's professional tee, however, was at the top of an overgrown sand dune that lay behind the first two tees. The tee was one of the highest points on the island. Scaling the top of the dune required negotiating a series of about thirty steep, wooden steps. Hunter guided Savannah down a cart path toward the steps.

"Where in the world are we going?" Savannah asked, slightly tipsy.

"You'll see in a minute!" Hunter responded merrily.

The young couple reached the bottom of the steps and Hunter motioned Savannah to climb up.

Savannah turned to Hunter and asked, "What's at the top, the Dalai Lama?"

Hunter laughed and responded, "No spiritual enlightenment, just the second-best view on the island."

Hunter and Savannah climbed the steps, Hunter with his arm around Savannah's slim waist, assisting her up the steep incline. The air was hot and muggy, but the gentle sea breeze increased as they went higher. The night was quiet as there were no other people around, since it was well after midnight. Only the pounding of the surf and the symphony of the crickets could be heard. As they reached the top, Savannah ran forward to take in the view, Hunter lingered back to allow Savannah her moment. Savannah ran to the edge of the golf tee toward the ocean. From this vantage point, one had a panoramic view of the coast line and a tremendous view of the moonlit sea. Windblown scrub oaks surrounded the flat tee on the south and west side, blocking the view from the condominiums and the Amelia Inn, making the tee a private amphitheater overlooking the ocean.

Savannah stood admiring the view, while Hunter stood at the top of the steps watching Savannah, her petite body silhouetted against the moonlit sea. Savannah was so happy that she twirled around in circles like a little girl, then she motioned to Hunter to come join her. Hunter walked toward Savannah and as he did, Savannah ran toward him and jumped into his arms, her legs wrapped around his waist. Hunter was surprised at how light Savannah was.

"Oh, Hunter, I've had the best time today," Savannah confessed.

"Well, the day's not over yet," Hunter responded, as he gazed into Savannah's eyes.

"Oh, yeah?" Savannah replied coyly. "What else is on the agenda?"

At that point, Hunter could no longer restrain himself. He kissed Savannah deeply as he continued to hold her up against him. Savannah responded passionately, her legs tightening around his waist. The young couple kissed hurriedly as if they were trying to consume each other, their passion rising to the surface. Hunter laid Savannah down on the soft, smooth grass of the golf tee as he continued to kiss her. Hunter began to remove Savannah's clothes and she did not resist. Soon, Savannah was naked in the moonlight. Hunter hesitated slightly to admire Savannah's body. Savannah was not in the mood for any delays and grabbed at Hunter's shirt and pulled it over his head. Hunter quickly undid his belt buckle and removed the rest of his clothes. The young lovers fell together and made passionate love under the stars, their bodies caressed by the gentle ocean breeze, the rhythm of the ocean swells pounding on the beach in the background.

After their love was consummated, Hunter and Savannah rolled onto their backs and gazed up at the star-laden sky. Savannah contently nestled in the crook of Hunter's arm as they lay recovering their breath.

"That was wonderful," said Savannah.

"Yes, it was," said Hunter assuredly.

"Do you believe in love at first sight?" asked Savannah, gazing questioningly into Hunter's eyes.

"I do now," confessed Hunter as he pulled Savannah closer to him.

The young couple lay there, naked, gazing up at the heavens, cuddling and talking. After only a short time, Hunter began to feel a stirring within him. Hunter wasn't sure if it was the environment or his love for Savannah or the combination of both, but soon he was ready for another round. This time Hunter and Savannah made love slowly and more profoundly, reaching a crescendo that exceeded even their first time. As they lay side by side, again trying to catch their breath, Hunter and Savannah were startled by the beep of a pager.

As they fumbled through their discarded clothes, Savannah discovered it was her pager and not Hunter's this time. Savannah thought this was strange because she was not on call at the hospital this week. Maybe it was Darrell. He probably was stranded somewhere and needed a ride home. If that was it, Savannah swore she would kill him, but as she read the number off the pager she saw it was the hospital that paged her.

"Who is it?" asked Hunter as he was putting on his pants.

"It's the emergency room," said Savannah puzzled. "Do you have your cell phone?" Savannah said as she was zipping up her dress.

"Yes," responded Hunter, pulling it from the back pocket of his pants.

Savannah dialed the number and Hunter watched as Savannah talked into the phone.

All of a sudden, Hunter saw Savannah's face change drastically in the moonlight. She sat down on the tee as the phone fell from her hand.

"What's happened?" said Hunter.

"It's Darrell," said Savannah dejectedly. "He's been in an accident."

Chapter Twelve

Savannah's feeling of extreme happiness was replaced by dread, fear, and anticipation. Hunter and Savannah drove to the hospital in Hunter's car. Savannah was quiet, staring without recognition at the landscape passing by in the night. Hunter did not know what to say, so he concentrated on his driving. Soon Hunter was pulling into his usual space in the parking lot. Savannah jumped out of the car and rushed inside the hospital. Hunter locked the car and followed Savannah in.

The front desk clerk informed both of them, first Savannah, then later Hunter, that Darrell was in the intensive care unit. Savannah continued her mad dash down the hall until she came to the ICU. Savannah burst through the double doors, startling the nurse on duty, Dora Stimpson. Dora was a pleasant woman in her early fifties who had worked in the intensive care unit for many years. Savannah knew Dora's reputation as a capable nurse and was relieved that Dora was on duty.

"Dora, where's my brother?" Savannah asked hurriedly.

"Over here," Dora responded, rising from her desk and leading Savannah to one of the beds in the ICU with a curtain drawn around the bed. Darrell lay motionless on the bed, hooked up to a breathing machine. Savannah ran to Darrell's bedside and put her head on his chest, comforted by the sound of him breathing. Dora spoke up, knowing what was going through Savannah's mind.

"He's in a coma, but he's stable," Dora said gently.

"What happened?" asked Savannah.

"It was a one-car accident. The two boys in the front seats were killed. Nobody was wearing their seat belts. According to the policeman who accompanied the ambulance, Darrell was thrown through the windshield from the back seat. The policeman said there were beer cans all over the floor of the car. The police have requested a blood test on Darrell's alcohol level," Dora added almost apologetically.

"Oh, Darrell," Savannah said with a sigh, realizing her worst fears had come true. Savannah sat on the side of the bed and brushed Darrell's hair from his forehead. Savannah thought Darrell looked kind of peaceful. If it wasn't for Darrell's labored breathing and all the equipment in the room, it would appear as if Darrell was just in a quiet sleep. Savannah, however, knew that it could be days, or it could take months or years for Darrell to come out of his coma. Savannah also knew that even if Darrell did come out of the coma, he might not be the same person she knew before, because there might be brain damage.

Savannah started to cry, a deep sobbing, as she laid her head on Darrell's chest. Hunter, who had also arrived at the bedside and had been standing off to the side, came forward to console Savannah. Hunter sat down beside Savannah and placed his hand on Savannah's back as she continued to cry over Darrell.

"It'll be all right," Hunter said, trying to comfort Savannah. Then Hunter added hopefully, "Darrell will come out of it soon."

"But what if he doesn't?" said Savannah, clearly distraught.

"Well, let's not think that way," Hunter said. Hunter knew the odds of a full recovery for Darrell were not good but he preferred to think optimistically for Savannah's sake. Hunter watched Savannah now, pouring her heart out for her brother, and Hunter could not help but feel empathy and love. Hunter was surprised at himself, for even in this tragic moment, he was in love with Savannah.

After an hour or so, Savannah tried to get Hunter to go home and get some rest. Hunter knew there was nothing for him to do here, but he felt this strong obligation not to leave Savannah alone. Hunter glanced at the monitors, and everything seemed stable for now.

"Is it all right if we stay?" Hunter asked Dora, knowing overnight visitors are not allowed in the intensive care unit.

"Of course," said Dora reassuringly.

Hunter and Savannah settled down for the night, Savannah curled up at the feet of Darrell's bed and Hunter squeezed into a nearby chair. Although the chair was uncomfortable, Hunter was numbed by the late hour and the events of the evening. He was very tired and quickly fell asleep. For Savannah it was to be the first of many restless nights as she began her vigil by Darrell's side.

Chapter Thirteen

The next couple of weeks were monotonous. Savannah used up all her sick time and vacation time so she could be by Darrell's side. Hunter was not involved with Darrell's care, since Darrell had signed up with a different primary care provider when Savannah had him insured through Medi-Most as her dependent, before Hunter's arrival. A host of specialists kept watch over Darrell's vital signs. Hunter was glad he wasn't directly involved; he didn't like treating family. Even though Darrell wasn't family, Hunter was in love with his sister and preferred his role of advisor and confidant to being directly responsible. Besides, Hunter knew in situations like Darrell's things could turn bad very quickly through nobody's fault, and Hunter did not want to be the doctor of record if Darrell died.

So as Savannah continued her vigil by Darrell's side, Hunter kept himself busy with his practice. Hunter would stop by at lunch and take Savannah to the cafeteria. In the evening, Hunter would again stop by and take Savannah to dinner either in the cafeteria or occasionally out for a quick bite in town.

Hunter met Savannah's parents during one of his visits to Darrell's bedside. Savannah's parents were a very handsome couple in their early sixties. The older couple was very kind and polite to Hunter even under the adverse conditions that involved Darrell's accident.

Savannah's mother, Virginia Jones, or Ginny as everyone called her, was a petite, silver-haired, ball-of-fire of a woman. Even in these trying circumstances, Ginny took control, comforting everyone and impressing Hunter with her positive attitude. Savannah's father, Robert, was a tall, stately man who had a quiet, easygoing manner. Robert was kind of reticent, particularly with Darrell in this condition, but his eyes brightened when Savannah told him that Hunter had played baseball at Mercer. Robert, a self-made man who built houses for a living, had never been to college but had played semipro baseball in Pennsylvania before moving to the South. Robert loved to talk baseball and in Hunter he had found a peer. Savannah's parents had retrieved Snickers from Savannah's townhouse because Savannah wasn't ever there to care for the dog.

There really wasn't much to do for Darrell, his condition pretty much remaining the same as when they brought him in from the accident. Hunter tried to get Savannah to go back to work to take her mind off the situation and to save some of her time off for later, in case Darrell came out of his coma and could recognize her. Savannah, however, insisted on being at Darrell's side every day, talking to him and reading to him, as if she could personally stimulate his brain back to normal functioning. Ginny told Savannah that she would be there if Darrell woke up, but Savannah wanted to be there also.

Hunter knew Savannah felt responsible since Darrell was staying with her and she had been unable to change his behavior. Hunter told Savannah that you cannot change people until they are ready to change themselves. Hunter tried to reassure Savannah that, in case Darrell made it through this accident, the accident might be an awakening that alters Darrell's behavior. Savannah was reassured by Hunter's comments but continued to hover over Darrell like a mother. Hunter realized it was fruitless to try and distract Savannah from Darrell's situation and quietly admired her loyalty and tenaciousness.

To keep himself busy on the lonely nights after he had left Savannah and her parents at the hospital, Hunter kept busy by researching Dr. Baker's records. Hunter was still bothered by Ben Johnson's death. Hunter felt responsible for Ben's death and felt the system had somehow failed the man. Ben should have had surgery sooner, as requested, Hunter thought, but he felt also that the system had failed Ben a second time in the intensive care unit after the stroke.

Hunter wanted to know what kind of care the hospital was giving, so he was doing a systematic search through Dr. Baker's old records looking for people who had been admitted to the hospital and subsequently died while in the care of the hospital. Dr. Baker had never computerized his records, so Hunter was having to go back through the charts one by one. Hunter felt that if he could gather some statistics proving the HMO's protocol was not effective, maybe he could change the system for the better. Hunter knew if he was going to try to change anything he would have to have the numbers to back it up, so even after a long day of seeing patients, followed by a visit with Savannah, Hunter would spend a couple of hours each night going through the records in his office.

At least Dr. Baker had separated the deceased files from the active files, so all Hunter had to do was read the last couple of pages of the deceased charts to see what had happened. Hunter entered into his laptop computer the names of the deceased for the last five years and also entered the cause of death. Hunter would go back later, after he compiled his list, and separate the deceased as to cause of death, then analyze the data to see if there was some kind of pattern.

After two weeks of working in his spare moments every day, Hunter had made it through all the files. If Hunter couldn't decide on a cause of death from his charts, he would put the file in the "undecided" stack. At the end of two weeks, Hunter had ten undecided files from two years ago, twenty-one files from one year ago and five undecided files so far this year, including Ben Johnson's chart.

Hunter noticed that, in all of these cases, the patients had been brought in with a serious medical problem like a stroke or heart attack, but all had been stabilized and seemed to have a chance for recovery when they all suddenly died. The cause of death listed was their original problem, which was handled, and then a second, catastrophic event appeared to be the true cause of death. Hunter also noticed that patients who were diagnosed with terminal cancer were only living about half of the average for their condition.

Hunter wasn't quite sure what to do with this newfound information. Hospital policies being what they are, Hunter didn't want to get anybody into trouble. However, if people were dying prematurely, or if some of the deaths were preventable, something must be done.

The obvious choice would be to go to Dr. Hockman with this information. Dr. Hockman, however, had not been very receptive on Ben Johnson's case and appeared to be more concerned with the HMO protocol and the bottom line than with good patient care. Hunter decided before he confronted Dr. Hockman with this information he better do some more fact-finding and have his facts straight. Therefore, Hunter decided he would recruit Savannah to find out from the nurses working the floor if they knew anything. Also, since all of these cases had belonged to Dr. Baker, Hunter would discreetly ask the other staff doctors if they had any similar cases. Hunter picked up the phone and called Savannah at the hospital.

Savannah was amazed when Hunter told her about his findings. Savannah worked in the emergency room, so she couldn't follow a lot of the cases, but she did remember a couple of instances where they had done great work in the emergency room saving somebody, only to hear later through the hospital grapevine that the patient had died shortly thereafter.

Savannah was grateful to have something to think about beside Darrell. Darrell had made no progress and was still in a deep coma. Savannah, who had been at Darrell's side, day and night, for over two weeks, was getting very tired of sleeping on the cot the staff had brought in for her. She was running out of vacation time and sick time, and the time had come when she knew she would have to go back to work the next day. While talking on the phone, Hunter convinced Savannah to go home for a good night's sleep. Savannah drove home and, exhausted, fell immediately asleep.

Savannah woke up the next day refreshed and able to return to work. As she drove into work Savannah felt relieved to be going to the hospital to work, instead of facing a long, uneventful day by Darrell's bedside. Savannah soon found the hectic pace of the emergency room was good for her as it kept her mind occupied so she didn't constantly think of Darrell. As lunchtime approached, however, Savannah thought about her conversation with Hunter the night before. Hunter had asked Savannah to do some snooping around with the nurses. Hunter knew that if anything was amiss at the hospital, the nurses would realize it first since they were the heart and soul of the hospital. Hunter had warned Savannah to be discreet, for obvious reasons.

At her lunch break, Savannah headed for the cafeteria. After going through the line, Savannah sat down with her tray of food with a group of nurses that she knew. Savannah eased into the conversation, which was mostly about men. The other nurses teased Savannah about her relationship with Hunter and let her know they were jealous. After awhile, Savannah manipulated the conversation around to ask of the group if they ever had any unexpected deaths on their shifts on patients that had been stable.

Rita Cruz, one of the ICU nurses, who was about five months' pregnant, spoke up. "When Medi-Most took over, they did not retain most of the nurses that previously worked in the intensive care unit. I, like the others, was fresh out of nursing school. The only person with experience was Dora, and Mrs. Healy, who has since retired. I got into nursing to save lives, but in the intensive care unit it seemed to me that we lost more people than we should. In fact, we nicknamed the intensive care unit Hotel California because, as the song lyrics go, 'You can check out any time you like, but you can never leave.' I used to be bothered greatly by one of my patient's deaths, but now I'm immune to it."

Savannah was shocked to hear Rita say what she did. The other nurses in the group did not seem to be concerned by Rita's comments at all. In fact, a couple of the nurses were nodding their heads in agreement.

Savannah knew Hunter would want to know about this information right away. Savannah excused herself from the group, as she had finished her lunch anyway. She made her way over to Hunter's office; it was still lunch time and with any luck

Savannah could catch Hunter between patients. Savannah found Hunter eating a sandwich at his desk while updating charts.

"Hi, gorgeous," Hunter said as Savannah entered his office.

"Just wait until you hear what I learned in the cafeteria," responded Savannah. Savannah sat down in a chair as Hunter wheeled around to give her his undivided attention.

"What's up?" asked Hunter.

"Well, you know how you asked me to snoop around with the nurses," asked Savannah.

"Yeah," responded Hunter.

"Well, I was just in the cafeteria with a bunch of nurses and one of them, Rita Cruz, said that ever since Medi-Most took over, they had been losing patients out of the intensive care unit that she felt were stable," reported Savannah.

"She said that?" asked Hunter incredulously.

"Yes," said Savannah, adding, "the weird thing is, some of the other nurses were in full agreement."

"Well, maybe there is more to this than I thought," remarked Hunter, pondering the ramifications of what Savannah had told him. "I need to talk to some of the other doctors and see if they have had any unusual cases. But I need to be careful. I don't want to step on anybody's toes."

Hunter knew how hospital politics worked. Even if a problem was exposed, the hospital would want to deal with it quietly so as to not to alarm the public or disillusion the staff. "Tomorrow night is the hospital staff meeting. I'll ask some of the doctors there," decided Hunter.

"Be careful," Savannah warned.

Deep in thought, the young doctor said, "I will."

Chapter Fourteen

Hunter showed up early for the staff meeting, hoping to talk to some of the doctors before the meeting started. The meeting wasn't to begin until six-thirty in the evening, but Hunter arrived at six. The meeting was held in the hospital cafeteria, which that night was closed to everyone but the doctors. From six to six-thirty the cafeteria staff would be regrouping, and at six-thirty the staff would serve appetizers for the doctors as they chatted. At seven the meeting would begin and dinner would be served at seven-thirty during the meeting.

When Hunter arrived, he found that he was the only doctor there, so he sat at a table and started doing some paperwork he had brought along, just in case. Fairly soon, Dr. Raja entered the room. Dr. Raja was an internist whom Hunter had spoken to once or twice before, but they did not know each other well. Dr. Raja glanced over at Hunter, nodding an acknowledgment toward him, then proceeded to the coffee machine to pour himself a cup of coffee. After Dr. Raja had prepared his cup of coffee, he came back to where Hunter was sitting.

"Another early bird," said Dr. Raja pleasantly.

"Yes," responded Hunter, then added, "I got through early so I thought I'd come on over."

"How is your practice coming along?" Dr. Raja asked.

"Very well," said Hunter truthfully. Then Hunter added matter-of-factly, "I did have one patient I lost that I don't think we should have."

"Well, when you first start out, every patient's death hits you especially hard, but after awhile you get used to death," said Dr. Raja.

"Well, this guy was on the waiting list for carotid surgery when he had a stroke," said Hunter. "Then, after surviving that, he was stable in the intensive care unit when they lost him."

"If the poor fellow had that bad of a stroke, maybe it was better that he died," responded Dr. Raja. "It's awfully hard on the patient's family to take care of that person for the rest of their lives," Dr. Raja added.

"That may be so, but we'll never know because the patient never made it out of the hospital," responded Hunter. "Have you ever had any patients that seemed stable, then taken a sudden turn for the worse in the intensive care unit?"

Dr. Raja's eyes narrowed and his demeanor seem to harden as he said, "Those are very sick people that get put in the intensive care unit. Of course, some of them are not going to make it out of there alive." Then Dr. Raja asked rhetorically, "Are the hospital and the intensive care unit staff doing a good job?" Then Dr. Raja immediately answered his own question, "Yes, I think they are doing a great job." After that Dr. Raja added sternly, "If you have any complaints I suggest you take them up with Dr. Hockman."

Just then, some other doctors entered the room and Dr. Raja excused himself and went over to greet them. Hunter went back to his paperwork but couldn't help but notice the occasional glance over in his direction by the group of doctors with whom Dr. Raja was talking. Hunter decided that he may have hit upon a sensitive subject and that he better not push his luck any further that night. Hunter spent the rest of the meeting quietly sitting in the back and not talking to anyone. Hunter didn't know what was going on, but something was amiss and he was going to find out what it was, for Ben Johnson's sake.

Chapter Fifteen

Savannah was working full time and spending all of her free time sitting with Darrell. The hectic schedule was beginning to take a toll on Savannah. Some nights Savannah would sleep all night in the intensive care unit. Savannah, who was naturally thin, was getting thinner, and dark circles were gathering under her eyes. Savannah's only brief respite was the dinners she had with Hunter.

One night after Savannah had read a chapter of a book to Darrell, she fell fast asleep in a chair next to his bed. Savannah might have been asleep an hour or so when she startled herself awake. The chair was very uncomfortable, and the discomfort had woken her from her sleep. Savannah was in the process of moving from the chair to the spare bed when she thought she saw something. Savannah was half asleep and kind of groggy, but she looked more carefully at Darrell's hand.

"There!" Savannah saw it again: an ever-so-slight movement of one of Darrell's fingers. Savannah moved closer for a better look, and she saw it again. One of Darrell's fingers moved.

Savannah pushed the buzzer to summon the nurse. The two nurses on duty happened to be Rita Cruz, who Savannah had spoken with in the cafeteria previously, and Dora Stimpson.

"Rita, I think I saw Darrell's fingers move!" Savannah said excitedly.

"Are you sure?" Rita asked, moving closer to the bed. The three women stood there staring at Darrell's fingers, watching intently for any kind of movement. The three nurses stood there for five, then ten minutes, but nothing happened. Rita and Dora looked at Savannah and Savannah felt their gaze.

"I wasn't dreaming!" Savannah said, knowing what Rita was thinking and trying to convince herself. "I'm sure I saw some movement," Savannah added.

Rita wanted to be reassuring, but noticing the dark circles around Savannah's eyes from lack of sleep, Rita was unconvinced.

"I'm sure you saw something," Rita said sweetly. Then Rita added, "But you look very tired. Why don't you go home and get some rest? I'll check on Darrell every fifteen minutes and if anything exciting happens, I'll call you," Rita said.

"But I want to be here if he wakes up," protested Savannah.

"Now, Savannah," Dora interjected. "You're a nurse. You know how long these things can take. It could be days or weeks before anything happens. What you saw may have been just a muscle spasm. Why don't you go home and get some rest and we'll call you if anything happens. Besides," Dora added, "if Darrell wakes up and sees you looking like this, you might scare him back into his coma."

Savannah managed a laugh and said, "Maybe you're right, Dora, maybe I'll go home and get some sleep." With that thought, Savannah realized how tired she was. The lack of sleep over the past couple of weeks was catching up to her, and she considered the possibility that she had hallucinated.

As Rita and Dora walked Savannah to the door of the room, Savannah glanced over her shoulder one more time at her brother. Darrell lay completely motionless, the small nightlight casting on eerie glow over his still body. But Savannah felt certain of what she had seen and she couldn't wait to get home and call Hunter to tell him about it.

Several hours later, at three o'clock that morning Rita headed over to the small alcove to make her and Dora some coffee. Dora, meanwhile, had excused herself to go to the bathroom down the hall, right outside of the intensive care ward. As Rita was making coffee in the little alcove, a figure made its way down the hall and into the main supply room that was connected to both the hallway and also to another door that made it accessible from the intensive care ward.

The figure entered the supply room and ambled over to the door that led into the intensive care ward. After peering through the slightly opened door to make sure Rita was out of sight, the figure eased into the intensive care ward and went directly to Darrell's bedside. With a practiced touch, the figure raised Darrell's gown and located his femoral vein. The person expertly emptied the syringe filled with a high potassium solution into the vein. The vein would eventually take the potassium to the heart where it would throw off the electrolyte balance of the heart, causing hyperkalemia and cardiac arrest. There would be just enough time for the person to leave and get back to work before the heart would fail and the monitors would go off.

As the person emptied the syringe into Darrell's femoral vein, Darrell's fingers on his left hand wriggled slightly. This caused the person emptying the syringe to flinch because Darrell was supposed to be comatose with no chance of recovery. But the figure had no time for remorse, so after the syringe was emptied and removed, the person hastily exited through the supply room.

Rita was stirring her coffee when she heard Darrell's heart monitor alarm go off. Rita hurriedly placed the coffee on the counter and rushed to Darrell's bed. Rita took one look at the flat line on Darrell's monitor and pushed the "code blue" button for an emergency. Rita quickly gave Darrell a shot of epinephrine and began to put gel on the resuscitation paddles hanging on the wall. Dora rushed into the room to help Rita and in less than a minute, the resident doctor on call and two other nurses were in the room. The group worked feverishly, trying to revive Darrell three times with the paddles, only to watch his heartbeat go back to a flat line each time. Finally, after about fifteen minutes, the doctor called off the effort. Darrell was dead.

Rita sat down in a chair and cried. Sorry now that she had sent Savannah home, Rita made her way back over to the nurses' station where she laid her head down on the desk to try to compose herself to make the phone call to Savannah. Dora asked Rita if she wanted her to call Savannah for Rita, but Rita shook her head. Rita told Dora that this stress was not good for her baby as she patted the protruding belly that contained her five-month-old fetus. Dora consoled Rita and after awhile Rita had gathered herself enough to reach for the phone and dial Savannah's number.

Savannah was in a deep and blissful sleep when the phone rang. Savannah had been dreaming that she and Darrell had been playing together as young children, fighting over a toy. At the sound of the phone, Darrell's hand left Savannah's as he won the battle over the toy.

Savannah was groggy when she picked up the phone and said hello. Savannah instantly recognized Rita's voice, however, which caused Savannah to sit up in bed and ask excitedly, "Did he move?"

Rita, having forgotten that she had promised Savannah she would call if anything exciting happened, was now even more distressed. "No, Savannah, I'm afraid I have some really bad news," Rita managed, fighting back the tears. "We did everything we could, but I'm afraid Darrell is gone," Rita continued reluctantly.

"What?" said Savannah in shock, her mood falling off a precipice after having expected good news.

"Darrell is gone," Rita repeated.

"How?" Savannah asked meekly.

"Heart failure," Rita informed Savannah.

"But I thought his body was in fine shape, only his brain was a problem," Savannah mumbled.

"I know, but somehow Darrell's heart gave out," Rita responded.

"Don't move him," Savannah said emphatically, then followed, "I'll be right there."

Savannah then called Hunter, waking him up. Hunter glanced at the clock and moaned, realizing it was almost four in the morning. But as soon as Hunter found out it was Savannah and what she had to say, he said, "I'll meet you at the hospital in twenty minutes."

Chapter Sixteen

Hunter met Savannah at the hospital. Savannah had arrived first and was sobbing beside Darrell's body when Hunter arrived at the intensive care ward. Hunter embraced Savannah when he arrived, her body shaking uncontrollably in his arms. After awhile, Hunter released his embrace and went to question Rita, Dora, and the resident doctor about what happened. It sounded to Hunter that the staff had done everything by the book and did all that was possible to try to save Darrell.

But what bothered Hunter was that here was another seriously ill but stable patient who took a sudden turn for the worse while in the intensive care ward. Was it coincidence or was something sinister at work here, Hunter asked himself. Hunter decided to ask Rita if she had seen anyone come in or out of the room. Rita truthfully told Hunter she had seen nobody come or go. Hunter asked Rita if she had left her post at any time to go to the bathroom or whatever. Rita responded she hadn't left the area but she did get a cup of coffee from the lounge area just before Darrell's alarm went off, while Dora had gone to the bathroom down the hall.

Hunter thanked Rita for her help and walked over to the lounge area where the coffee pot was located. Standing in front of the coffee pot, Hunter could plainly see the nurses' station and the double doors leading into the intensive care ward. Hunter noticed that from this position Rita could not see where Darrell's bed was located, but she would have clearly seen anybody come in through the main doors.

Hunter walked around the wall separating the lounge area from the main room of the intensive care ward. Hunter looked to see if there were any other entrances into the intensive care ward. The only other door in the entire intensive care ward besides the main double doors was a small door in the back of the ward near Darrell's bed that looked like it led to a closet. Hunter walked over to the door and opened it, revealing a supply room about eight feet by ten feet, filled with shelves and supplies. Hunter was about to close the door when his eye caught another door on the right side of the room. Hunter entered the supply room and walked over to the second door to see where it led. Hunter opened the door and discovered it led to the main hallway outside the intensive care ward.

Hunter realized that a person could enter the intensive care ward through the supply room and be undetected as long as the nurses on duty were not sitting at their desks. Hunter went back through the supply room and into the intensive care ward. Savannah was still at Darrell's side, too distraught to noticed Hunter's wanderings. Hunter gave Savannah another reassuring hug and told her he was going to examine the body. Hunter gently asked her to go have a cup of coffee with Rita, while he looked at Darrell.

"What are you looking for?" Savannah asked between sobs.

"I'm not sure yet," Hunter answered truthfully.

"Now be a dear, and go sit with Rita for a minute," Hunter gently prodded, walking Savannah in Rita's direction at the desk. Hunter assisted Savannah to a chair beside Rita. Feeling guilty about sending Savannah home earlier, Rita offered to get Savannah some coffee.

Hunter returned to Darrell's bedside and removed the sheet that was now covering him from the neck down since the gown had been torn away. Hunter could see the burns on Darrell's chest where they had tried to revive him. Hunter looked carefully at Darrell's arms for puncture wounds. There was a large puncture wound on Darrell's right arm where there had been an I.V. hook-up. There was another puncture wound location where Rita had said she gave him a shot of epinephrine. Other than that there were no other puncture wounds on the arms. Noticing that Rita, Dora, and Savannah had gone around the wall separating the coffee machine from the intensive care ward, Hunter pulled the sheet off completely to examine the rest of Darrell's body. Hunter's eyes wandered down to Darrell's right hip area. There Hunter saw what appeared to be a fresh puncture wound. The hole was very small, as if made with a small-gauge needle, but there was a small coagulation of blood at the wound area, which made it more noticeable.

Hunter noticed out of the corner of his eye Rita, Dora, and Savannah emerging from behind the wall, so he pulled the sheet back up to Darrell's chin. Hunter walked over to where Rita and Savannah were sitting and put his hands on Savannah's shoulders.

"Rita, you said that the only medications Darrell had were an I.V. in his arm and an injection of epinephrine when his heart failed," Hunter noted.

"That's right," responded Rita. "Why?"

"Just wanted to be sure," Hunter said, smiling disarmingly. Hunter did not want to alarm Savannah yet and he was not sure of Rita's involvement, so Hunter quickly changed the subject.

"Why don't we go to the cafeteria and discuss our options?" Hunter said to Savannah, referring to what to do with Darrell's body and wanting to be with her alone so he could talk more frankly.

"All right," Savannah mumbled weakly, numbed by her loss. Hunter took Savannah's hand, and after they had thanked Rita and Dora, he led Savannah out of the intensive care ward and toward the cafeteria.

The cafeteria was empty at this early hour except for two cooks in the back who were beginning to make breakfast. Hunter went over to the vending machines, bought them both Cokes, and then he and Savannah sat down in the deserted eating area.

"Savannah," Hunter began, clasping her hands. "We need to think about what to do with Darrell's body."

"Yes, I know. We have to think about which funeral home to send him to," said Savannah.

"Actually, I think we need to send him to the pathologist for an autopsy," said Hunter.

"What?" responded Savannah incredulously.

"I think Darrell was murdered," responded Hunter as gently as he could.

"But how?" Savannah asked, intently looking at Hunter.

"I think someone came in through the supply room and gave Darrell a shot of something that killed him," the young doctor replied. As Hunter said this, Savannah shook her head in disbelief. Hunter continued, "There is a door leading from the main hallway into the intensive care ward from the supply room. Darrell had a puncture wound in his right femoral vein that looked like it came from a syringe. I think someone came in through the supply room while Rita wasn't looking and Dora was in the bathroom and killed Darrell."

"But why?" Savannah asked.

"Well, I think Darrell's situation fits into the pattern that I have been researching: seriously compromised but stable patients that have suddenly died in the intensive care ward. What I had thought to be a failure of the system or negligence on someone's part may be a systematic attempt to get rid of certain patients," Hunter reported.

"That's crazy, who would do such a terrible thing?" asked Savannah incredulously.

"I'm not sure," responded Hunter, "but we need some proof and that's why we need to do an autopsy and not by a pathologist connected to the hospital."

"Oh, I don't know," said Savannah, shuddering at the thought of Darrell being dissected.

"We must have this done," said Hunter, grasping both of Savannah's hands with his own hands and gazing intently into her eyes.

Savannah nodded in agreement, then said sadly, "If we must."

Hunter pulled Savannah to him and gave her a hug and then a kiss to reassure her.

"I guess you're right," responded Savannah.

"I'll make all the arrangements," Hunter said. Seeing the pained expression on Savannah's face and the dark circles around her red, puffy eyes, he followed with, "Now you go home and try to get some rest. I'll tell the emergency room you're not coming into work today."

Hunter helped Savannah up from her chair and walked her to her car in the parking lot. Hunter kissed her good-bye and watched as Savannah drove away, hoping she would be able to sleep. Hunter himself had plenty to do before he starting seeing patients in a little over an hour.

Hunter hastily walked back to his office and looked up the phone number to the pathologist's office in Jacksonville. Hunter placed the call, but only heard the answering service. There wouldn't be anybody in the office for another hour. Hunter left a message and then went to the cabinet behind his desk to retrieve the Polaroid camera he used to document injuries in suspected abuse situations. Hunter walked back over to the intensive care ward where he found that Rita and Dora had just been replaced by other nurses after a shift change. This was fortuitous because Hunter wasn't sure how to explain to Rita and Dora why he was taking a picture. Hunter did not know the new nurses on duty, so he introduced himself and explained to them about the arrangements he had made for Darrell's body and that Savannah, who the nurses did know, had asked Hunter to take one last photograph of her brother. The nurses thought this was kind of strange, but they didn't question it and went to get a cup of coffee.

Hunter quickly made his way back by Darrell's bedside. Hunter took one picture of Darrell's entire body, then he took a close-up picture of the area where the puncture wound was located. Hunter completed the task as quickly as possible before the nurses came back into view. Hunter covered Darrell up with the sheet and then he waited beside the bed as the pictures developed. The pictures turned out all right so Hunter left, thanking the nurses as he left the ward.

Hunter walked down the hall, looking intently at one of the photographs. The doctor turned the corner and bumped into a large man. Hunter almost dropped the photographs, barely managing to hold on to them. Hunter quickly thrust the pictures into his pocket and looked up to see who he had run into. Hunter noticed it was the large man he had seen coming out of Dr. Hockman's office the day Hunter went to talk about Ben Johnson. Hunter quickly apologized to the man and went around him and hurried down the hall. After a few steps, Hunter glanced back at the big man who was just disappearing around the corner. What a strange-looking guy, thought Hunter to himself. Hunter glanced at his watch. He had only fifteen minutes before he started seeing patients. Hunter quickened his pace and headed for his office.

Chapter Seventeen

During the next few days while waiting for the pathologist's report, Hunter kept himself busy seeing patients and consoling Savannah. Hunter tried to get Savannah to take a few days off from work, but after one day off, which Savannah spent almost entirely in a sedative-induced sleep, the dedicated nurse returned to work. Savannah went back for two reasons. First, she had already used up all of her vacation and sick time, and, second, she couldn't just sit at home and be consumed by thoughts of Darrell. It was better for Savannah to be at work, helping others, keeping her mind occupied. Hunter admired Savannah's strength, but also saw how vulnerable she was away from work.

Hunter would meet Savannah after work every day. Usually Hunter and Savannah would go over to Hunter's place, change clothes and then go for a walk on the beach. It was after Labor Day now, most of the tourists had gone home, and Savannah and Hunter had the beach nearly to themselves. After a long walk and a therapeutic talk, Hunter would either make Savannah dinner at his place or they would go down to the casual restaurant at Main Beach and have dinner on the terrace overlooking the ocean.

After dinner, when it was dark, Hunter and Savannah would sit outside on Hunter's deck. Hunter would nurse a bottle of beer, Savannah a glass of wine, as they gazed at the stars above and the lights of the shrimp boats working the ocean in front of them. After awhile, Hunter and Savannah would retire to the bedroom. Savannah, having decided she did not want to be alone in her apartment with memories of Darrell, had brought some of her clothes over to Hunter's to stay with him for awhile. The young couple would make love, sweetly and gently, then fall asleep in each other's arms. Sometimes, as they were falling asleep, Hunter would feel a tear fall on his chest where Savannah had laid her head.

As Hunter lay there, he couldn't wait to see the pathologist's report. Hunter promised himself that for Savannah's sake he would find out what happened to Darrell. Hunter would tighten his embrace of Savannah, and they would drift off into sleep.

After about one week, Hunter received the pathologist's report in his office. Between patients, Hunter found time to open the package excitedly. After reading the report, however, Hunter was dismayed. The pathologist's report did not reveal any drugs that killed Darrell. Darrell died of cardiac arrest, and there wasn't anything unusual in his bloodstream. The only slight abnormality was that his potassium levels were higher than normal. Hunter didn't know how he was going to tell Savannah. But then again, maybe it would be easier on Savannah if Darrell had died of natural causes; that it was destiny.

Then Hunter started thinking about Darrell's potassium levels. Hunter knew that if a patient's electrolyte balance was too far out of line, heart failure would result from interference in the electrical impulses in the heart. Hunter wondered what would happen if someone injected a high potassium solution into a victim's femoral vein. Hunter assumed it would cause cardiac arrest, but to be sure Hunter decided to call Dr. Steve Mathews, a young cardiologist that had befriended Hunter during Hunter's residency at Emory University Hospital in Atlanta.

Hunter placed a call to Dr. Mathews, noting it was almost lunch time and hoping to catch him between patients. Dr. Mathews' receptionist told Hunter that the cardiologist was still in the cath lab but that she would have him return Hunter's call when he came out of the lab. Hunter thanked the receptionist and then went to see his last patient before lunch.

Hunter walked briskly down the hall to retrieve the chart from the little plastic holder beside the door leading to exam room number two. The chart in the holder beside the closed door to the exam room meant the patient had already been worked up by Sheila and was ready to be examined by Hunter. Eager to get done with this last patient so he would be free to take Dr. Mathew's call when the cardiologist returned Hunter's call,

Hunter grabbed the chart from its holder and quickly glanced over the pertinent information.

According to the record, Lolita Gomez was a thirty-year-old unmarried woman who thought she had discovered a lump in her breast. Hunter looked on the chart to see if the woman was on any medications, which she was not. Then Hunter looked under past family history and saw that the patient had reported that her mother had died of breast cancer. Knowing he was going to have to do a physical examination, Hunter walked back down the hall to find Sheila so she could accompany Hunter during the examination. Not spotting Sheila in any of the open exam rooms or work-up area, he asked Rosa, who was working at the desk in the reception area, if she knew where Sheila was.

"Sheila has taken Mr. Wiley over to the X-ray department at the hospital," responded Rosa. "She'll be back after lunch," Rosa added.

"Where's Bonnie?" Hunter asked.

"I let her go to lunch early because we had to squeeze a patient in at ten minutes until one o'clock, and I wanted her back in time to work up that patient," explained Rosa. Then Rosa added, "Is there anything I can help you with?"

Hunter knew he should have a female assistant present during the exam, but Sheila and Bonnie were not available and Rosa was by herself watching the front desk and overseeing the phone. Dr. Mathews would be calling back in a few minutes and Hunter wanted to be done with this exam by then, so Hunter decided to go ahead with the exam alone.

"No thank you, Rosa, just listen out for the phone, please," Hunter responded as he walked down the hall to the exam room. Hunter opened the door and greeted a fairly attractive Hispanic woman with raven-colored hair and a smooth, olive complexion. The woman, already dressed in just a paper gown, was sitting on the edge of the examination table and greeted Hunter warmly as he entered the room.

"Hello, I'm Lolita," offered the woman.

"I'm Dr. Davis, Lolita. It's very nice to meet you," said Hunter, shaking the woman's hand as he sat down on the stool with her chart in his other hand.

Getting right to the point, Hunter said, "It says here that you may have discovered a lump in your right breast?"

"Yes. Due to my mother's history, I try to do a self-examination at least once a month. The other day while I was checking myself, I think I felt a hard place," the woman said matter-of-factly as she brushed her dark, shoulder-length hair away from her face.

"Well, let's check a few things," Hunter said as he put on some latex gloves. The basics, like blood pressure, had already been taken and noted on the chart, so Hunter proceeded to the physical exam. Hunter walked around behind the woman and placed his stethoscope earpieces in position, then slipped the end of the stethoscope through the gap in the back of her gown onto her back to listen to the woman's breathing.

"This is going to be cold," said Hunter. The woman jumped slightly as the cold metal rim touched her skin.

Hunter instructed the woman to take several deep breaths as he listened intently to the sound. After checking each lung and satisfied that the sound of the breathing was normal, Hunter untied the top of the woman's gown and slipped it over her shoulder so he could examine the right breast.

Hunter walked around the table so he was beside the patient and had her swing her legs over the end of the examination table so he could stand right next to her. The woman was cooperative as Hunter gently palpated the right breast trying to locate a lump or inconsistency in the feel of the breast. Hunter had performed breast exams hundreds of times between between his internship, residency, and his practice and his thoughts were always clinical even if the woman was attractive, but as Hunter continued to probe, the woman seemed to start enjoying herself. The woman arched her back slightly and reached over and pulled her hair over her left shoulder, exposing a long, slender neck, and glanced over at Hunter with a bit of a sly smile.

Hunter immediately stopped the examination, regretting his impulsiveness in going ahead without a female assistant.

"I don't feel a lump, maybe you were mistaken," Hunter said.

"Why don't you take your gloves off? You might feel it better," the woman said, staring Hunter squarely in the eye.

"I don't think that will be necessary," continued Hunter. "I think we will get a mammogram, which is a more sensitive test anyhow, particularly with your family history. I'll go make the arrangements with Rosa," Hunter said as he quickly exited the room eager to get out of that situation.

Hunter shook his head at himself as he walked down the hall to the front desk. Hunter knew better than to allow himself to get in that position but he was so eager to get through with that last exam to wait for his phone call that he had allowed his judgment to become impaired. Hunter arrived at the front desk and leaned over the desk to give Rosa the patient's chart and instructions on what to do for the patient. While Hunter was giving Rosa the orders for the mammogram, Ms. Gomez, fully clothed now, approached the desk.

"I want to thank you, doctor, for being so thorough," Ms. Gomez said provocatively, with a flip of her hair and looking quite stunning in a short black leather dress and red high heels.

Rosa and Hunter, who had been finishing their instructions, both stopped and turned to look at the woman. Rosa's mouth was wide open and all Hunter could mumble was a mild, "You're welcome."

Since the woman was on Medi-Most insurance, Rosa told her they would file her insurance for her, but she had a five-dollar co-pay. The woman pulled a five-dollar bill out of her small black purse and said to Rosa with a wink, "That's the best five dollars I've ever spent."

Then the woman turned and, with a practiced walk, sauntered out of the office.

"Don't say a word," Hunter warned Rosa, knowing the inquisitive office manager would want to know all the details.

"It's not what you think," Hunter added. Then changing the subject, Hunter said, "If Dr. Mathews calls, I'll be in my office."

Rosa nodded open-mouthed, as Hunter disappeared down the hall before Rosa could ask any questions.

Still shaking his head over his last patient, Hunter returned to his office and called Savannah. Hunter had to tell Savannah he wouldn't be able to meet her for lunch because he was expecting an important phone call. Hunter didn't go into too much detail with Savannah but he did tell her it had to do with Darrell's death. Savannah said she would grab some sandwiches at the cafeteria and bring them to Hunter's office so he would have something for lunch. Hunter thanked Savannah, suddenly realizing how hungry he was and then hung up the phone to wait for the call.

If Steve was on call in the cath lab, Hunter knew it could be hours until he might get a chance to call Hunter. Hunter picked up that morning's mail and started to go through it when Rosa buzzed Hunter over the intercom saying Dr. Mathews was on line one. Hunter excitedly picked up the receiver.

"Hello, Steve?" Hunter said.

"Hunter, I can't believe they are actually letting you practice medicine down there in Florida," Steve Mathews said through the phone, laughing.

"Well, I haven't killed anybody yet, that I know of," Hunter responded good-naturedly.

"To what do I owe the honor of your calling? Are you coming to visit Atlanta?" Dr. Mathews asked.

"As much as I'd like to see a Braves game, that's not the reason I'm calling. I've got another reason. I've got a medical question," said Hunter.

"Shoot," responded Dr. Mathews.

"What would happen if somebody injected a syringe filled with a high potassium solution into a person's femoral vein?" asked Hunter.

"Well, you should know that, Hunter. The solution would travel up the vein directly back to the heart and cause, almost immediately, cardiac arrest," responded Dr. Mathews. "Are you planning on killing someone, Hunter?" Dr. Mathews asked.

"No, no," responded Hunter laughing. "I'm just trying to get to the bottom of something going on here at the hospital," said Hunter nonchalantly.

"Which hospital is that? The Little Shop of Horrors?" Dr. Mathews said sarcastically.

"That's it," said Hunter going along with the joke. "Well, it looks like the Braves are going to win their division again," said Hunter, changing the subject.

"Yes, it does. I just hope their relief pitching holds up through the playoffs this year," said Dr. Mathews. "If I get any playoff tickets, I'll give you a call. Maybe you can come up for a game."

"That would be great!" responded Hunter. "Well, thanks for the information, Steve. Let me know if you get any tickets. Going to the games with you guys is the one thing I miss about Atlanta, compared to living here."

"Well, don't spend too much time at the beach, buddy, it's bad for your skin," answered Dr. Mathews.

Both men said good-bye and hung up their phones. Hunter sat there, leaning back in his chair pondering his next move, when Savannah arrived with their sandwiches.

"Special delivery," said Savannah, knocking gently at the edge of the door.

"Perfect timing. Come on in," said Hunter.

"Did you find out anything?" Savannah asked as she made her way to Hunter's desk to put down the food and drinks.

"Well, I got back the pathologist's report and it did not show any abnormal drugs in Darrell's system. The only thing that was out of line was his potassium levels. The report showed that Darrell died of cardiac arrest. So I called a cardiologist friend of mine from my residency to confirm what would happen if someone shot a high potassium solution into a person's femoral vein, and the answer was cardiac arrest," said Hunter.

"So, you do think Darrell was murdered?" asked Savannah.

115

"Yes, I do," responded Hunter. "The only question is who would want to do that, and why."

"Do you think it is related to the other cases of patients dying unexpectedly?" asked Savannah, not wanting to believe that idea.

"It could be," responded Hunter.

"Why would anybody want to do this?" asked Savannah, shaking her head in disbelief.

"Maybe whoever it is thinks they're an angel of mercy, maybe they think they are doing these people a favor by putting them out of their misery," offered Hunter.

"That's absurd," shouted Savannah. Then Savannah said, "Some of these people may have recovered. Darrell, I know, was going to recover."

With that thought, Savannah started crying. Hunter stood up from behind the desk where he was eating and walked around the desk to console Savannah.

"I'm sorry about Darrell, I know how close you two were," said Hunter, apologetically, as he placed his hand on Savannah's shoulder. "I promise you I will find out who did this to Darrell," said Hunter emphatically.

"Aren't you going to notify the police?" asked Savannah.

"About what?" Hunter asked. "All we know so far is Darrell died of heart failure. We have no proof," said Hunter dejectedly. "I need to do some more investigating. In the meantime, I don't want you to say anything to anybody. We don't know who may be involved," followed Hunter earnestly. "Got that?" Hunter questioned Savannah.

"Yes," responded Savannah. "But promise me you will be careful also," Savannah said, her large, teary eyes demanding an answer from Hunter.

"I will," said Hunter reassuredly.

"I couldn't stand to lose both of you," Savannah said sadly as she rose from her chair to embrace Hunter.

"Don't worry, you won't," said Hunter as he returned Savannah's embrace, wondering what his next move would be.

Chapter Eighteen

That night Hunter sat at the computer in his office, staring at the screen. Previously Hunter had entered the entire hospital's schedule for employees. Hunter had acquired a disk containing the employees' schedule earlier that afternoon from Myrtle Jenkins, a kindly older lady who worked in administration. The ernest, young doctor had told Mrs. Jenkins that he was doing some postgraduate work in hospital efficiency to acquire an MBA to go along with his medical degree. Mrs. Jenkins copied the hospital employees' schedule for the year on a disk for Hunter.

Hunter had previously noted the dates of suspicious cases and was cross-referencing employees to see who was working on that date and on the shift when the patients had died. Hunter had been at the screen for about four hours and he was growing tired. Hunter had talked to Savannah earlier in the evening to tell her he wouldn't be able to meet her for dinner. Now after four hours, the weary doctor had only found one name that matched the criteria.

That name belonged to an orderly named Kendall Brill. Hunter did not consider Kendall Brill a good suspect because he did not work on the floor where the intensive care ward was located and would not have routine access to the intensive care ward where most of the deaths had occurred.

Hunter was down to the last couple of employees and had just about given up when he found another match: Dora Stimpson, the older nurse that had been on duty with Rita the night Darrell died. Dora's work schedule matched all the dates on Hunter's computer. He hurriedly checked the last employee on his list and quickly found that employee did not match, so Hunter returned his attention to Dora Stimpson.

Dora Stimpson's file revealed that she had worked at Medi-Most Hospital since its inception a few years ago. The file showed that Dora had been hired as the nursing coordinator for the entire hospital originally, but a couple of years ago she had been demoted to head nurse of the intensive care unit with a corresponding pay cut.

That's a possible motive, Hunter thought to himself, referring to the demotion and loss of pay. Maybe Dora is trying to get back at or embarrass the hospital. After speculating for awhile, Hunter decided he would let Savannah do some investigating with the nurses before he proceeded with any action.

Hunter shut off his computer, locked up his office, and headed home. Savannah was waiting up for him when Hunter arrived back at his apartment. Over a late-night dinner Savannah had prepared earlier, Hunter filled Savannah in on what he had learned. Savannah was aware of Dora's reputation as a good and competent nurse and was skeptical of Dora as a suspect even though she did not know Dora that well. Savannah conceded to Hunter's wishes, however, and promised she would try to find out more about Dora Stimpson. Some of the nurses were having a baby shower for Rita Cruz this Thursday night, Savannah remembered. She had planned to back out of going due to Darrell's death, but now Savannah realized the shower would be a perfect opportunity to try and find out some information, and possibly take her mind off Darrell.

Thursday night rolled around before Savannah realized it. Savannah had barely had time to go out and get a gift. Savannah had used her lunch hour the day before to buy a gift for Rita's unborn baby. It had been a strange sensation for Savannah to stand in the baby department of a local discount store. Surrounded by all of the baby paraphernalia, she had begun for the first time in her life to seriously think about what the future held for her. Previously, Savannah had been wrapped up in her career. Also, with her previous bad experiences with men, Savannah had not thought much about the future, only the present. But, then, surrounded by baby blankets, cribs, and mobiles, Savannah couldn't help to think how nice it would be to have a baby with Hunter. As Savannah browsed the aisles looking for just the right present, she had wondered what their children would look like. If it was a boy, Savannah hoped he would look like Hunter, strong and lanky, and move with the same athletic grace that Hunter did. Savannah also hoped if she and Hunter did get married and had a son, they could name him Darrell. Then, in some small way, Darrell, her brother, could live on, at least in name.

Savannah had shaken off those daydreaming thoughts, however, as she realized she must make a decision on a present and get back to work. Savannah decided on a cute little baby blanket with bears and balloons. Savannah rationalized that you can never have too many baby blankets and maybe, just maybe, this blanket would become the baby's favorite and become that object of security that some toddlers retain until early childhood and beyond.

Now, as Savannah drove to the baby shower with her present neatly wrapped, she felt a little guilty about her mission. Savannah did not know Dora that well but from her limited experience with the older nurse, she could not picture Dora being involved in anything sinister. Hunter, however, had persisted that Savannah attend the shower, particularly since Dora was hosting the shower at her house. Hunter had said it was the perfect opportunity for snooping around, but Savannah felt uneasy with her clandestine role. Nurses were there to save people, she thought to herself, not to accelerate their deaths. Savannah couldn't imagine one of her sisterhood, who fight so hard to help people, being on the other side of the game.

Savannah had followed the directions that Betty had given her to Dora's house and pulled her car off of Atlantic Avenue and drove up the small hill on North Fifteenth Street. This neighborhood was an older area of Fernandina Beach with its majestic old oak trees and small, neat brick houses. Savannah drove down the other side of the hill and further down Fifteenth Street until she saw a house surrounded by cars, and she knew that must be Dora's house.

Savannah parked on the side of the street in front of one of Dora's neighbor's houses, since there was no room in Dora's driveway or in front of Dora's house. After locking her car, Savannah walked through the maze of cars in Dora's driveway and reached the front door. Still a little reluctant about her task at hand, Savannah hesitated slightly before ringing the doorbell. After a deep breath, and remembering that Betty was coming, Savannah mustered up the courage to ring the doorbell.

The door was opened by a smiling and gracious Dora, who motioned for Savannah to come in and join the circle of nurses gathered around Rita, who was already opening baby gifts. The other nurses and hospital employees stopped briefly to acknowledge Savannah's arrival, then quickly returned to their work at hand.

Savannah was grateful that everyone was preoccupied by "oohing" and "aahing" over the baby presents. Savannah slipped into the circle of women in between Betty, who Savannah was glad to see was already present, and Bonnie, who worked in Hunter's office.

"It won't be long before we are giving you one of these," Betty said to Savannah with a wink.

"Isn't it customary to be married first before having children?" Savannah countered sarcastically.

"That doesn't stop many of our patients," Betty said with a laugh.

Bonnie, who was listening, interjected, "Oh, I've seen how Dr. Davis acts when you come to the office. I don't think it'll be long before he gets down on one knee."

"Oh, you girls stop it. You'll have Hunter and I married with four kids before I leave this party," Savannah said in protest.

Savannah curled up on the floor between Betty and Bonnie, who were sitting in chairs, and watched as Rita continued to open her presents. Savannah recognized most of the women at the party as employees of the hospital. There were a few ladies she did not know who she assumed were friends of Rita's but not connected with the hospital. There seemed to be a constant flow of baby presents from diapers to baby bottles, to a crib, then a stroller. Savannah never realized how many material things are necessary just to care for a little baby.

Savannah noticed that Dora was being the perfect hostess, ushering the stragglers, like Savannah, in the door, bringing refreshments to everybody, and putting everyone in a jovial mood. Savannah could not imagine that this kind, older nurse would be involved with anything unseemly at the hospital.

As more and more presents were opened, Savannah was pleased that nobody else had given Rita a baby blanket. Maybe because the choice was so basic, everyone opted for something more exotic. Some of the presents were even gag gifts, including a see-through red negligee to ward off the Madonna Syndrome after the baby was born. But Savannah was happy that nobody else gave Rita a baby blanket, so maybe Savannah's present might become that favorite blanket after all.

After all the presents were opened, the women sat around talking about babies, work, sex, and men. One of the nurses asked Rita if she would be returning to work right after having the baby. Rita responded that she was going to take off six weeks to bond with the baby, but after that she was going to return to work. Another nurse asked Rita who was going to watch the baby. Rita told the group that she was fortunate because her sister, who stayed at home with two young children of her own, was going to be able to watch the baby also. The other women nodded in the affirmative, knowing how hard it is to get someone you trust to watch a newborn.

"Well, if you're returning to work I guess you won't be breastfeeding," responded Sally Register, a nurse who worked in pediatrics who was known to be a big proponent of breastfeeding.

"I will at first, but, yes, if I go back to work, I'll have to get the baby to take a bottle," Rita said defensively.

That opened up the door to what Savannah knew would be at least a thirty-minute debate on the pros and cons of breastfeeding versus bottle feeding. As several women spoke up at once to offer their versions of what is best, Savannah stood up and made her way to the kitchen where Dora was cooking and holding court for the small group of people that at parties always seem to congregate in the kitchen.

"A lot of you girls are too young to remember the good days of nursing before the HMO's took over," Dora was saying as she pulled some hot chocolate chip cookies from the oven.

After putting the tray of cookies on top of the stove to cool, Dora took a sip of wine and continued, "It used to be we practiced medicine at the highest level without regard to cost, and we did whatever the doctor and nurse felt was best. Now we have to follow protocol and there is so much paperwork, it's getting more and more burdensome. The responsibility on nurses is also getting greater as the decision making process is getting pushed further down the medical tree from doctors to physicians' assistants to the nurses due to time and money constraints. For all these extra responsibilities we get paid the same or less," Dora continued as she shook her head in bewilderment, and the other nurses nodded in agreement.

Another nurse, Cathy Highsmith, spoke up, "Yeah, we used to keep patients in the hospital until they were well, but thanks to the Balanced Budget Act of 1997, which was designed to reduce the budget deficit by reducing the rise in Medicare spending, we are sending patients home from the hospital as soon as possible, sometimes too soon."

"Yeah, maybe they should have called the bill the 'Geriatric Reduction Act of 1997' since it's sending some of our senior citizens to their graves," said another nurse whose quip brought laughter from the group of women, most of whom were drinking wine.

"Well, it's certainly led to a boom in the home health-care industry. I can't believe the number of nurses going to work for home health-care companies. It seems like all my classmates are going to work for them," said Betsy Winters, a young nurse from the hospital.

"That's not real nursing," responded Dora, who then added, "maybe I'm old fashioned, but real nursing is done in the hospital."

"How long have you been nursing?" asked one of the young nurses of Dora.

Dora shot the nurse a condescending look and then said, "Well, let's just put it this way: it was before HMOs, home health care, and before all the other bullcrap."

The cookies had sufficiently cooled so Dora was able to transfer them from the cookie trays to a plate.

"So, why do you keep working?" Betsy asked innocently of Dora, obviously in reference to her advancing age.

Dora turned around, a plate of cookies in each hand as she prepared to deliver them into the living room. "Because I like helping people," Dora said to Betsy with a wink of her eye so that Betsy did not know if Dora was serious or not.

Savannah stayed in the kitchen for a minute or two trying to digest all that she had heard, then she followed Dora into the living room. Dora was busy distributing the cookies to her guests so Savannah wandered around the room looking at photographs on the table and walls.

Savannah spotted a photograph of Dora's wedding. Dora was quite beautiful at that time in her splendid wedding gown. Dora was still trim and professional looking at her age now, which Savannah guessed to be in her early fifties, but Dora appeared to be quite a knockout when she was younger. The man beside her in the picture also looked handsome in his formal army uniform. Savannah left the table of wedding photographs and followed a trail of pictures down a hallway. The pictures provided a chronological history of the development of a young man who Savannah guessed must be Dora's son. The pictures started with baby photographs, progressed to toddler pictures, then youth football and baseball pictures, then prom pictures, high school graduation pictures, and finally college graduation. At the end of the photographs was a framed college diploma that declared Tommy Stimpson had graduated from Georgia Tech with a degree in electrical engineering.

As Savannah reached the end of the photographs near the edge of a doorway to a bedroom, she noticed somebody inside the bedroom looking at the photographs on top of a dresser.

"You aren't being nosy, are you, Betty?" Savannah asked of her older co-worker.

"Well, you never know what you are going to learn," responded Betty, motioning for Savannah to join her.

Savannah went inside the bedroom with its neatly made bed and mementos on the walls and dresser. From the looks of it, this bedroom was the master bedroom belonging to Dora and her husband, although this house was built before the days of walk-in closets and big master baths. There was just one small closet and a cramped, old-fashioned bathroom connected to the bedroom.

Betty motioned for Savannah to sit beside her on the bed. Savannah did so, and as she sat next to Betty she could tell Betty was slightly tipsy.

"It's amazing what can be learned after a couple of glasses of wine," Betty began in a hushed tone as if she were carrying world secrets. "Yeah, a little tongue oil and you can learn all kinds of things," Betty continued. Savannah knew Betty's favorite pastimes were benignly gossiping and meddling, so Savannah politely turned to hear what Betty had to say.

Betty glanced apprehensively toward the doorway of the bedroom to reassure herself nobody else was listening, then started speaking, slightly above a whisper.

"Well, I was talking with one of Dora's long-time friends and we were talking about men, money, and those sorts of things. Anyway, she told me Dora's whole life history. Do you want to hear it?" Betty asked of Savannah.

Savannah generally did not believe in gossiping, but anything she could learn about Dora might be helpful, so she encouraged Betty to continue.

"Dora grew up in Yulee," Betty began, referring to a small, rural, unincorporated area on the mainland just west of Amelia Island. "Dora's father worked for the railroad and her mother did clothes alterations. When Dora was seventeen, she got pregnant by her boyfriend, who was joining the army. They got married and had a son. Dora got her nursing degree by taking college courses at whichever base they happened to be stationed at that time. When her husband got out of the army, he went to work at the paper mill here in Fernandina, while Dora went to work at the old hospital here. Well, between their two modest salaries, they were able to get this house and raise their little boy, Tommy, who by the way, turned out to be a pretty smart kid and now works up in Boston for some big company. Anyway, after Tommy left for college, Dora jumped ship from the old hospital to Medi-Most when it was first built to make more money and to be its first nursing director.

"This is where it starts to get good now," Betty interjected, then continued. "It seems that Dora and her husband started having problems around that time. It might have been the stress of a new job, having been married too young, or the empty-nest syndrome, but get this now: Dora had an affair with Dr. Hockman!"

"No!" said Savannah in disbelief, shocked that anyone could find Dr. Hockman appealing.

"Yes!" said Betty gleefully, pleased that her revelation brought such a strong response from her audience.

"And there's more!" said Betty with relish. "Very quickly, Dora became remorseful and broke off the affair, but Dr. Hockman wanted to continue, and he was so mad at Dora that he demoted her to the I.C.U."

"Well, that explains why Dora works the I.C.U. instead of being nursing director. I thought it was because she didn't like dealing with the personnel issues. But why didn't he just fire her?" asked Savannah incredulously.

"Well, that would open him up to a sexual discrimination suit," replied Betty.

"Then why didn't she just quit?" asked Savannah.

"Because she had left the old hospital in a lurch when she jumped ship to Medi-Most and she couldn't go back," responded Betty.

"Why didn't Dora go to Jacksonville and find a job?" asked Savannah.

"Well, because Dora didn't want to commute the hour each way to work in Jacksonville, and because she doesn't like driving on the highway," explained Betty.

"No wonder Dora acts kind of bitter," said Savannah.

"You'd be bitter too if you got demoted and still had to work with a boss you never wanted to see again," retorted Betty.

"But why doesn't she just quit working?" asked Savannah incredulously.

"Because Dora's husband doesn't make enough money at the paper mill. He only works in the wood yard. Dora makes almost as much as he does. Their income would fall almost in half if she quits and she's too young to retire and get any benefits," explained Betty, proud that she had heard the full story.

"Well, that is quite interesting," said Savannah, shaking her head, trying to absorb it all so she could relay the information to Hunter later.

"Yes, it is. Even if I say so myself," said Betty with satisfaction.

"Well, I'd better be going. It's getting late," said Savannah.

"Oh, don't leave. The night is young and we still have dirt to dig up," said Betty, fueled by the wine and the success of her revelations to Savannah.

"No, I really must go. Hunter is waiting for me," said Savannah anxiously.

"I really created a monster with you two," said Betty proudly, referring to the fact that she helped set them up. "If I had a young stud like that, I'd be leaving too," added Betty, clearly influenced by the wine.

"Are you sure you are going to be okay driving home by yourself?" asked Savannah.

"Oh, sure, darling. Don't you worry your pretty little head about me. I've done this many times and haven't failed to make it home yet. Besides, I do not have very far to go. I only live about a mile away," reassured Betty.

The two women stood up and Savannah hugged Betty, then left the room leaving Betty free to continue her snooping around. Savannah walked into the living room, which was only about half-filled with people now. Savannah found Dora and thanked her for the evening and then hugged Rita and wished her luck with her first baby. Savannah then excused herself and walked out into the fresh air. Savannah breathed deeply the slightly cool, but fresh, night air, just now realizing how thick the cigarette smoke had become in the small, cramped house. Savannah was glad that she had come and walked hurriedly to her car, for she could not wait to tell Hunter what she had learned.

When Savannah arrived at Hunter's house, she found Hunter still up waiting for her, reading a book in the living room. Savannah plopped down on the couch beside Hunter and hurriedly told Hunter what she had learned earlier this evening.

Hunter listened attentively and when Savannah was done, he sat back and spoke.

"Well, it looks like Dora doesn't like Medi-Most and she certainly doesn't like Dr. Hockman. It can't be easy for her working for a company she doesn't like and a boss she probably despises. Maybe Dora is killing patients to make the hospital or Dr. Hockman look bad. Maybe it's her way of getting back at them," Hunter wondered aloud.

"Oh, I don't know," started Savannah. "Dora just doesn't seem the type to do something so unethical, so evil," continued Savannah.

"Yeah, well, that's probably what Jeffrey Dahmer's neighbors said until they started finding body parts in his freezer," responded Hunter with a sly smile.

"Oh, Hunter, you're incorrigible," responded Savannah, giving him a light punch in the arm.

"I'm going to bed," Savannah retorted, suddenly realizing how tired she was after working all day, attending the shower, and drinking a couple glasses of wine.

"I thought you would never ask," said Hunter mischievously, as he followed Savannah toward the bedroom.

Chapter Nineteen

Hunter woke up early the next day. Sleep was not easy when he had so much going on in his mind. Dora had access, opportunity, and reasons for committing the acts upon the patients. Now all Hunter had to do was prove that Dora was doing the deed.

Hunter's mind raced as he thought about ways of proving Dora was doing harm to her patients. Hunter thought about going to Dr. Hockman and relaying his suspicions and asking for a security camera to be installed in the I.C.U. ward to monitor what was going on in there. Dr. Hockman, however, had not been receptive to any of Hunter's ideas so far, and Hunter was a little bit intimidated by the man, so Hunter decided he needed to have more evidence than just hunches and suspicions.

Hunter decided as he lay in bed that he would track down Rita and try to wean any information out of her about what exactly occurred during each episode. Hunter forced himself out of bed to shave and shower. After eating a bowl of cereal, Hunter headed to the hospital. Hunter knew Rita would be completing her shift around seven o'clock in the morning and Hunter waited by Rita's car in the hospital's parking lot in order to catch Rita alone.

Hunter arrived at the parking lot at ten minutes until seven. Then he located Rita's car, parked near it, and turned off the motor and listened to the car radio until Rita arrived.

Soon Hunter spotted Rita weaving her way through the cars in the parking lot on the way to her car. Hunter turned off his radio and got out of his car to intercept Rita. Just as Rita had stopped beside her car, fumbling to find her keys in the bottom of her purse, Hunter approached her.

"Good morning, Rita," Hunter began pleasantly.

"Oh, hi, Dr. Davis," Rita acknowledged, then added, "You're getting an early start this morning."

"Well, I was hoping I might get a word with you. Could I buy you some breakfast in the cafeteria?" Hunter inquired.

Rita looked at Hunter inquisitively, wondering why Dr. Davis would want to talk to her. "I don't know. I'm kind of tired," said Rita hesitantly.

"It won't take long, and you must be famished after working all night," Hunter countered.

Rita was hungry and didn't want to make breakfast before she went to sleep so Rita reluctantly agreed, her stomach overruling the need for sleep.

Rita and Hunter walked toward the cafeteria, making small talk along the way. Rita kind of enjoyed being in the company of the handsome doctor, relishing the envious glares from the other nurses as she entered the cafeteria. Hunter escorted Rita to a table and went through the cafeteria line to retrieve his items and the items that Rita had requested.

Rita watched the other female hospital workers steal glances at Hunter as he made his way back to their table. Rita felt very important that Dr. Davis wanted to have breakfast with her. Hunter sat down beside her and smiled at her reassuringly, realizing that he needed to use his charm to get the information he desired. Since Hunter had already had a bowl of cereal, all he had on his tray was a bagel and a cup of black coffee. Rita, however, coming off the night shift was starving and sat down to a tray of scrambled eggs, bacon, grits, and toast.

Hunter held back from starting the conversation as he watched Rita attack her breakfast. After he noticed Rita slowing down slightly, Hunter began to speak.

"Rita, I'm doing some research on hospital efficiency," Hunter began, trying to flash his best smile. "I'm doing some postgraduate work at the University of North Florida to add a hospital administration degree, and I'm doing a paper on the mortality rates of the different hospitals in the Jacksonville area," Hunter lied, but remained smiling at Rita as she continued to eat her breakfast. Rita looked up briefly from her breakfast and nodded acknowledgment to Hunter.

130

"Now my research shows that Medi-Most Hospital has a relatively high mortality rate over the last couple of years compared to other hospitals in the area," Hunter continued, trying not to be direct.

"Our rates are higher?" Rita asked as she munched on her toast.

"Yes, significantly so for a hospital this size," Hunter lied, not knowing the exact numbers but wanting to elicit a response from Rita.

"Well, I always felt we were losing more than our share, but being new to the I.C.U. I just thought that was normal, since the patients were so compromised," Rita responded, shaking her head.

"Do you have any theories why Medi-Most's mortality rates would be higher in the I.C.U. than they should?" Hunter asked earnestly.

"Well, I don't know, Dr. Davis, I always thought Dora and I were pretty competent nurses," said Rita.

"Nobody is saying it is the nurses' fault, Rita. The nursing care is just one of the parameters involved. It could be the equipment, the protocol, the type of patients, or just plain bad luck. But it is important to analyze the situation to see if there is a causal effect. Now, think hard, are there any similarities between the cases that have happened on your shift?" implored Hunter.

"Well," Rita began, "Dora and I usually work the night shift, so all the cases I've been involved with happened at night. It's just Dora and I working the I.C.U. alone. Usually it's pretty quiet since most of the patients are on medication and unconscious. We obviously have the most severe cases, so they are more likely to take a turn for the worse and meet their demise, but I've always felt we keep a close watch on them. Dora particularly seems to be very conscientious and is always hovering over them."

Hunter nodded his head, as he listened attentively to what Rita was saying, then he asked, "Are you and Dora both present in the ward all the time together?"

"Of course," Rita responded, indignant at Hunter's question. "What do you think we do? Take turns sleeping while the other one takes watch?" Rita asked sarcastically.

"No, I didn't mean to imply that," Hunter said apologetically. "I just wanted you to think if there ever was a time when you were distracted or out of the room," Hunter said in explanation.

"You're not suggesting that Dora does something to the patients while I'm out of the room, are you?" Rita asked incredulously.

"No, no," Hunter responded instantaneously. "I'm just trying to establish if there is any sequence of events that is coincidental with these occurrences."

"Dora couldn't be connected with these deaths, because, if my memory serves me correctly, a lot, if not all, of these occurrences have happened on our coffee break about three o'clock, when Dora usually goes down the hall to use the bathroom, while I fix the coffee," Rita said emphatically.

This information struck Hunter like a lightning bolt, knowing that Dora could have walked out of the I.C.U. on the pretense of going to the bathroom, then snuck back in to the I.C.U. by the way of the supply room—unseen by Rita if Rita was over at the coffee machine. Dora would have had time to administer an injection, then rush back into the hallway through the supply room to enter through the main entrance to the I.C.U. just as the monitors would go off.

"Yes, I see your point," Hunter answered to give Rita the appearance that he didn't believe Dora could be involved while at the same time confirming to himself that Dora was his prime suspect.

"Well, thank you for your time, Rita," Hunter said flashing his best smile. "I'm sure those occurrences are probably just unrelated incidences involving unhealthy patients. I was just

132

hoping to establish some underlying cause to help my paper on hospital efficiency. I know that you and Dora do a good job, and I didn't mean to imply anything else. I'm sure, like a lot of things, these things go in cycles, and the I.C.U. is just having a statistical anomaly right now. Thanks again for your time."

Hunter stood up and shook Rita's hand. Rita thanked him for the breakfast and then, realizing how tired she was following her shift, hurried off to go home to her nice soft bed. Hunter, meanwhile, sat back down to finish his coffee and glancing at his watch noticed he had about twenty minutes before he needed to head to his office to start seeing patients.

Hunter stared into his coffee cup, more convinced than ever that Dora had access and motive to be carrying out these deeds. Dora's conspicuous absence during the cardiac arrests gave her a perfect alibi while at the same time providing her with the time to sneak through the supply room to inject the potassium. If the scheme was ever found out, it would be Rita implicated, not Dora. It was a very clever scheme, Hunter admitted to himself, but there was one thing that bothered Hunter. In the couple of brief conversations Hunter had had with Dora, Hunter couldn't imagine this pleasant and stately woman being capable of the evil intent behind these occurrences. But Hunter quickly put these thoughts aside, knowing that appearances and first impressions are often deceptive. Besides, Hunter thought, as the saying goes there is nothing worse than a woman's spite, and Dora had plenty to be spiteful about.

Chapter Twenty

That evening after Hunter and Savannah had completed their day's work at the hospital, the young couple met back at Hunter's beach house. Hunter had gotten home first and was just coming back from a run on the beach when he spotted Savannah's car coming down the road to his house as he walked around the front yard, cooling down from his run. Hunter and Savannah both had been too busy at work to meet for lunch, and Hunter was dying to tell Savannah about his conversation with Rita.

Savannah pulled her car into the sand driveway beside Hunter's rental home and Hunter walked up to the driver's side door.

"Hey, beautiful," Hunter said pleasantly as Savannah opened her door, grabbed her purse, and started out of the car. Hunter stood with one hand on the open door and the other hand on the roof of the car and kissed Savannah as she exited the car.

"Oooh, how did you get so sweaty?" Savannah asked seductively, running a finger down Hunter's chest.

"Well, I've been thinking about you," Hunter said mischievously.

"Yeah, I bet," Savannah responded, then added, "and that five-mile run you just completed didn't have anything to do with it, did it?"

"Well, maybe, but I was still thinking about you," Hunter responded as Savannah locked her car door and they walked the short distance to the house.

"How about a little shower together?" Hunter asked of Savannah with a gleam in his eye.

"Oh, that running has raised your endorphin levels, hasn't it?" Savannah said with a smile. But then Savannah added, "Why don't you go ahead and take a shower while I get dinner ready? It's been a long day for me."

Hunter nodded disappointedly, then remembering his conversation with Rita said, "Wait until you hear what I learned today."

"O.K., go now and get your shower and I'll hear all about it over dinner," Savannah said as she turned toward the kitchen while Hunter headed to the bathroom.

After his shower, Hunter entered the small dining room wearing a fresh pair of gym shorts and a clean T-shirt. Savannah, still in her nurse's uniform, was putting the finishing touches on the dinner she was laying out on the dining room table. As Savannah was lighting the lone candle on the dinner table, Hunter sneaked up behind her, wrapped his arms around her, and after giving her a sweet kiss on the cheek, whispered into her ear, "You're the best."

"I bet you say that to all the girls," responded Savannah with feigned sarcasm.

"Only to girls in nurses' uniforms that fix me dinner and whom I live with," said Hunter reassuringly.

"Well, let's eat," said Savannah, then added, "I'm starving. I didn't have a chance to eat all day, we were so busy."

"Good idea," said Hunter as he sat down at one end of the table. "Wait until I tell you what Rita said today," Hunter offered.

"Do we have to talk about work?" Savannah said, exhausted from her day's activities.

"Don't you want to know if Darrell was murdered?" asked Hunter incredulously.

"Well, of course I do," Savannah muttered. "But I'm tired of the hospital. I think we should go away somewhere and get away from all of this," Savannah said wearily.

Hunter got up from his chair and walked over to Savannah and, putting his arm around her shoulder, knelt down beside her. Hunter gazed into Savannah's eyes, who was taken aback by Hunter's serious approach. Hunter looked directly at Savannah and said, "I'm getting tired of this also. But think about Darrell and Ben Johnson and all the others past and possibly in the

135

future. If what is going on at the hospital is what we think is going on, then we have to stop them. Our only problem is finding out who exactly is behind this. Now, Rita had some interesting things to say today. Would you like to hear them?" inquired Hunter.

"Of course I would," responded Savannah. "But promise me, when this is over, we will go somewhere and forget that Medi-Most ever existed," added Savannah.

"That's a deal," responded Hunter merrily, giving Savannah a kiss on the cheek as he rose to return to his seat. As Hunter sat back down to resume eating, he began to speak.

"Rita had some very interesting comments today. You know how you found out at the baby shower that Dora had a motive for revenge against the hospital and Dr. Hockman? Well, I think Rita may have told us how Dora is doing it," Hunter expounded as Savannah sat listening intently.

"Usually there are two nurses on duty in the I.C.U. at all times, so it would be hard for one to do something to the patients without the other noticing, right?" Hunter asked as Savannah nodded in affirmation. "Well, Rita said that they usually take a coffee break around three o'clock in the morning and that Dora goes down the hall to the bathroom while Rita makes coffee."

"So?" asked Savannah, wondering the significance of that statement.

"Well, that gives Dora the opportunity, under the pretense of going to the bathroom, to go out in the hall and then sneak back through the supply room into the I.C.U. and inject the potassium."

"Wouldn't Rita see her come back in through the supply room?" asked Savannah.

"Not if she is at the coffee machine," responded Hunter. "Remember, it is around the corner in the little alcove. The beds in the I.C.U. are not visible from the coffee machine area," explained Hunter.

"You're right!" exclaimed Savannah. "I never noticed that before, but you're right. You can't see what's going on in the rest of the I.C.U. from the coffee machine area."

"That also gives Dora a perfect alibi if the deaths were found to be suspicious. She could say she was in the bathroom when the event occurred and the blame would fall on Rita, if anybody," Hunter reported.

"I can't believe Dora would do this, but it's sure looking that way," agreed Savannah. "But how do you know it's not Rita injecting the patients while Dora is out of the room?" asked Savannah.

"I don't know for sure," answered Hunter. "But Rita seems too sincere and naïve to be behind this. I think she is just a pawn being used by someone else, who is taking advantage of her newness and naïveté," continued Hunter.

"Well, how are we going to find out if Dora's really doing it?" asked Savannah.

"I have been thinking about it," responded Hunter, "and I have come to the conclusion that we need to do a stakeout."

"A stakeout?" Savannah exclaimed. "Who do you think we are? Starsky and Hutch? I think you have been watching too much late-night television," Savannah added. "Why don't we just go to the authorities with our suspicions?" Savannah implored.

"Because that's all they are, suspicions," Hunter answered. "We need some proof," countered Hunter.

"Just how do you plan on getting that proof?" asked Savannah, not really wanting to hear the answer.

"Well, we know what time these events occur. We just need to be at the hospital, outside of the I.C.U., right before three o'clock in the morning," answered Hunter.

"You must be kidding," responded Savannah wearily. "I'm tired now from working all day at the hospital. Now you expect us to spend our nights there also?" Savannah said shaking her head from side to side.

"No, we don't have to both go every night, we can take turns," said Hunter. "I'll take the first night so you can catch up on your rest, then we will alternate. If we go to bed early, we can get five or six hours of sleep then get up at 2:30 and be at the hospital before three," explained Hunter.

"And just how would we do this without them seeing us spy on them?" asked Savannah, still not willing to go along with this plan.

"I've already scouted this out and, if you remember, the X-ray department is right across and slightly down from the supply room. The small reception area has a window facing into the hall with a great view of the supply room door. We just have to sit in there with the lights down and then we can videotape through the window anybody entering the supply room," explained Hunter.

"Yeah, but how do we know they plan to strike again? It could be weeks before another episode happens and I am so tired already," Savannah said, not fully recovered from her vigil with Darrell.

"That's true," admitted Hunter reluctantly. "But in my gut, I feel something is going to happen. Let's give it a couple of weeks and if nothing happens, I promise, I will call it off," Hunter added.

Savannah was bone weary. The last few weeks had really sapped her strength. Savannah stared at Hunter across the table. How could he be so energetic after all they had been through lately, Savannah thought to herself. Hunter stared at Savannah, with pleading eyes not unlike a puppy waiting for a bone. As tired as she was, Savannah couldn't bring herself to disappoint him. Besides, she knew if she didn't participate, Hunter would do it by himself and eventually become so tired his practice would suffer.

"O.K., we'll do it," Savannah reluctantly agreed.

"Great, I'll take the first watch tonight," Hunter said eagerly.

"Tonight?" asked Savannah incredulously.

"No time like the present," Hunter answered energetically as he finished his dinner. "Besides," Hunter said, looking at Savannah mischievously, "it's a great excuse to go to bed early."

And with that remark hanging in the air, Hunter rose from the table, took Savannah's hand and led her into the bedroom.

Chapter Twenty-One

Hunter woke up with a startle. The alarm clock had rudely awakened him from a nice dream he was having about being marooned on a tropical island. The island however was not deserted. In fact, it had a small hotel on it with a bar, restaurant, and a beautiful white sand beach, and it was full of people who had been marooned there but had no desire to be rescued. The weather was always perfect and the days were always alike, with snorkeling and windsurfing followed by umbrella drinks in the hammock.

Hunter hit the button on the alarm clock so it wouldn't wake Savannah. Hunter stared at the time on the clock: 2:27 A.M. Hunter was tempted to just roll over and continue his dream. It had been three weeks since he and Savannah had started this schedule and it was wearing both of them down. Hunter did not know how much longer they could keep this pace going. Savannah particularly was having problems with sleep deprivation, particularly after her long vigil with Darrell. Hunter himself noticed that he was nodding off between patients and being grouchy to his staff.

Hunter glanced over at Savannah, who in her deep slumber had been undisturbed by the alarm clock that Hunter had purposely set on a low volume. Hunter was usually a light sleeper, but even he almost slept through the alarm clock's incessant beeping. Hunter laid his head back down on the pillow one last time before making the final decision that he must get up.

Hunter finally arose from the bed and stumbled into the bathroom to throw cold water on his face and bring himself back to reality. Hunter stared into the mirror at his reflection and seeing the tired, sad face staring back at him wondered if going to the hospital was worth it. Hunter and Savannah had alternated for three weeks now, and it could be another few weeks or even months before something happened. But right when Hunter thought about returning to bed, Ben Johnson's face flashed before Hunter's eyes and Hunter knew what he had to do.

Hunter splashed some more water on his face, combed his unruly hair and put on his scrubs so it would appear he was checking on a patient if he encountered anybody at the hospital. Hunter clipped his identification card to the pocket of his scrub shirt and quietly exited the bathroom. Hunter glanced at Savannah, who was peacefully in a deep sleep. The pale moonlight was sneaking between the curtains and casting a glow upon Savannah's face. Savannah was laying on her side with her hair stretched out on her pillow. In her white satin nightgown, with the moonlight playing upon her, Hunter envisioned Savannah to be an almost angelic form. Hunter felt his love for Savannah filling his soul and he desperately wanted to return to bed and put his arms around her slim waist. But Hunter didn't want to disturb Savannah and he had a job to do, so he turned and headed for his car.

The roads were deserted this time of night and Hunter quickly made it to the hospital. Hunter parked in the nearly empty employees' lot and briskly walked into the side entrance of the hospital. The hospital had a limited staff at night and Hunter developed a path to the X-ray department that would keep Hunter and Savannah away from the staff that was on duty on the night shift. With him, Hunter carried a clipboard with some notes on it and a briefcase with the video camera inside. If Hunter did encounter the occasional security guard or nurse, he would just glance at his clipboard, then at his watch, and walk purposefully past that person as if he was headed to some important rendezvous with a patient.

Fortunately, this night Hunter did not see a soul as he made his way to the X-ray department. Hunter took a circuitous route so as to reach the X-ray department without having to walk past the intensive care ward. Hunter glanced at his watch as he walked down the hall, seeing that his watch said it was eight minutes to three o'clock in the morning. Hunter quickened his pace. Finally arriving at the X-ray department door, Hunter slipped through the unlocked door and entered the small reception area. Hunter quickly placed his briefcase on the small table that was under the fairly large window with mini-blinds that faced across the hall toward the supply room of the intensive care ward. Hunter reached up and closed the mini-blinds until there were only small slits to look through. The door of the supply room was almost directly across the hall, just a little bit to the left. The main entrance to the intensive care ward was further down the hall to the left and could be seen by standing just to the right of the little table and looking at an angle down the hall. Hunter retrieved the video camera from the briefcase, removed the lens cap, and turned the camera on to the ready position. Hunter glanced again at his watch, it was now two minutes until three o'clock. Peering through the slats, Hunter waited for Dora to exit and head for the bathroom. In the three weeks since Savannah and Hunter had started their surveillance, Dora had faithfully gone on a bathroom break at three o'clock. However, each time when Dora returned from the bathroom she went directly back into the intensive care ward.

After a couple of minutes, Dora emerged from the intensive care ward, right on time. Hunter moved from his position of looking through the narrow slats in the mini-blind at the window to his filming position, which was through a small rectangular window that was head-high on the door to the X-ray room and almost directly across the hall from the supply room door. Hunter turned the camera to record and let the camera run as he focused on the supply room door.

If this wasn't another false alarm, Hunter would soon see Dora come into his viewfinder from his left and enter the supply room door. But while Hunter was still adjusting his focus, a figure suddenly entered his viewfinder from the right and disappeared through the supply room door.

Hunter, caught by surprise, had no time to recognize the figure but he could tell that the person was tall and male. Hunter felt the hair on the back of his neck stand up. "This is it. It's starting to happen," Hunter thought to himself as he focused the camera on the door across the hall to get a good picture of whoever emerged. Maybe it wasn't Dora after all, thought Hunter, or maybe this person was just getting supplies out of the supply room and it was another false alarm.

Suddenly the door to the supply room came open. Hunter had to move the camera up slightly because the man was so tall. The man, dressed in orderly clothes, hesitated briefly to look both ways down the hall and then quickly disappeared to Hunter's right. It was that tall, ugly man that Hunter had seen in Dr. Hockman's office.

Hunter kept the camera rolling, moving its focus down the hall toward the front entrance of the intensive care ward in the direction from which Dora would return from the bathroom. Soon Hunter could see Dora come into the viewfinder as she headed back to the intensive care ward. Dora was wiping her hands with a paper towel and was just a few feet from the doors to the intensive care ward when the late-night silence was broken by the intercom.

"Code blue I.C.U. Code blue in the I.C.U. All necessary personnel please respond, stat!" Hunter could hear Rita's panicked voice blasting throughout the hospital.

Hunter kept the camera rolling as first Dora disappeared through the double doors to the intensive care ward, then after a minute or so delay, the resident doctor followed by a couple of nurses. After the commotion in the hallway had died down as everyone was in the I.C.U. trying vainly to save some poor patient's life, Hunter hastily slid the camera into the briefcase and headed down the hall. Hunter was suddenly overcome with guilt, realizing his own ambition to acquire evidence came possibly at a price of a human life. Hunter briefly thought about turning around and joining the team fighting for the patient's life, but if the events occurred as Hunter had theorized then it was too late for that patient anyhow. As Hunter hurried through the hospital on his way back to his car, Hunter rationalized to himself that he couldn't have gone to the authorities earlier, he just had no proof. But now he wanted to rush home and review the tape and see if he had the proof that Hunter needed. It just wasn't the person who he thought. Instead of Dora, it was the orderly. But that doesn't mean Dora wasn't involved because she was always conveniently out of the room when these events occurred. Was Dora's going to the bathroom just a habit or was it part of the plot, Hunter wondered to himself.

As Hunter reached his car he glanced at his watch. It was only three-thirty in the morning. Things had happened so fast, not much time had elapsed. Hunter had time to go back to his apartment and catch a couple of hours of sleep before he had to be at his office to see patients. But Hunter didn't know if he could go back to sleep. Hunter was too wired from the events that occurred. It was a full moon so Hunter put the top down on his car and took the scenic route back to his apartment along the beach road.

As Hunter drove along the beach road with the bright full moon shining from the west at this late hour, casting an eerie white shimmer out on the ocean to the east, it made Hunter think about an event that occurred one summer while he was working as a lifeguard at Amelia Island Plantation. Shouts from some tourists about one hundred yards up the beach from Hunter's large, wooden lifeguard chair had startled Hunter from his usual daydreaming as he sat in his chair surveying the ocean before him. It was about noon and the heat was becoming oppressive, since the sea breeze had yet to begin for that day. Hunter had looked over at the tourists, which consisted of a man, his two young daughters, and an elderly couple. The younger man was pointing at something in the sand above the high-water mark and excitedly talking to his daughters. When the man looked up and saw Hunter looking at them from his chair he motioned for Hunter to come over to see something.

Hunter had begrudgingly descended from the wooden lifeguard chair, thinking to himself it was probably some dead jellyfish or stingray that the tourists had never seen before and thought was so interesting, but to Hunter it just meant he would have to walk up to the beach club and fetch the shovel to bury the creature so nobody would accidentally step on it with their bare feet and injure themselves with either the stinging tentacles of the jellyfish or the sharp barb of the sting ray. But as Hunter got closer to the tourists and as more people gathered around, Hunter saw what looked like from a distance a line of oversized ants making its way down toward the water line. As Hunter got closer, he saw that the line of creatures wasn't oversized ants, but baby sea turtles that had just hatched from their nest under the warm sand above the high-water mark. That was a rare sight in the daytime, as usually the nests hatch at night in order to give the hatchling sea turtles a better chance of reaching deep water before being snatched up by seagulls and other birds. Also, the hatchlings are guided to the ocean at night by the moonlight reflecting off its surface, which makes it brighter than the land.

As Hunter drove along the beach road admiring the late-evening/early-morning moonlight that was giving the ocean a beautiful glow, Hunter thought about the tremendous odds these young hatchlings faced in order to become an adult sea turtle. The large female loggerhead and green turtles, some weighing as much as four hundred pounds, emerge from the sea and waddle up above the high-water mark, dig a deep nest in the sand with their flippers, and then deposit a clutch of more than one hundred eggs about the size of Ping-Pong balls. After covering the nest with sand, the mother turtle returns to the sea, leaving only its crawl tracks as evidence it was there, and those tracks would be mostly washed away by the next high tide.

If the nests were not discovered by animals, such as raccoons or opossums, and eaten, or lost to storms or even, lately, run over by four-wheel drive vehicles, the nests would hatch about seven to nine weeks after being laid, due to solar incubation. The large number of eggs were necessary because only a few of the hatchlings would ever reach the adult stage. Hunter and the tourists had been eyewitnesses to the biological law of "survival of the fittest," or in the case of the hatchling sea turtles, survival of the luckiest and a war of attrition. What had started as a miracle of birth with the cute, little babies emerging from their hidden sand nest soon turned into a feeding frenzy. While the tourists had been busy gathering some wayward hatchlings and putting them in line with the others heading down toward the water line, a seagull alarm had sounded and soon there was a flock of seagulls in position over the hatchlings' path to the sea with reinforcements arriving every few seconds for the natural seafood buffet. Unaware of the gauntlet they were beginning to run, the young sea turtles headed instinctively toward the sea with inbred determination.

The two young girls who had discovered the nests as the baby sea turtles emerged from the sand watched in horror as the cute little hatchlings, about one to two inches long, were attacked by ghost crabs making an appearance from their holes in the sand, and once they reached the waters edge, they were also descended upon by the seagulls. Some of the poor hatchlings, less than a minute into their short life, were snatched and eaten up by the seagulls and other birds, like the skimmers: graceful white and black birds who flew at high speeds barely above the shallow water with their lower beak in the water to snatch up unsuspecting prey. After watching the massacre for a few moments, Hunter and the tourists tried to form a human wall on each side of the group of turtles to keep the birds away. Hunter still could remember the determination of the little hatchlings. Despite overwhelming odds and despite being constantly tossed back by waves, the hatchlings swam for their lives, once they reached the water. Hunter watched one particularly determined hatchling swim frantically to gain three or four feet toward the ocean depths only to be caught by a wave and tossed like a bobbing cork in the white water and pushed fifteen feet back toward the shore. As soon as the turtle righted itself, it started swimming frantically again toward the deeper water. Hunter watched three or four more waves buffet the poor baby sea turtle, negating any progress it made between waves. The waves were scattering the hatchlings beyond the boundaries of the protective people and the birds were quick to pounce on any sea turtle that was not right next to a human. Hunter had decided to give this turtle a fighting chance and scooped him and a few others up into his hands and waded out beyond the waves to release them. Hunter had noticed the hatchlings never stopped trying to swim even when he cradled them in his hands, so strong was their instinct to swim away from danger. After reaching deep water, Hunter watched as they tumbled out of his hands and immediately dove out of sight in the translucent water.

Hunter hoped he had helped a few of the sea turtles survive, but as he made his way back to the edge of the water he turned around and noticed that the predatory fish had arrived. Hunter knew that the jack crevalle, blues, and Spanish mackerels would take their toll on the young hatchlings. Hunter even thought he saw the wake and silver flash of a tarpon who had joined the feast. Hunter watched for awhile, knowing that the few hatchlings that did get past this gauntlet would still have to get past that biggest predator of all. While the sea turtles, once they reached a certain size and with their hard shells, would be safe from all the other predators in the sea, they were not fast enough to swim away from the shrimp nets pulled behind the large shrimping trawlers and caught as by-product in other commercial fishing nets as well.

This rumination got Hunter thinking about the laws of natural selection: how the weak, old, and genetically inferior die off to ensure the propagation of the species, that only the strongest survive. Hunter thought how man is changing all the rules that have existed since the beginning of nature. Nature is now not the only force in determining which species survives. Man, by his predatory ways and also changing the environment is determining to some extent which species survive and which do not. Even within our own species we are changing the rules to suit ourselves, Hunter further thought to himself. Advances in medical care are allowing us to expand the parameters on who can survive. From allowing very premature babies to live to allowing elderly people's bodies to live past their mind's life span, man is altering the laws of nature. Hunter wondered to himself that if man's constant tinkering with his place in nature would be his eventual downfall as a species. Would this constant quest in medical care to save everyone no matter how compromised or handicapped or elderly eventually weaken the gene pool and cause the demise of man?

Hunter thought back to a patient he had seen recently. The patient was a rather plain woman around thirty years old. The patient had come in with two children in tow and also brought a friend who had driven her to Hunter's office. The patient had come to Hunter's office to confirm what she had already guessed, that she was pregnant with her third child. With symptoms of nausea in the morning and recent weight gain, it was an easy diagnosis soon confirmed by a quick in-office test. After ordering a urine sample taken for a more formal test, Hunter was reviewing the medical history with the patient when the patient reported that she suffered from a hereditary eye disorder that limited her vision to the 20/200 level even with correction and that was also present in her mother and two children. Hunter also noticed on the chart that the woman was on Medicaid and unmarried.

The woman anxiously asked Hunter if he thought this next child would also be afflicted with vision problems. Seeing that the previous children were both a boy and a girl, and knowing that the disorder did not skip a generation, Hunter knew the disorder was a dominant trait and felt sure the next child would suffer from the same problem.

"I'm sorry," Hunter had said to the woman, incredulous that the woman was not already aware of the consequences of her action. Hunter remembered at the time just shaking his head to himself thinking about the cost to society this ill-informed woman was incurring. Hunter then referred the patient to an OB-GYN who was on the Medi-Most panel with the recommendation that the woman's tubes be tied after delivery.

Now, as Hunter drove along the beach road near his apartment, Hunter realized how tired he was, his mind taking off in strange directions. Hunter thought about the woman and her children and realized that in prehistoric times these people would not have survived. With their poor vision, these people would have perished, falling prey to some large animal or perhaps fallen off a cliff. Nature would have run its course, ensuring the survivability of the clan. Today, however, these unfortunate people will be raised by the government with money, food, job training, etc., which is good, so they can hopefully become productive members of society, but somewhere there should be some genetic counseling thrown in so that the laws of natural selection are not totally disobeyed.

This line of thought got Hunter thinking about what was going on at Medi-Most Hospital as he neared his apartment. Originally, Hunter had thought Dora was responsible for these acts in order to embarrass the hospital or Dr. Hockman. Now Hunter had proof these deaths were apparently caused by the tall orderly, although Dora could still be an accomplice since she was always conveniently out of the room at the time of the occurrence.

Hunter pondered what the motives might be for this man to kill these people. All of the patients were severely compromised, most with neurological problems in which they were unlikely to make a full recovery. Maybe these were mercy killings, Hunter thought to himself. Maybe Darrell and Ben were better off dead than in some form of vegetative state. Maybe this guy was doing society a favor, taking the place of nature by killing off the weak and old.

As Hunter reached his apartment and turned into the sand driveway, Hunter snapped out of this train of thought realizing how ludicrous it was. These acts were still murder, he thought. We were talking about taking a human life no matter how compromised it was. These people had a chance for recovery. No one should play God, deciding that another person's time is up. Hunter would find out why this man was doing this, but for right now all he could think about was sleep.

Hunter quietly stumbled into his apartment trying not to wake Savannah. Hunter would have loved waking Savannah up and revealing the night's events but he knew how tired Savannah had been after the past few weeks, so Hunter eased into the bed next to her without disturbing her sleep. Hunter reset the alarm for six-thirty in the morning, giving him another couple of hours of sleep, and laid back contentedly. Things had taken an unexpected turn, but at least he was closer to his goal of finding out what was going on and who was behind it. Tomorrow he would check out the tall, ugly orderly, but for now a tired wave of darkness was washing over him.

Chapter Twenty-Two

Hunter was awakened by the rude ringing of the alarm clock. Hunter sat up in the bed, unrefreshed but determined to find out what was happening at the hospital. Hunter glanced over at the empty space on the bed where Savannah had slept and realized Savannah had snuck out without waking him since she had to be at the hospital at seven and Hunter did not have to be at his office until eight.

Hunter was anxious, however, to get to his office and do some research on his computer about the man he had filmed last night going into the supply room of the I.C.U. Hunter was going to have to get going if he was going to get to his office in time to do that research before seeing patients. Hunter had slept fitfully that last two hours, too many thoughts running through his mind. The orderly's ugly face kept appearing in Hunter's mind as he tried to sleep. After stumbling into the bathroom, Hunter quickly shaved and took a shower to revive himself. Hunter then hurriedly got dressed, had a bowl of cereal and some black coffee, then headed to his office.

Hunter arrived at his office at seven-thirty. This gave Hunter thirty minutes before his first patient and he eagerly turned on the computer and, after it came on, clicked into the personnel files that he had borrowed from Mrs. Jenkins. Hunter brought up Kendall Brill's file onto the screen and he quickly recognized Kendall Brill's face as belonging to the big man he saw coming out of Dr. Hockman's office one day. That's his man, Hunter thought to himself, now all he had to do was prove the man guilty. Thankfully, it was Friday; Hunter only saw patients until noon on Friday. The doctor would have the whole afternoon to try to dig up some more proof. Hunter printed out a copy of Brill's file, complete with picture identification, and then exited the computer and turned it off. Hunter leaned back in his chair and glanced at his watch. It was almost eight o'clock now and soon Hunter would have to see his first patient. Extremely tired,

Hunter closed his eyes to try to catch a quick little catnap before beginning work.

After a very brief catnap, Hunter began seeing patients. Even though he was busy, the morning seemed to drag on forever as Hunter had other things on his mind. After thirty patients, and what seemed like forever, Hunter was finally done.

Hunter had called Savannah earlier in the morning in a spare minute between patients and had arranged to meet her in the cafeteria on her lunch break. There, in the cafeteria over lunch, Hunter explained to Savannah his suspicions about Kendall Brill and that he was going to try to find some proof. Savannah thought Hunter should go to the police at once, but Hunter felt he needed some solid evidence first. Savannah asked Hunter how he planned to go about doing that. Hunter admitted he wasn't sure what he was going to do, but he figured he would start by snooping around the orderlies' room. Savannah begged Hunter to go to the police, or, at the very least, go to Dr. Hockman, since he was chief of staff and hospital administrator, and let him investigate. Savannah didn't want anything to happen to Hunter, particularly after what happened to Darrell. Savannah realized how completely alone she would be if something happened to Hunter.

Hunter stubbornly refused Savannah's advice, feeling he must have more than just the videotape of Brill going into the supply room, but he reassured Savannah that he would be careful. Savannah had to return to work since her lunch break was over. Before she left, however, Savannah bent over and kissed Hunter gently and whispered into his ear.

"Promise me you will be careful," Savannah said softly.

"I will," said Hunter.

Savannah returned to work and Hunter, after sitting for a few minutes, decided he would go look for some evidence.

Hunter followed the hallway, making a couple of turns until he came to the orderlies' room. The door was half open, and Hunter knocked lightly as he peered inside the room. An old man in an orderly's uniform was putting supplies on a shelf. Hunter recognized the orderly as Ben Johnson's friend who had spoken to Hunter briefly after his death.

"Can I help you, doctor?" said the man kindly.

"Well, I guess so," Hunter said hesitantly. "Do you know an orderly named Kendall Brill?"

"Yeah, but he's not here right now, he works the night shift," said the man. Hunter already knew Brill's schedule from his contact at the front desk. Hunter was looking for information on Brill.

"Oh, that's too bad," Hunter lied. "I wanted to thank him for helping me with a patient."

The elderly orderly looked at Hunter with a perplexed look on his face. Hunter, not being used to espionage, struggled for something else to say. Hunter, spotting the man's name tag, said, "Sam, how well do you know Brill?"

"Well, personally, I try to stay away from him," Sam said, returning Hunter's look.

"Why's that?" Hunter asked.

"That's one weird fellow," said Sam, shaking his head.

"What do you mean?" Hunter said, trying to get Sam to elaborate.

"Have you even seen the man?" Sam said. "Just looking at him gives me the creeps. There is just something about him that bothers me. I asked to work the day shift just so I didn't have to work with him."

"Yes, I have seen Brill and he does look kind of strange, but has he ever done anything weird?" asked Hunter innocently.

"Well, I try to stay away from him as much as I can, but I did open up his lunchbox by mistake one day," Sam reported.

Then Sam motioned for Hunter to come closer. Hunter followed Sam over to a refrigerator in the corner of the orderlies' room. Sam opened up the refrigerator and retrieved a lunchbox.

"Now, I'm not one to get anybody into trouble," Sam began. "But I'm not one to turn my back on something I think is wrong either," continued Sam. The older man put the lunchbox on the counter and opened it.

153

"Drugs killed my son and I'm just not going to tolerate it here at work," Sam continued as he reached into the lunchbox. After pushing aside a banana and an old sandwich, Sam showed Hunter what was at the bottom of the lunch box.

"This is Brill's lunch box and this belongs to Brill also," Sam said, showing Hunter a syringe filled with a fluid at the bottom of the lunch box.

"Now I ain't no drug expert, but I think the boy is on heroin," Sam said, looking at the syringe. "Maybe that explains the way the guy looks," Sam said as he sucked in his cheeks to give his face a hollowed-out look.

Hunter immediately recognized that the solution was not heroin, but probably the potassium solution that Hunter needed for proof.

"Do you mind if I have that?" said Hunter as he moved closer, reaching for the lunch box.

"You can have it, just don't tell 'em how you found it," said Sam, handing the lunch box to the doctor.

Hunter took some latex gloves from his pocket and put them on his hands and took the syringe out of the lunch box.

"Thank you," said Hunter, hoping Sam had not handled the syringe, thereby smudging Brill's fingerprints with his own.

"I got to go get some beds ready now," said Sam as he squeezed past Hunter to go out the door.

Hunter looked at the syringe trying to decide what to do. Hunter could have taken the syringe to the lab and had it analyzed, but knowing that blood work had to be done on all deceased patients, Hunter surmised that the lab should have found elevated potassium levels on all of the suspicious deaths if his theory was correct. This meant the lab was either incompetent or in on the conspiracy. Finally, Hunter decided to bypass the lab and take the syringe to Dr. Hockman and explain his suspicions to the chief of staff as Savannah had suggested. Hunter placed the syringe in the pocket of his lab coat and walked through the hallways to Dr. Hockman's office. Hunter entered Dr. Hockman's outer office where he encountered Dr.

Hockman's secretary. Hunter explained to the secretary that he needed to see Dr. Hockman as soon as possible on a very urgent matter. The secretary told Hunter to have a seat, while she checked with Dr. Hockman. The secretary disappeared into Dr. Hockman's office for a minute and then reappeared at the door and motioned for Hunter to come into the inner office. Dr. Hockman stood up from behind his desk and greeted Hunter with a handshake and motioned for Hunter to take a seat in a chair across the desk from him.

"What can I do for you today, Dr. Davis?" asked Dr. Hockman with a friendly tone.

"I'm afraid I have a very grave matter to discuss," began Hunter, realizing the unintended pun of his words. "In fact, I believe it is literally a grave matter because I believe somebody is murdering certain seriously ill patients," Hunter spurted forth.

"Murder! In my hospital?" exclaimed Dr. Hockman. "Where do you get such a ridiculous idea?"

Hunter pulled the syringe out of his pocket and the color left Dr. Hockman's face.

"Where did you get that?" asked Dr. Hockman, referring to the syringe.

"I got the syringe out of a lunchbox belonging to an orderly named Kendall Brill," answered Hunter. "I think Brill has been sneaking into the intensive care ward and shooting the contents of this syringe into patients when nobody is looking. I think if you have it analyzed by an independent lab, you will find that it contains a high-concentration solution of potassium, leading to cardiac arrest in those patients," said Hunter calmly.

"May I see that?" Dr. Hockman said as he leaned forward to take the syringe from Hunter. Dr. Hockman leaned back in his chair, staring at the syringe he held in both hands.

"Are you familiar with the laws of natural selection, Dr. Davis?" Dr. Hockman said wistfully as he continued to lean back in the chair and stare at the syringe.

"Well, of course, I studied the laws of nature during high school," said Hunter, mystified at Dr. Hockman's question.

155

"Then you know about 'survival of the fittest' and the natural law that the weak, sick, and old die off for the eventual benefit of the rest of the group," continued Dr. Hockman.

"Yes, I remember my high school biology, but I don't understand what that has to do with our situation," said Hunter, beginning to get annoyed.

"Do you know how much this country spends on trying to save patients that cannot be saved?" asked Dr. Hockman rhetorically. "You know how the game is played, Dr. Davis. In medical school and residency they teach you to do everything possible for every patient without regard to cost. If a patient is diagnosed with cancer, even if the situation is probably terminal, chemotherapy and/or radiation therapy will be done to buy some time. The patient might get a few extra months but the end result is the same; the patient dies and there is a huge bill to the insurance company. The doctors and the family of the patient feel no guilt because they did everything medically possible and the insurance company is left with the tab.

"Now in the past few years, things have changed," continued Dr. Hockman, pointing the syringe at Hunter, who sat in amazed silence. "When Bill Clinton first got in office, he and Hillary made medical care reform the top of their agenda—which, by the way, was like putting doctors in charge of tort reform, both of them being lawyers and all. Well, anyway, politics being what they are, Bill and Hillary's efforts failed, but the insurance companies saw an opening that they went through like Barry Sanders running on Astroturf."

Dr. Hockman stood up and walked over to the window, clearly riled up by his own monologue. "The insurance companies have won the war, boy. The patients and doctors have lost the battle. Now, we have managed care, which means the insurance companies tell the patients and the doctors what to do and what they can't do."

"You're crazy," said Hunter, shaking his head and remembering Dr. Hockman's obsession with this issue on their first visit together.

156

"Am I?" snapped Dr. Hockman as he turned from the window to face Hunter. "Must I remind you of our bonus situation with Medi-Most? The insurance company has put some burden of risk on our shoulders. Some of Medi-Most's plans are capitated, meaning the hospital network gets paid a set amount to take care of a group of people, no matter what the actual costs are. A few very expensive cases can eat up the allotted medical dollars for the entire group. To use our analogy of the herd, we may spend too much on the few unsalvageable members of the herd at the expense of the stronger majority of the herd. Therefore, in the last two years, myself and most of the doctors I have recruited have worked to identify these expensive, unsalvageable patients who represent a financial detriment to the group as a whole," said Dr. Hockman as he watched Hunter for a reaction.

"You are all crazy!" exclaimed Hunter, remembering Dr. Raja's expression in the cafeteria. "You are talking about murder."

"I prefer to call it clinical euthanasia; besides, we are talking about patients that are going to die anyway or be so mentally or physically handicapped that death is the preferred option," continued Dr. Hockman.

"But Darrell could have recovered," Hunter blurted out.

"If you are referring to the young man from the car accident, the doctor on the case assured me the prognosis was very poor. If and when the young man came out of his coma, the doctor told me he would be severely impaired," Dr. Hockman said matter-of-factly.

"You are playing God," remarked Hunter.

"Quite correct," said Dr. Hockman. "In the animal kingdom, God allows the weak, sick, or slowest to be taken by the lions or whatever to the ultimate benefit of the herd. Why should mankind be any different?"

Hunter had to admit, in a twisted sort of way and following the laws of natural selection, what Dr. Hockman was saying made sense.

"Why don't you join us, Hunter? I was planning on recruiting you anyhow, and now is as good a time as any," said Dr. Hockman as he sat back down in his seat, waiting for Hunter's reply.

Hunter couldn't believe what Dr. Hockman was asking of him. Never did Hunter believe when he took the Hippocratic Oath upon graduation from medical school that he would be asked to blatantly ignore the main theme of the oath: "above all else do no harm." Hunter wanted to blurt out, "You're a crazy and cynical old man that belongs in jail," but something in Dr. Hockman's icy stare warned Hunter that he needed to be careful. "I need some time to think about this," responded Hunter, trying to act confused.

"Sure, Dr. Davis," said Dr. Hockman confidently. Then Dr. Hockman added, "I just want to leave you with a couple of thoughts while you mull this over. First of all, I'm going to dispose of this little syringe that Mr. Brill left so carelessly in his lunchbox. In addition, an autopsy of the involved patients will not reveal any illicit substances at this late date. Therefore, there is no evidence linking us to any involvement. All of the cases will show natural causes.

"Second, just in case I needed to guarantee your cooperation at some future date, I sent you a special patient a couple of weeks ago. I won't tell you her name, but I will tell you that she is a pretty young woman who loves money and is willing to testify that you made unwarranted sexual advances on her during your examination. You know how this type of controversy can ruin a doctor's reputation and follow him throughout his career even if it's untrue, which is difficult to prove one way or the other. So you think long and hard about this, Dr. Davis. I trust you will make the wise decision," Dr. Hockman said confidently as he walked around to Hunter's side of the desk.

Hunter rose from his chair and they both walked toward the door.

"Oh, by the way," Dr. Hockman said as he ushered Hunter to the door. "Give my condolences to Nurse Jones, she must be distraught over the passing of her brother," said Dr. Hockman with feigned concern. "We wouldn't want to give Nurse Jones anything else to worry about, would we? It might be bad for her health," said Dr. Hockman smiling. Then Dr. Hockman whispered in Hunter's ear, "Nobody else knows about our little situation, do they?"

Hunter turned toward Dr. Hockman for an instant, then gathered himself to look into Dr. Hockman's earnest gaze while he lied, "No, nobody."

Dr. Hockman looked at Hunter intensely for a couple of seconds, then shook Hunter's hand firmly. "Think hard, Dr. Davis, think hard," Dr. Hockman said as he released Hunter's hand and Hunter passed through the doorway.

Hunter knew exactly which patient Dr. Hockman had sent him, Lolita Gomez. Hunter cursed himself for being so careless. No wonder the woman acted the way she did and said what she said to Rosa. The veiled threats about Savannah's health also concerned Hunter greatly. Dr. Hockman it would seem, was willing to do anything to keep his scheme quiet.

Hunter stood motionless on the other side of the closed door. Dr. Hockman's receptionist politely asked Hunter if he was all right. Hunter nodded his head in affirmation and walked slowly out into the hallway. Hunter staggered down the hallway, his mind abuzz with what had just transpired.

The ramifications of what Hunter had just learned were beginning to sink in. Not only were Hunter and Savannah in danger but Sam the orderly was also. Hunter needed some solitude to think out his options. Hunter glanced at his watch. It was four-thirty in the afternoon. He decided to go back to his office, which had closed earlier in the day, to consider his options.

Chapter Twenty-Three

That next day, Sam Blackmun cast his line again, trying to get closer to the shore. Sam was sixty-seven years old and had a rugged, weather-beaten face that made him look even older. Sam had come by his weather-beaten looks honestly, having spent most of his life outdoors. Sam had been born back in the 1930s to Joshua and Wilma Blackmun. The Blackmun family lived in a Florida cracker house on a small homestead in Chester, Florida. Chester wasn't really a town, just a bend in the dirt road with a few families scattered about in the woods.

Sam's father, Joshua, tried just about anything to support the family. Joshua, at one time or the other, was involved in turpentine, shrimping, and farming trying to make a living. Sam's father was gone a lot doing his various jobs, so it was up to Sam's mother, Wilma, to raise Sam and his two younger brothers and three younger sisters. The kids were brought up to be independent and hardworking. To feed themselves, the Blackmun family raised chickens and pigs and also had a vegetable garden. With their father being gone a lot, it was up to the children to do many of the chores around their small farm. It was up to the kids to feed the pigs, gather the eggs, and weed the vegetable garden. As Sam got older, he learned how to hunt and fish to supplement the family fare. At that time there was plenty of game in the woods. Dove, quail, squirrel, rabbit, and an occasional deer or turkey . . . all made it to the Blackmun table. Fishing added variety to the Blackmun diet, and Sam became an expert in taking sea trout, redfish, and other species from the Bell River. The Blackmun family didn't have much money, but they did eat well by taking advantage of what nature offered them.

Growing up, Sam's best friend had been Ben Johnson. Ben's family lived about a half mile down the dirt road from the Blackmun homestead. The two boys did everything together; fishing, hunting, and going to class at the small school in Yulee.

160

When the boys turned eighteen, they even enlisted in the army together. It was a few years after World War II and patriotism was still running high, but the world was at peace when the boys joined the army. After boot camp, however, the boys found themselves halfway around the world in an escalating situation they didn't understand that was soon to be called the Korean War.

The two boys ended up in the same unit in Korea, but with very different jobs. Ben had been made a cook, but Sam, thanks to his deftness with a rifle, was made a sniper on the front line. Sam spent the next year dodging death. It was a year-long nightmare of going from one foxhole to another trying to shoot a foreign figure several hundred yards away who was trying to shoot you. Sam would never forget the sound of mortars and the shelling, wondering if the incoming sound was the one with his name on it that would spell his demise. The only respite Sam got was on those rare occasions when his unit was granted leave. On those special occasions, Sam and Ben would get together, partaking of Korean beer and women like there was no tomorrow.

Tired of the cold and the killing, Sam's unit was finally recalled back to the States. Honorably discharged, Sam and Ben returned to Nassau County. With some of their money saved while in the army, Sam and Ben purchased an old logging truck and went into the pulpwood business. It was hard and hot work dragging the pine trees out of the low-lying, swampy land around North Florida and South Georgia and transporting the logs to the paper mills in Fernandina Beach, Florida, or St. Marys, Georgia.

The money was up and down depending on the demand from the paper mills and it was very hard work. After a good week, the young men would head to the Palace Saloon, their pockets full of money. The Palace was Florida's oldest continuously operated saloon. The two-story brick building on the corner of Second Street and Centre Street in downtown Fernandina was built in 1878. The building housed a shoe store until 1903 when it was converted into the classiest saloon in Fernandina. In its early years, the Palace's stunning murals, decorative tin ceilings, and hand-carved bar featuring a pair of bare-breasted mermaids, attracted wealthy vacationers from Cumberland Island such as the Carnegies, Rockefellers, Du Ponts, Goodyears, Pulitzers, and Morgans. During Fernandina's downturn in tourism during the 1950s, the Palace was more frequented by the shrimpers, pulpwooders, and paper mill workers than the occasional tourist. The Palace, however, remained a great place for drinking. After entering through the wooden swinging doors at the entrance, the Palace ambiance was of a New York tavern crossed with an Old West saloon with a pinch of Florida thrown in.

In order to distinguish the Palace Saloon from the twenty-two other saloons in Fernandina in 1903—which were the usual seamen's dives, rife with random violence and prostitution—Louis G. Hirth, a German immigrant, Florida entrepreneur, and friend of Adolphus Busch of Anheuser-Busch fame, decided to open an elegant gentlemen's saloon worthy of ship's officer, railroad tycoons, old guard yachtsmen, and wealthy industrialists on winter vacation. With Aldophus Busch's help, Hirth had a custom-made English oak bar fixture made in the St. Louis "Exposition" style complete with two undraped mermaids. Hirth paid fourteen hundred dollars, a princely sum at the time, for the oak and mahogany bar, and Aldophus Busch even oversaw its installation. Hirth also wainscoted his barroom in Italian marble, and Fernandina artist Roy Kennard painted a series of four murals on the upper walls which were action scenes from timeless works of fiction such as Dickens. The old tile floor, which was perfect for dancing, coupled with the low-hung antique ceiling fans and red velvet curtains gave the Palace an aura of timelessness that made every night seem like a reoccurring dream.

Ben and Sam would enter the Palace early on Friday evening, take their respective spots at the end of the bar, and spend the rest of the night alternatively draining their longneck beers or dancing with whatever available women that were there

162

that night. Sometimes, around midnight, after the beer had set in, Sam would think back to his recent days in Korea and remember his buddies that were blown away with a mortar blast or killed by a sniper's bullet and wonder about the vagaries of life in which two men are in a foxhole and one man gets half his head blown away and the other gets to go back to the other side of the world to resume his previous life.

During the day on the weekends, Sam and Ben would head down to the beach to watch and participate in car racing. The wide, flat beach with its hard-packed sand at low tide provided a great surface for car racing. Taking its cue from its neighbor to the south, Daytona Beach, Fernandina Beach was a haven for car racing on the beach during the fifties.

Most races were set up on a half-mile oval course with two barrels serving as the markers to go around on each end of the oval. Most races were casual with just small wagers and pride on the line. Once or twice a year there would be an official race with sponsors and prize money. Sam and Ben were a team using Sam's old Pontiac. Sam was the driver and Ben was the mechanic and crew chief. Sam and Ben won their fair share of races as Sam knew distinctly how to walk that fine line of going fast on sand without spinning out, and Sam and Ben always split any money that was won.

It was at one of these informal racing events that Sam met his future wife. Joy Butler was a farm girl from Millwood, Georgia, who had driven down to Fernandina Beach with some friends from Waycross, Georgia, to spend the day at the beach. The girls had watched the car racing event briefly with Joy noticing the tanned, shirtless young man driving the number nine car, but the girls being bothered by the raucous crowd and the noise of the cars decided to drive down the beach aways to find some solitude and to do some sunbathing.

Sam had also noticed the girls in the small crowd, particularly a fair-skinned brunette with a trim figure. Sam had watched the girls drive down the beach and after the racing was over, he and Ben got in Sam's car and drove down to where the girls were laying out on their blankets. The girls started giggling as Sam and Ben pulled up in Sam's old Pontiac. These young and naïve farm girls were no match for the tanned young men in the car, and Ben and Sam soon won them over and joined them for the rest of the afternoon. Sam kidded Joy that with her fair skin combined with the hot sun, she would soon be the orange-pink color of a Georgia peach. Joy cleverly countered that Sam's tanned and weather-beaten face reminded her of the saddle on her horse back home, and Sam knew he had found his soul mate.

After a three-month courtship, and with the blessing of her parents, Joy and Sam were married. Joy moved to Fernandina Beach where she and Sam eventually settled in a small house on North Eighteenth Street. Sam realized that he now needed a more stable income than pulpwooding, so he sold his interest in the pulpwood business to Ben and went to work in the wood yard at one of the paper mills. The work, unloading logs from the trucks and getting them ready to be sent into the mill to be made into pulp and eventually paper, was not exciting but it was stable. Sam worked at the mill for thirty-five years, and he and Joy raised three children. Now, all of Sam's children were raised and gone to other areas of the country. Sam had retired from the paper mill a few years ago, with the idea that he and Joy would buy an old camper and travel around to see some of the country, but Joy was diagnosed with breast cancer and they spent his first retirement year going to doctors instead of to different states. Joy died at the end of that year and Sam could not take sitting around in the old house on Eighteenth Street with all of its memories, so he sold the house and bought a mobile home and placed it on the small remaining parcel of land that he had inherited out in Chester. Sam also felt he needed to go back to work because he had worked all of his life and he felt worthless sitting around. Sam was too old to go back to the mill, but with all of his visits to the hospital taking care of Joy, he had become pretty friendly with the staff and they offered him a job as an orderly when he went back and applied for a job. Sam only worked three days a week but it gave him something to do so he could enjoy his time off without feeling guilty.

In order to enjoy his time off, Sam had bought a small aluminum boat with a twenty-five-horsepower outboard engine. The area around Chester was too crowded with people now to go hunting, but fortunately for Sam the miles of marshes in the area still provided plenty of solitude for fishing. The area just west of Fernandina was a saltwater estuary formed by the confluence of the Bell, Jolly, and St. Marys rivers. This large, triangular saltmarsh area divides Florida and Georgia and is several miles across at its base toward Fernandina and eventually narrows down to a single river, the St. Marys, at its apex, which is about ten miles to the west. A wide variety of different species of fish could be caught within a day's fishing trip from Sam's launch site in Chester. From Chester eastward toward the salty Atlantic Ocean, saltwater species could be had, such as spotted sea trout, redfish, or drum. Heading west from Chester led to brackish water and striped bass. West of where Interstate 95 crosses from Georgia to Florida leads to freshwater conditions and largemouth bass.

Early on this Saturday morning, Sam decided to head west in search of striped bass, or stripers, as they are known locally. Sam had headed down the Bell River staying on the outside curve of the meandering river since, as every local knew, the currents kept the outside half of the river deep while the sandbars tended to form on the inside of each curve. After leaving the Bell River behind with its small collection of houses with docks protruding into the river, all of the land on the Florida side between here and the interstate was undeveloped. Sam turned left past the point of land where the Bell River merges into the St. Marys River. Sam followed the St. Marys River for another mile or so past Rose's Bluff, a place where the river cuts into the land, resulting in a stretch of thirty-foot-tall white sand cliffs. Another mile or so past Rose's Bluff was Crandall, a private retreat that was rarely used by a large timber company. About one-half a mile past

165

Crandall, Sam navigated the boat into the entrance of a small creek where there was one of Sam's secret fishing holes.

Sam had been casting his plug there for over one hour and had caught seven nice stripers when he heard another boat approaching. Sam was up the small creek a little bit and since it was low tide he was hidden from view from the river by the tall marsh grass except when he looked straight down the creek to the river. Sam saw a flats boat with a big outboard and two men aboard zoom by heading up the river, the outboard throwing up a large roostertail of water.

"Damn those big engines," Sam mumbled to himself, hating being buzzed by the new fast boats running up and down the river these days, almost swamping the old geezers like himself with their old-fashioned boats.

Sam heard the big outboard's engine change pitch and saw the roostertail of water circle back around, then heard the outboard engine throttle down to an idle. Pretty soon Sam saw the boat come into view and head up the creek right towards him.

"I wonder what these yahoos want," Sam thought to himself. Sam reeled his line in as the other boat approached. As the other boat got nearer, Sam saw there was one big guy driving the boat and another older guy in the bow of the boat. Both of the men were dressed for fishing with khaki pants, long-sleeved shirts, and hats with hooks in them. Both men also had sunglasses on so at first Sam didn't recognize them.

"Hey, there. We were wondering if you had any fish we could buy from you?" said the man in the bow.

Sam thought he recognized the voice but he wasn't sure since the man had on a hat and sunglasses.

"Dr. Hockman?" Sam queried.

"Sam? Is that you?" Dr. Hockman responded as if he didn't know.

"Yes, it is," confirmed Sam, as he recognized the other man as being that big goon of an orderly, Brill.

"We've been out here fishing all morning and haven't gotten a bite," said Dr. Hockman dejectedly. Then Dr. Hockman continued, "It's going to be embarrassing if we go home empty-handed, so we were wondering if you had any luck and would be willing to sell us some fish?"

"Well, I've got more than I need for myself. I've caught seven stripers and I only need two for myself. You're welcome to the other five, for free," responded Sam, proud of his catch and glad to help out Dr. Hockman, who he knew was an important man at the hospital.

Sam stowed away his pole, now that he had retrieved all of his line, in the rod holder along the side of his boat. Sam told Dr. Hockman to grab a bucket and come aboard as he walked to the bow of his boat to pull up his stringer of fish. As Sam had caught his fish, he had placed each one on his stringer by running the string through the mouths and out the gill and thrown the fish back overboard attached to the boat by the string to keep them alive and fresh. Sam pulled up the string of fish, proudly showing the collection of fish to the other two men who nodded their heads approvingly.

Dr. Hockman was now in the bow of the small boat next to Sam. After he handed the bucket to Sam, Dr. Hockman watched as the experienced old fisherman filled the bucket with water and placed it on the flat part at the very front of the boat. Sam was bent over the bow, kneeling on the flat part of the bow and was just about finished transferring the last fish from the stringer to the bucket when he felt a sharp, jabbing pain in his right buttock like being stung by a bee.

When Sam wasn't looking, Dr. Hockman had pulled a syringe from a small cooler on his boat. The syringe contained succinylcholine chloride, an ultrashort-acting, depolarizing skeletal muscle relaxant. The white, odorless, slightly bitter powder, which is easily soluble in water, causes a rapid (less than a minute) onset of flaccid paralysis that lasts four to six minutes. Since succinylcholine chloride is used as an adjunct to general anesthesia, to facilitate tracheal intubation, and to

167

provide skeletal muscle relaxation during surgery or mechanical ventilation, Dr. Hockman was well aware of its effects.

As Sam felt the sting in his buttocks, he started to turn around and face Dr. Hockman. Dr. Hockman knew, however, if this was going to appear to be accidental drowning he needed to get Sam into the water before the chemical affected Sam's diaphragm so he would take in some water. As Dr. Hockman knew, the chemical would affect the levator muscles of the face first, then the muscles of the glottis, and then, finally, the intercostals and the diaphragm and all the other skeletal muscles.

Before Sam's body could go limp, Hockman put his foot on Sam's backside and pushed Sam over the bow of the boat, knocking the bucket over and spilling the fish into the creek. Sam came to the surface and he started to swim toward shore but he only took a couple of strokes before his arms started to feel leaden. Sam struggled to keep his head above the surface of the water, he kicked his legs as hard as he could, but they began to not respond. After going up and down above the surface a few times, Sam lost the battle, his skeletal muscles now useless.

Dr. Hockman looked on with irony as the previously doomed fish hurriedly scurried away to their newfound freedom, while the man slowly sank to his doom with bubbles coming out of his mouth.

Sam's skeletal muscles were completely paralyzed and he was unable to save himself, but his mind was intact and he could have kept breathing if he could have kept his head above water.

Sam's boots and the large fishing knife in its holder on his belt weighed him down and he slowly sank below the surface as his clothes became wet. As he spiraled downward, Sam was able to see Dr. Hockman out of the corner of his eye staring down at him. Sam's rage was great and if his body would have responded, he would have burst out of the water with his fishing knife in hand and slit Dr. Hockman's throat. But Sam's body would not respond, and he changed his focus to the blue sky and scattered clouds behind Dr. Hockman's head as Sam realized he was headed to join his buddies from the Korean War. He took comfort in the fact that he had almost forty bonus years since their unfortunate demise.

Chapter Twenty-Four

Later that same day, Hunter leaned back in his chair weighing his options. Hunter had spent a sleepless night thinking about his predicament. After leaving Dr. Hockman's office the previous day, Hunter had called Savannah and feigned that he was feeling ill. Savannah offered to come over and take care of him and make him dinner, but Hunter, fearing for Savannah's safety, had put Savannah off, telling her he was too nauseated to eat and that he just wanted to go to bed early after taking some medications. Savannah reluctantly acquiesced to Hunter's wishes and Hunter felt terrible having to lie to Savannah, but he knew it was in her best interest. He knew he couldn't go along with Hockman's scheme, regardless of the blackmail attempt. Hunter cringed at the thought of the headlines that would come out in the local paper if he was charged with misconduct with the female patient. Hunter pictured Lolita Gomez on the witness stand at his trial exuding sexuality, and Hunter knew every man on the jury would believe her story. Hunter thought of the embarrassment this would cause his parents.

Hunter also had doubts that he could prove that murder was being committed at the hospital, because Hunter no longer had the syringe that would have helped prove the case. Hunter was mad at himself for being so naïve and stupid. Hunter realized that he should never have touched the syringe but instead left it in Brill's lunchbox and called the police. He still had the videotape showing Brill going into the supply room, but Brill could say he was just going into the room to get supplies and it was just a coincidence it was close to the time the patient died.

Hunter could go to the police now with the tape and without the syringe, but even if Hunter could convince the police to exhume the bodies for autopsies, if what Dr. Hockman said was true, there may be no evidence of murder. Also, when Hunter was in Hockman's office, he had noticed a photograph on Hockman's desk of a golfing foursome. In the foursome, besides

Hockman, Hunter recognized Jack Wheeler, the regional director of Medi-Most with whom Hunter had played golf, and also the chief of police whom Hunter had recognized from local newspaper articles. The fourth person Hunter did not recognize. Hunter was not certain how long the tentacles of the conspiracy at Medi-Most Hospital reached. Hunter did not want to repeat the tactical error of confiding in the wrong person as he had with Dr. Hockman. Hunter was unsure if the photograph indicated the two men were involved in Dr. Hockman's scheme or whether it was just a social outing, but it did tell Hunter he needed to proceed carefully.

After almost a full day of contemplation, Hunter decided he would call Billy Reilly, the childhood friend who was on the city police force who had almost given him the traffic ticket when Hunter first moved back to town. Hunter knew he could trust Billy. Hunter felt that even if the police chief was somehow involved, Billy would never be a participant in a scheme of this nature. Hunter pulled out his wallet and looked for the card that Billy had given him when he had pulled Hunter over shortly after his return.

Hunter found the card and looked for Billy's phone number. Hunter tried calling Billy's home phone number but it yielded a recording. Hunter next called Billy's work number and spoke with the police dispatcher. Hunter asked the dispatcher if she could pass a message through to Officer Reilly to have him call Hunter at his office as soon as possible. The dispatcher responded that Officer Reilly was on patrol in the north end of the island and that she could radio a message to him. The dispatcher then asked Hunter if it was an emergency, because she could send another officer to see Hunter if necessary. Hunter told the dispatcher it was not an emergency, but he did need to speak to Officer Reilly concerning an urgent police matter as soon as possible. Hunter left his name and number, and the dispatcher confirmed that she would radio Officer Reilly right away to give him the message. Hunter leaned back in his chair to await Billy's call.

Dr. Hockman, meanwhile, was sitting in his office wondering what Hunter was going to do. After returning from his morning's adventure with Sam the orderly, Dr. Hockman had taken a shower and then returned to his office. Now the tired, old doctor was sitting at his desk wondering about how things were getting out of control. It was one thing to ease damaged people into the afterlife, quite another thing to commit cold-blooded murder. Dr. Hockman kept seeing Sam Blackmun's face as it disappeared into the murky water. But Barry Hockman was a survivor, and he shook off any more thoughts of remorse and concentrated on what he had to do to survive this situation unscathed.

The older doctor's thoughts turned to Dr. Davis. Hunter Davis didn't appear to Dr. Hockman to be somebody that would be easy to control, his being so idealistic and headstrong. Dr. Hockman had given up his idealism for reality a long time ago. Surely the young doctor could see the pragmatism of what Dr. Hockman was doing.

While Dr. Hockman planned his next course of action, he switched on the police scanner that he kept in his office. Dr. Hockman's father had been a policeman and Dr. Hockman enjoyed the police terminology that he heard over his scanner. The scanner was also useful in predicting when the emergency room was going to get busy after there were car accidents.

Today, as he sat at his desk pondering what to do, Dr. Hockman was listening for something more ominous. Dr. Hockman had a bad feeling that Dr. Davis was not going to play his game and Dr. Hockman was going to have to do something about it.

The scanner had been pretty quiet, Fernandina being a small town and all. Dr. Hockman had been listening to the usual banter when the dispatcher broke in, "Officer Reilly, please contact an individual, named Hunter Davis, at 555-4561 immediately. He reports it's an urgent police matter."

Dr. Hockman stiffened in his chair, his worst fears realized. Fortunately for Dr. Hockman, he had anticipated this kind of situation. First of all, Dr. Hockman had called Brill and told him to stay by the phone in case Dr. Hockman needed him. Secondly, before Dr. Hockman had hired another doctor to work that office after Dr. Baker died, Dr. Hockman had a line run from that private office to his private office so he could eavesdrop as needed.

Dr. Hockman waited for the light to light up on the special phone he had installed. When the light came on Dr. Hockman waited until the instant the light stopped blinking and picked up the receiver.

"Hunter, what's up?" Billy Reilly began. "The dispatcher said you had an urgent police matter. Somebody run over your dog?" Billy said jokingly.

"This is no joke, Billy," said Hunter sternly.

"What's going on?" asked Billy, immediately serious.

"Well, I don't want to say too much over the phone," began Hunter. "But it involves murder at the hospital."

"Murder?" said Billy in disbelief.

"Yes, we need to meet somewhere secure, so I can fill you in on the details," said Hunter. "Meet me at the southwest bastion at Fort Clinch in thirty minutes," continued Hunter.

"But that is out of my jurisdiction, that's state land," protested Billy.

"Just do it," said Hunter firmly. Then, remembering the photograph on Dr. Hockman's desk, Hunter added, "Don't tell anyone where you are going. Your police chief may be involved."

"What, are you kidding me?" responded Billy.

"No, I'm very serious," said Hunter solemnly. "Just be there," commanded Hunter.

Hunter hung up the phone. Hunter knew he could trust Billy. They had been best friends growing up, and even though they had gone their separate ways in adulthood Hunter still felt a bond with Billy.

Dr. Hockman also hung up his phone, albeit a bit more slowly. Dr. Hockman knew what he had to do. The stakes were getting unpleasantly high. Dr. Hockman picked up the other phone, the one with an outside line. He dialed the phone and heard Brill's gruff hello on the other end of the line.

"Don't worry about coming into work tonight, Brill," Dr. Hockman began. "I've got something more important for you to do," said Dr. Hockman.

Chapter Twenty-Five

Hunter spent a few minutes printing the list of patients that were involved in the suspected murders and other information he felt germane to the case. After gathering the information and placing it into a briefcase, Hunter walked to his car in the parking lot. The early September air was still hot and humid in northeast Florida even though it was about five-thirty in the afternoon.

Hunter pulled the top down on his car and threw the briefcase into the back seat. Plopping down in the driver's seat, Hunter started the ignition. Hunter realized he should tell Savannah what he was doing but he didn't have time to walk over to the emergency room, and also didn't want to be seen talking to Savannah. Therefore, Hunter reached for his car phone and dialed the back number to the emergency room as he backed up his car and then pulled out of the parking lot. The phone rang and another nurse answered the phone. Hunter asked for Savannah, but was told by the nurse that Savannah was working with a patient. The nurse asked Hunter if he wanted her to interrupt Savannah, but Hunter said it wasn't necessary and hung up the phone. Deciding he would call Savannah later, Hunter pulled out on Will Hardee Road to begin the lengthy drive to Fort Clinch.

Officer Reilly, meanwhile, had been on patrol out in Old Town, which was near the back entrance to Fort Clinch State Park. The area was called Old Town because it was the original site of the town of Fernandina when it was first settled by the Spanish. After awhile, another peninsula of land across the marsh from the original site became the present town of Fernandina, leaving the old site to be called Old Town, which had become a somewhat run-down, disheveled neighborhood, over the years but recently had shown a bit of a revival.

Officer Reilly drove his patrol car over the small bridge that spans Egan's Creek, stopping just short of the metal swinging gate that blocks access to the road leading into the state park. Billy turned off his car and fumbled through his key chain looking for the key that unlocked the gate. Billy remembered when he had joined the force he had been told he had a key to the gate in case of emergency, but Billy had never had a reason to use the key. Billy wasn't sure which key was the proper one, so he tried several, finally finding the right one. Billy swung the gate open, drove his patrol car past the gate, and then got back out of his car to close the gate. After closing the gate, Billy got back in his patrol car and began driving down the half-mile-long road that would lead to the entrance of the fort itself. This was the same shortcut that Billy and Hunter had used as kids to sneak into the state park without paying. Driving down this road brought back fond memories to Billy. Billy remembered how the boys on their bikes would play a cat-and-mouse game with the park rangers.

The boys, however, rarely rode their bikes through the front entrance of the fort because there were three good reasons for sneaking in the back entrance to the park. First, to go in the front gate required a circuitous route from the boys' homes of over eight miles, while the back entrance was a more direct route of only two miles. Second, the boys couldn't afford the fifty cents admission price. Third, and perhaps the best reason, was the adventure of hiding from the park rangers. To the boys, it was a higher stakes game of tag or hide-and-seek, with the park rangers being the pursuers.

Billy remembered that this straight, wide-open stretch of road leading into the park from the back gate was the most crucial stretch of road to traverse without detection. If spotted on this stretch of road by a passing park ranger, the park ranger knew the boys had snuck in because this road was closed to the public. If spotted on this road the boys had two choices. One was to make a mad dash back out of the gate hoping that they could reach the gate before the ranger could catch up with them. The other choice was to duck into the woods beside the road, but the dearth of good trails off the road usually made this a poor choice.

176

Billy laughed at the irony that now he was the authority figure and that mischievous boys would run from him. Billy had switched sides in the game. After coming to the end of the road that led in from the back gate, where it intersected with the road that led from the fort to the campground, Billy turned right onto the road that led to the main road and eventually led to the fort's parking lot. After parking the patrol car in one of the many empty spaces—the parking lot was nearly deserted, since it was getting near closing time—Billy stepped out of his patrol car and walked across the grassy field that led to the fort. Soon Billy came to the old drawbridge that transverses the now-dry moat that surrounds the fort. Billy walked across the drawbridge through the large brick archway that forms the entrance to the fort. The officer walked down the long cobblestone ramp that leads from the entrance to the large grass field at the center of the fort. At the bottom of the ramp, Billy turned left and walked past the old jail to the entrance of the tunnel that leads to the southwest bastion.

The tunnel was a brick-lined archway with a slate floor about forty yards long that leads through an earthen berm built to protect both the interior buildings and soldiers going to and from the bastions. Billy's footsteps echoed in the solitude as he walked through the tunnel to the bastion. The tunnel gave way to two doorways on each side, right before the bastion. From the two doorways led paths that followed the back side of the four-foot-thick brick walls that connected each bastion. Every few feet there was a rifle port in the thick walls where a rifleman could shoot at an approaching enemy.

The bastion was quiet and appeared empty as Billy walked into the room. Billy glanced around; realizing Hunter would have to come in the longer front entrance to the park, Billy sat down at base of one of the Civil War cannons facing out the cannon ports to wait for Hunter. After smoking three-fourths of a cigarette, Billy heard some footsteps approaching. Jumping to his feet expecting to see Hunter, Billy saw instead it was a tall, strange-looking man wearing a hat and a trench coat. The man had a camera around his neck and was holding a map of the fort.

"Do you work here?" the stranger asked, pointing at Billy's uniform.

"No," Billy began, before being interrupted by the stranger.

"Could you show me where the officer's quarters are?" said the stranger extending his map, undeterred by Billy's answer.

Billy started to protest, then decided it would be easier just to tell the man where the quarters were. Billy stepped beside the stranger and took the map to point out the spot on the map indicating the officer's quarters. As Billy stood slightly in front of the man pointing at the map, he did not see the stranger reach into his pocket to retrieve something. Billy was saying, "It's right there," when he felt a sharp pain in the right jugular area of his neck. Brill emptied the contents of the syringe as Billy saw a white flash before his eyes. That white flash would be the last thing that Billy would ever see.

Brill lowered Billy to the floor and removed the syringe. Brill dragged Billy's body to the side of the room and laid him on the floor beside one of the cannons and near the dark, open doorway of the gunpowder room. Brill stepped into the darkness of the gunpowder room with its silent, sand floor and pulled another syringe out of his pocket to wait for Hunter. Brill felt no remorse for what he had just done. Life had been unfair to Brill and if it was unfair to somebody else, so be it. Life was cruel; death was easy. In a way Brill felt he was doing people a favor, sending them into an afterlife that had to be better than the one he knew on Earth.

Brill didn't like this silence, though; it gave him too much time to think. Kendall Brill was a tall man and as ugly as they come; his shaven head made his angular features even more dramatic. Small children would sometimes point at Brill, tugging their mother's skirt, petrified by his looks. As a small child himself, Brill was taunted by the other children because of his appearance. As a child he lived under the double curse of being poor as well as ugly. Not surprisingly, Brill became a loner and learned to fight.

As Brill became older he graduated from beating up kids, to mugging older people, and finally to armed robbery. During a convenience-store robbery, Brill's striking appearance worked against him, as he was soon identified and eventually sentenced to five years in the state penitentiary.

Brill came out of prison a hardened man, but he did not want to return quickly to incarceration, so he temporarily gave up his life of crime. Brill joined a traveling carnival as a barker for the sideshow. It was a good job for Brill, being around people even stranger looking than himself, but after about six months Brill's unlucky life took another turn.

When the carnival was passing through Nassau County, Brill began arguing with another man over a girl. Brill received about a four-inch cut to his abdomen when the other man produced a pocket knife during their altercation. Brill was brought to the Medi-Most hospital back when it had first opened, and Dr. Hockman had closed the wound.

During Brill's recovery in the hospital, Dr. Hockman was very friendly to him on his visits during rounds. This was the first time that anybody had been nice to Brill in his pathetic life, so when Dr. Hockman suggested he stay on as a hospital orderly after his recovery, Brill agreed.

After about two weeks of cleaning bedpans and helping old people have sponge baths, Brill was ready to go back to his life of crime. Anything had to be better than doing this for a living. It was about that time that Dr. Hockman suggested they have a meeting. Dr. Hockman suggested they meet at a bar near the beach called the Shark's Den. The Shark's Den was a nondescript, one-story establishment that was frequented by a slightly rough crowd.

It was a Monday night when Dr. Hockman and Brill had met at the bar. The Shark's Den was dark and deserted that night except for a bartender and two guys playing pool. Dr. Hockman was already there when Brill arrived. Dr. Hockman was sitting in a booth near the back, by a counter that said Amelia Island Barbeque. The one redeeming quality about the Shark's Den was that it housed an independent, African-American-owned carry-out barbecue business in the back of the bar. The barbecue business was run by a longtime, local black family and the food was excellent. It was a strange mix: a black-run business that catered to mostly white patrons, including the biker crowd. But patrons didn't have to go inside the Shark's Den and encounter the roughnecks to pick up a to-go order, thanks to a window that led to a dirt parking lot in the back. Well-heeled patrons in the know would call in their order, pick it up from the outside window, and carry it home for a delicious meal.

Over a meal of mustard-based barbecued ribs, brown-sugared baked beans and French fries, Dr. Hockman made a proposal to Brill. Dr. Hockman had told Brill he had certain patients who were suffering and who were going to die anyway that were costing the hospital a lot of money. Dr. Hockman had told Brill that if he wanted to supplement his minimum wage, he would pay three thousand dollars for every patient Brill assisted on. Dr. Hockman then told Brill he would be doing the patient a favor, since they were suffering, and a quick death was preferable over a slow, lingering death. Dr. Hockman said he would identify the patients and instruct Brill on how to give an injection that would make the patient peaceably pass away.

Dr. Hockman was trying to sugarcoat the act, but Brill didn't have any problem with the ethics of the task. To Brill, three thousand tax-free dollars per patient was a fortune, and life had been so cruel to him that he didn't have a problem easing anybody into their afterlife. The next life had to be better than this one, Brill had rationalized. Now, a couple of years later and after a couple of veiled threats of exposure to Dr. Hockman, Brill was up to six thousand dollars per patient.

Brill thought about the night not long ago when he had helped that young man into his afterlife. Remembering that night, Brill had made his way down the hall, dressed in his orderly's uniform. Even though the sight of him in the hallway would be common at that hour, Brill had walked quietly, not wanting to be seen in this vicinity by anyone in case of problems later. Brill had ducked into the supply room, which was accessible both from the hallway and also from another door that led to the intensive care ward.

Brill had glanced at his watch: the time was five minutes until three o'clock in the morning. Brill knew that at three o'clock one of the nurses on duty would usually take a coffee break while the other would take a bathroom break. The coffee machine was in a little lounge area, just around the corner from the nurses' station. The nurse that was making the coffee could still hear the monitor alarms from there but would be unable to see what was going on in the ward. Brill had cracked the door leading from the supply room into the intensive care ward slightly so he would have a view of the nurses' station.

After a few minutes, Brill saw the nurse, Rita, get up from her station and head to the lounge area and Dora headed to the bathroom. As soon as Rita and Dora were out of view, Brill had eased through the door, syringe in hand. Brill then had made his way very quickly to Darrell's bed. Dr. Hockman had informed Brill of which bed Darrell would be in and what his name was. Brill had been slightly taken aback by Darrell's age. Up to that point all of the patients that Brill had "assisted" on were elderly patients. Brill had checked the chart at the end of the bed, the name was correct. Also, as far as Brill could see Darrell was the only patient in the ward at this time.

With a practiced expertise, Brill had raised Darrell's gown and located his femoral vein. Brill expertly emptied the syringe, filled with a high potassium solution, into the vein. It was then that Brill had noticed the young man's fingers moving, which had spooked Brill, causing him to jump and nearly pull the syringe out before it was completely empty. But Brill had settled himself, finished the job, and got out of there as quickly as he could.

But all of this killing was beginning to bother even Brill. Originally, Brill's deal with Dr. Hockman was to help some sick,

181

elderly patients ease painlessly into the afterlife, but now this had become out-and-out murder. Killing the young man in the hospital was bad enough, but now he had murdered a policeman and was about to get rid of the young doctor. Brill realized he had enough of this killing and had made enough money to disappear. Key West was a place Brill had always wanted to go, so Brill figured this would be a good time to head down there where he would fit right in with the other characters.

After what seemed like an eternity, Brill heard footsteps, faint at first, then growing increasingly louder. Standing beside the dark doorway where he could not be seen, but he could see Billy's body, Brill heard the steady footsteps come to a stop, then a shuffling as the person looked around. Brill heard a few hesitant steps forward and then several quickened steps as Hunter rushed to Billy's side.

Hunter was checking for Billy's pulse when Brill made his move. Hunter did not hear anything at first, but when Brill's sand-covered shoes hit the slate floor, Hunter spun around just in time to prevent Brill from plunging the syringe into Hunter's neck. Hunter caught Brill's right wrist with his left hand and Brill's left wrist with his right hand, but Hunter had been caught off balance and tripped over Billy's body, falling against the cannon yet still holding onto Brill's wrists. Brill pinned Hunter against the cannon and, towering over him, pushed the needle slowly closer to his neck. Hunter released Brill's left wrist so his right hand could join his left hand on Brill's right wrist. The maneuver stalled Brill's advance momentarily, but due to Brill's height and leverage advantage, the needle regained its slow advance. Brill placed his free hand on Hunter's right shoulder to pin him in place.

Hunter, realizing his situation was desperate, glanced around for some method of escape. Out of the corner of his eye, Hunter spied a stack of cannonballs beside the cannon. With the needle just an inch from his neck, Hunter released his right hand and in one swift motion reached over and grabbed the top cannonball and struck Brill on his left temple. Brill, momentarily stunned,

182

fell backward on the floor. Realizing that he was free, Hunter made a mad dash toward the entrance of the tunnel leading from the bastion. Brill, sitting on the floor, reached into the pocket of his trench coat and retrieved a small handgun with a silencer.

"I should've used this in the first place," thought Brill groggily to himself, but he had not wanted to leave any blood behind as evidence. Brill squeezed off a shot at the fleeing doctor, but Hunter's blow had induced some temporary double vision in Brill and the shot whizzed past Hunter's ear, striking the roof of the tunnel. Hunter, at the sound of the gunfire, instantly ducked through one of the doorways separating the bastion from the entrance of the tunnel and ran down the path that led along the inside of the walls. Hunter was about halfway to the cover of the brick walls of the old latrine area when a bullet kicked up sand on the hill just to his right. Brill had staggered to his feet and made it to the doorway, but he was still suffering from blurry vision and the bullet had missed its mark again.

Just as Hunter reached the open doorway to the latrine, another bullet splattered on the left side of the doorway. Hunter glanced to the right where there was a perpendicular tunnel leading to the open, central field and eventually to the front entrance and probable safety. Hunter, however, thought about Darrell and Billy, and, not wanting Brill to get away, decided to lead his pursuer into a trap. Hunter continued on straight toward the northwest bastion. Just before Hunter reached the safety of the next bastion, Hunter heard the muffled sound of another shot. Hunter ducked instinctively and another bullet narrowly missed, striking the brick as Hunter dove through the doorway.

Hunter ran immediately to the powder room in back of the bastion and stepped over the little step up and into powder room. Hunter was completely blinded by the darkness in the small windowless room. Breathing heavily, Hunter felt his way along the wall until he felt the ledge just to the inside right of the doorway. The doctor pulled himself onto the same ledge from which he had scared Savannah and waited in a crouch, letting his eyes adjust to the darkness and trying to calm his breathing. Soon Hunter heard Brill's heavy footsteps and labored breathing. Hunter could hear Brill's footsteps slow down and advance cautiously. Hunter closed his mouth and tried breathing through his nose to quiet his breathing; soon he could hear Brill's heavy breathing at the entrance to the powder room. Hunter could see Brill's shadow in the faint light at the edge of the doorway and the silhouette of Brill's hand holding the gun.

"Come on, come on in," pleaded Hunter silently to himself. Brill started to turn away from the doorway, when Hunter picked up a pebble and threw it against the opposite wall from the ledge. Hunter saw Brill's shadow snap around and advance back toward the doorway. Hunter's eyes had sufficiently adjusted to the dark room where he could just make out forms like the walls and the floor. Hunter knew that Brill, as soon as he stepped completely out of the light and into the room, would be temporarily blinded by the darkness.

Brill stepped forward out of the light into the darkness of the powder room and Hunter leaped from the ledge. Hunter knocked the gun from Brill's grasp with his right hand and his body knocked Brill into the far wall. Hunter landed on his feet and caught Brill ricocheting off the wall and hit him square in the jaw with his right fist.

Expecting Brill to fall over from the blow, Hunter was surprised when Brill just shook his head and advanced toward Hunter, blindly trying to grab him. Hunter knew he would soon lose his advantage as Brill's eyes became dark-adapted to the blackness of the room. Putting his anatomy training to use, Hunter kicked Brill in the groin, causing the big man to double over in pain. Barely noticing a loose brick on the sand floor in the gloom, Hunter picked it up and clobbered Brill over the head. Brill fell like a toppled redwood, falling face down onto the sandy floor. After quickly removing his belt and securely tying Brill's hands to his feet behind Brill's back, Hunter looked for Brill's gun but it was too dark in the room to find the weapon against the sand floor. Hunter walked out of the gunpowder room and down the tunnel leading to the central field looking for a park ranger. Usually there was a park ranger out in the field near the kitchen area dressed in a Civil War uniform. As Hunter entered the central courtyard, however, no one was visible. Hunter yelled hello, his voice echoing off the deserted fort walls. Maybe Brill did away with the park ranger, Hunter grimly thought to himself. Hunter decided to run for the parking lot and drive to the ranger station at the main entrance. Hunter dashed to the parking lot, which was now deserted except for his car, cranked the ignition and roared out of the parking lot, beginning the long, winding drive to the fort entrance.

Hunter reached down and grabbed his car phone to call Savannah to fill her in on what was going on and to have her alert the state police. Just as he was trying to dial the numbers, a jolt from behind made him drop the phone. Hunter looked into his rear-view mirror and was shocked to see Dr. Hockman in his Mercedes coupe approaching to ram him again. Hunter slammed down the accelerator of his Z-car just in time to avoid another collision. The two men raced down the narrow and winding tree-lined road, tires squealing at every curve. As Hunter slowed down to take the curves, Dr. Hockman's car would gain on Hunter, trying to ram his rear and make him spin out. Hunter's smaller BMW was just a little bit quicker through the turns, however, and each time Dr. Hockman advanced, Hunter would pull away in the turns. This jockeying back and forth went on for nearly a mile, and several times Hunter thought his car was going to fly off the road into the nearby trees that formed the canopy over the road.

Eventually the two cars roared into a straightaway and the trees gave way to a sand dune area on the left side of the road. Dr. Hockman's heavier but more powerful car was able to pull alongside the left side of Hunter's car on the straightaway. Dr. Hockman jerked his steering wheel to the right and barged into Hunter's car, trying to force him off the road. The collision knocked Hunter's car to the very right edge of the road, but Hunter expertly kept the car under control. Before Dr. Hockman could come across for another attack, Hunter decided to take the offensive and rammed Dr. Hockman's car. This maneuver caught Dr. Hockman by surprise, and his car left the road sideways through the sand. Hunter looked over his left shoulder to watch Dr. Hockman's car as it went spinning out of control.

Hunter laughed to himself over his victory but he knew a turn was coming up so he turned his head around just in time to see a large recreational vehicle coming around the turn straight in front of him blowing its horn. All Hunter had time to do was to swerve to the right, but the RV was too close and Hunter hurtled off the road straight for a tree.

A blinding white light was all Hunter saw as his car rammed into a tree at nearly fifty miles an hour. Fortunately for Hunter, he had his seat belt fastened and the airbag inflated after impact, but he was unconscious and although he didn't know it, his left tibia and fibula were broken.

Meanwhile, Dr. Hockman had regained control of his car and witnessed the accident in front of him. Dr. Hockman stopped his car on the sand beside the road and grabbed his doctor's bag from the back seat. The driver of the large, white recreational vehicle, a stout man in his mid-sixties wearing a Hawaiian shirt, shorts, and a ball cap, had stopped the camper in the middle of the road between Dr. Hockman and Hunter's car. The man saw Dr. Hockman walking toward him and immediately started talking.

"There wasn't anything I could do," the man began excitedly. "I came around the corner and there he was," the man followed, gesturing toward Hunter.

"I know," said Dr. Hockman. "I saw the whole thing. That guy just passed me and he was driving like a maniac, forcing me off the road," Dr. Hockman lied.

"It looks like he's hurt," blurted the man, pacing in confusion.

"I'll take care of this, I'm a doctor," said Dr. Hockman reassuringly, holding up his doctor's bag.

"Oh, thank God," said the man, clearly not comfortable in crisis situations.

The two men walked over to Hunter's car, which was hissing steam from a busted radiator. Hunter was slumped against the air bag, blood running down his forehead from a small cut above his left eye.

Dr. Hockman had hoped Hunter had perished in the crash, but much to his dismay, Hunter had a very strong pulse when Dr. Hockman checked it.

"Do you have a phone in your vehicle?" Dr. Hockman asked the man.

"Yes, I do," responded the man affirmatively.

"Why don't you go call 911?" Dr. Hockman suggested.

"Good idea," said the man, then rushed off to do so.

Dr. Hockman lifted Hunter out of the car and laid him on the grass next to the road. Different possibilities raced through Dr. Hockman's mind. He could suffocate Hunter, but that cause of death could be determined with an autopsy. Dr. Hockman also thought about trying to break Hunter's neck since this image would be consistent with a car wreck, but Dr. Hockman didn't know how to do this, only having seen it done in movies. Dr. Hockman decided to give Hunter a sedative to knock him out for a couple of hours. The ambulance would be here soon and Dr. Hockman would direct them to take Hunter to the Medi-Most Hospital where Dr. Hockman would have time to figure out what to do with him. The doctor searched in his black doctor's bag, found the proper syringe and gave Hunter a shot in the arm.

The man from the recreational vehicle returned, saying the ambulance was on the way. Dr. Hockman noticed Hunter's breathing slowing down as the drug took its effect. The man and Dr. Hockman waited until the ambulance arrived. After their arrival, Dr. Hockman introduced himself to the emergency medical technicians and directed them to take Hunter to the Medi-Most Hospital and not the county hospital.

After the ambulance pulled away, Dr. Hockman left the old man to talk to the park rangers to explain what happened and then drove back to the fort to see what had happened to Brill. Dr. Hockman was careful not to drive past the rangers as he left lest they notice the mild scrapes on his car from his encounter with Hunter's car. After an extensive search of the fort, Brill, now conscious, had answered Dr. Hockman, calling his name. Dr. Hockman admonished Brill for his incompetence, untied him, and explained to Brill that he was going to take care of Dr. Davis himself. Now, Dr. Hockman explained, they needed to get to the hospital and finish the job.

Chapter Twenty-Six

Savannah had just returned to her townhouse from her long shift at the emergency room when Betty Williams called on the phone. Savannah was tired and didn't pick up the phone, opting to let the answering machine take the call, as she began to get undressed. As soon as Savannah heard part of the message Betty was beginning to leave on the answering machine, Savannah raced to the phone to pick it up.

"Hey, Betty, I'm here," said Savannah anxiously into the phone after she had raced to snatch the phone off its holder.

"Oh, Savannah, I'm so glad I caught you," said Betty with concern in her voice. "They just brought in Dr. Davis, he's been in a car accident," continued Betty. "I thought you would want to know, so I called you right away," Betty said, knowing Savannah didn't deserve any more bad news after Darrell's situation.

"What?" said Savannah in disbelief. "Is he hurt badly?"

"I don't think so," said Betty. "But he is unconscious and they just took him into X-rays to determine the extent of his injuries," continued Betty. "Fortunately, Dr. Hockman came along right after the accident, so Hunter was in good hands," Betty added.

Realizing the ramifications of what Betty just said and not trusting Dr. Hockman, Savannah told Betty she would be right there. Savannah put back on the nurses uniform she had just taken off, grabbed her car keys, and rushed out her door. Jumping into her car, Savannah drove as quickly as she could but she was not a great driver and didn't want to get into an accident herself. Luckily, Savannah didn't have that far to go, and the traffic on the island was light since it was past the summer season.

Soon Savannah was at the hospital. Savannah parked her car quickly and ran up to the electronic double doors used to enter emergency patients from the ambulances. Running as fast as she could, Savannah had to pause to give the automatic doors a chance to open. Once the doors opened, Savannah raced inside, looking around anxiously. Spotting Betty, Savannah rushed over to where Betty was working behind the counter.

"Where is he?" Savannah inquired of Betty desperately.

"Calm down, Savannah," Betty said reassuredly, noticing that Savannah looked distraught.

"Hunter's going to be alright. The tests show he only has a broken leg and a possible concussion," said Betty calmly.

"Where is he?" Savannah again demanded.

"Well, they set Dr. Davis' leg and put it in a cast and he is resting in room 202," said Betty, wondering why Savannah was so agitated.

"They admitted him to the hospital?" Savannah asked in dismay.

"Yes, Dr. Hockman felt it was best to keep Dr. Davis here under observation since he was still unconscious," answered Betty.

"Oh, no," said Savannah as she ran down the hallway to the elevator as Betty looked on open-mouthed. Savannah pounded repeatedly on the elevator button and soon the elevator arrived. Savannah rushed through the elevator doors and pushed the button for the second floor. After what seemed an inordinate amount of time, the doors closed and the elevator was on its way. As soon as the elevator doors cracked open on the second floor, Savannah squeezed through and made her way down the deserted hallway. Savannah was just about to enter room 202 when she heard a voice inside. The door was cracked ever so slightly and Savannah paused to listen instead of pushing it open.

"We could have been business partners, you know," Savannah heard Dr. Hockman saying. "But you were too young and naïve, weren't you?" continued Dr. Hockman as he walked toward Hunter with a syringe in his hand. "Too bad you won't get a chance to get old and cynical like me," said Dr. Hockman as he sat down on the edge of the bed and squirted the air out of a syringe. "Regrettably, some partnerships are not meant to be, so consider our partnership dissolved," Dr. Hockman said maliciously as he advanced the needle toward Hunter.

At that moment, Savannah burst into the room. Savannah did not know if Dr. Hockman knew of her and Hunter's relationship, so she tried to bluff one by Dr. Hockman since she was still in her nurse's outfit.

"Dr. Hockman, there has been a bad explosion at one of the paper mills," Savannah lied with her best poker face. "Several workers have been badly burned and they are bringing them in now. Betty Williams sent me to round up all the doctors in the building; you're needed immediately," Savannah continued to lie, making things up off the top of her head.

"That's strange. I haven't heard anything over the intercom," remarked Dr. Hockman.

"Oh, you haven't heard?" asked Savannah in mock surprise. "The intercom has been broken since this morning. They are working on it now," said Savannah reassuredly, smiling as sweetly as she could.

"All right," relented Dr. Hockman. "Just let me finish this injection."

"Oh, let me do that," said Savannah stepping forward, placing her hand on Dr. Hockman's wrist and her body brushing Dr. Hockman slightly. "It's the least I can do, since you were so helpful after Dr. Davis' car wreck," said Savannah, facing Dr. Hockman wearing her most seductive smile.

Dr. Hockman gazed into Savannah's brilliant green eyes trying to size her up. Dr. Hockman hesitated for a moment, then decided what could be better than Dr. Davis' girlfriend administering the fatal dose. Dr. Hockman allowed Savannah to raise his wrist as she took the syringe with her other hand. Dr. Hockman took one more inquisitive glance at Savannah as he was leaving the room. Savannah turned her back to Dr. Hockman as if she was administering the dosage and he left the room.

Savannah ran to the door to make sure Dr. Hockman was headed to the elevator. Peering through a crack in the door

Savannah saw Dr. Hockman enter the elevator, and she immediately ran back over to Hunter.

"Hunter!" Savannah whispered loudly into Hunter's ear, slapping him lightly on the cheek. "Hunter!" Savannah said again a little more loudly, pinching his cheek to see if there was a response. The drug that Dr. Hockman had given Hunter was beginning to wear off, but the only response from Hunter was a slight moan and mild jerk of the head. Savannah knew she had only a small window of time before Dr. Hockman discovered her ruse and would be back at the room. Savannah had to move fast, so she ran into the hallway to find a wheelchair. Fortunately, there was an empty wheelchair outside the adjacent room. Savannah retrieved the chair and rushed it to Hunter's bedside. All of those years of helping patients combined with Savannah's athletic build came in handy as Savannah swung Hunter off the bed and into the chair. Hunter moaned slightly at all the jostling but was still unaware of what was going on and slumped sideways in the chair. Savannah pushed Hunter toward the open door of the room, made the corner and started for the elevator at the far end of the hall. Just then the elevator doors opened and Dr. Hockman and Brill stepped out of the elevator and into the hallway.

Savannah saw the two men just as they spotted her. Savannah whirled the wheelchair around and headed in the opposite direction. The two men immediately began to give chase. Brill pulled his handgun out of his pocket and started to raise his arm toward Savannah. "Not in the hospital," Dr. Hockman said as he placed his hand on Brill's arm and shook his head.

Savannah and Hunter burst through some swinging double doors and turned down another hallway. Savannah was pushing Hunter as fast as she could but she knew she wasn't going to be able to outrun the two men. Savannah's mind raced trying to think of a method of escape.

About halfway down the hallway, Savannah spotted a laundry chute. Savannah pushed the wheelchair toward the laundry chute as fast as she could. Savannah pulled up at the chute, then stuck her head in to see if there was a basket below. Luckily, on the floor below, there was a large laundry basket about six foot by eight foot that was nearly filled with sheets and blankets from the hospital beds. Savannah reached under Hunter's armpits and grasped her hands behind Hunter's back and squatting with her legs, raised him up out of the wheelchair as she had been taught to do.

The opening of the chute was large enough for a person to fit through so Savannah stuck Hunter's upper body through the opening, then grabbed his legs and Hunter slid easily through the chute and fell headfirst toward the laundry basket below. Savannah thought briefly that the fall might break Hunter's neck since he was nonresponsive and he might land at the wrong angle, but Dr. Hockman and Brill burst through the double swinging doors at the end of the hallway so Savannah had no time for second guessing.

After Hunter fell to the basket below, Savannah immediately stuck her upper body through the chute opening, then pushed with her feet expecting to fall to the basket below. Instead, Savannah had not got enough of her weight forward in the chute and she got stuck halfway into the chute. Savannah violently wiggled and kicked her feet trying to get her weight forward and dislodge herself so she would fall to the basket below.

Brill ran toward Savannah's kicking legs and just about made it there when Savannah's legs started disappearing through the chute as she began to fall. Brill got there just in time to grab onto one of Savannah's feet as she slid through the chute. Brill tried to pull Savannah back up but her shoe came off in Brill's hand and Savannah fell to the basket below. Savannah tried to miss landing on Hunter and stretched her arms out to break her fall. Fortunately, her landing was surprisingly soft due to all of the sheets and blankets in the basket and due to the fact that she missed Hunter completely.

Brill was left standing in the hallway above holding onto Savannah's shoe. Dr. Hockman stuck his head through the chute just in time to see Savannah climb out of the basket and drag it out of the way.

"Come on," Dr. Hockman barked at Brill. "We've got to go the long way." The two men raced back toward the elevator.

Meanwhile, Savannah had located another wheelchair and brought it back to the edge of the basket. Savannah jumped back into the basket and yelled at Hunter to wake up. There was still no response so Savannah flung Hunter over the side of the basket. Hunter hit the floor and emitted a groan. Savannah jumped out of the basket and lifted Hunter into the wheelchair. Savannah continued to talk to Hunter, trying to arouse him out of his drug-induced haze. Hunter would moan and briefly open his eyes but he always slipped back into his slumber.

Savannah raced out of the laundry area, pushing Hunter down the hall. Savannah and Hunter came to the main hallway and Savannah took a right toward the emergency room and the exit to the employees' parking lot. Savannah reached into her pocket as she ran to retrieve her car keys, but they were not there. Savannah realized that when she wiggled head first down the laundry chute her keys must have fallen into the laundry basket. Savannah was wondering if she had time to retrieve them when she spotted Dr. Hockman and Brill step out of the elevator at the far end of the hall.

Savannah whirled Hunter around, ducked around a corner of the hallway and made a dash toward the emergency room exit where they brought in patients transported by ambulance. Savannah bust through the double doors into the emergency room area, just as some emergency medical technicians were bringing in a heart attack victim through the doors at the other end of the room leading to the parking lot. Savannah spotted the ambulance backed up to the entranceway, its back doors wide open and the engine still running. Savannah made a mad dash through the emergency room, passing the attendants as they feverishly worked on the heart attack victim.

Betty Williams stood dumbfounded behind the counter watching Savannah race by, pushing Hunter in the wheelchair.

"Savannah, wait!" Betty said as Savannah raced out the open doors toward the ambulance. Betty came out from behind the counter and followed Savannah and Hunter toward the ambulance.

"What in the world are you doing, Savannah?" Betty asked as Savannah had pulled the wheelchair up to the back of the ambulance and was struggling to get Hunter out of the wheelchair and into the ambulance.

"No time to explain," Savannah said breathlessly. "Help me get him into the back of the ambulance," Savannah commanded between gulps of air.

With Betty on one side and Savannah on the other, the two women lifted Hunter forward, placing his upper body in the back of the ambulance and then grabbing his legs and pushing him further into the ambulance. The two women slammed the back doors shut and Savannah exclaimed to Betty, "Stall them."

Savannah ran to the driver's side of the ambulance while Betty turned to see Dr. Hockman and Brill racing through the emergency room. Betty took a few steps toward Dr. Hockman and Brill with her arms outstretched in a halt signal, but the two men brushed past her twirling her around and knocking her to the floor.

Savannah hopped into the driver's seat, slamming the door and putting the lever in drive. Savannah jumped on the gas pedal and the ambulance lurched forward throwing Hunter against the back doors. Hunter was beginning to wake up, and as he banged his head against the back door he started to come to his senses. Dr. Hockman and Brill tried to grab at the back of the ambulance so they could jump on the back bumper but the ambulance sprung forward just in time to elude their grasp. The two men then ran toward Dr. Hockman's car in the parking lot to continue the chase. Hunter, meanwhile, continued to tumble in the back of the ambulance as Savannah weaved her way out of the parking lot in the cumbersome ambulance.

"Who taught you how to drive?" Hunter remarked from the back of the ambulance, still groggy from the drugs, but his sense of humor intact.

"Hunter!" Savannah exclaimed, glad to see that he was responsive. "Dr. Hockman and the big ugly orderly are chasing us. I'm heading for the police station," Savannah reported, as she turned down Lime Street heading for Fourteenth Street. Hunter was still coming back to reality and his leg was throbbing, but he remembered about the city police chief's possible involvement.

"Head to the county's sheriff's headquarters," Hunter commanded.

"But that's a lot further," Savannah protested.

"Just do it," Hunter yelled as he looked through the back window, spotting Dr. Hockman's car pull onto Lime Street.

Hunter was trying to get to his feet but the cast on his lower left leg and the lack of a hand hold were preventing Hunter from doing so. Hunter had almost risen to his feet when Savannah slowed down dramatically, sending Hunter sprawling to the floor again.

"The light's red!" Savannah exclaimed as they approached the intersection of Lime Street with Fourteenth Street.

"Hit the siren," Hunter suggested as he pulled himself to one knee only to see Dr. Hockman's car gaining through the back window. Savannah found the siren lever and flicked it to the on position. The lights started flashing on the ambulance and the siren began its loud wail. Savannah hesitated to make sure the cars headed through the crossroad had stopped before wheeling the heavy ambulance into the intersection and turning left on Fourteenth Street.

Dr. Hockman's Mercedes had raced down Lime Street and had caught the ambulance at the intersection. Dr. Hockman pulled through the intersection right on the back bumper of the ambulance and the two vehicles continued their race down the undivided four-lane road. Hunter peered out of the back window.

"Don't let him pass you," said Hunter, realizing the only way Dr. Hockman's car was going to stop the heavier ambulance was to get in front and slow down.

Savannah pressed the accelerator to the floor as they sped down the straight four-lane road. There were other cars on the road but thanks to the siren they were pulling over to the side.

The Mercedes was faster than the ambulance, but thanks to Hunter's commands while looking out of the back window, Savannah was able to keep the ambulance in front of the swerving car.

The two vehicles approached a side street that led from a shopping center that had a red light. There was a car stopped at the red light in the left-hand lane going in the opposite direction from which the ambulance approached.

Dr. Hockman saw an opening and ducked to the left of the car at the red light, going through the open right-hand lane of the northbound lane heading in the opposite direction. As the two vehicles made it through the intersection, Dr. Hockman's car and the ambulance ended up side by side. Dr. Hockman swerved his car over to ram into the side of the ambulance. Savannah screamed at the collision and the ambulance was knocked from the left lane to the right lane but Savannah maintained control. "Go right," Hunter suggested pointing at a road that headed diagonally off Fourteenth Street and could be used as a short cut to Eighth Street, which led off the island and to the sheriff's headquarters. Savannah swerved the ambulance onto the side road, leaving Dr. Hockman's car heading straight down Fourteenth Street. Hunter and Savannah celebrated at their good fortune, but Hunter knew all Dr. Hockman had to do was to turn right at the next red light on Sadler Road and he could cut them off.

"Keep going as fast as you can," said Hunter as the ambulance neared the stop sign at Eighth Street, its siren still wailing. Savannah kept pushing on the horn to further warn cars on the busy Eighth Street of their approach. The last thing

Savannah needed was to be broadsided by a logging truck delivering pulpwood to the paper mills.

The ambulance cleared the intersection without incident and headed toward the red light at the intersection of Sadler Road and Eighth Street. As the ambulance approached the intersection, Hunter and Savannah could see Dr. Hockman's car zooming down Sadler Road trying to intercept them.

"Faster," Hunter demanded.

"It's on the floor," Savannah retorted, her foot pressing the accelerator firmly to the floor. With all the strength in his arms Hunter pulled himself into the passenger's side seat and buckled his seat belt for the impending collision. Both vehicles reached the intersection at the same time and appeared to be ready to collide broadside, when Dr. Hockman yanked his steering wheel to the left. The right side of Dr. Hockman's car hit flat with the left side of the ambulance and knocked both vehicles out of control temporarily. The ambulance went off the right side of the road as Dr. Hockman's car veered into the divider on the left. Both drivers jerked their vehicles back onto the four-lane road which was now called Highway A1A and which led to the bridge off the island. Both vehicles continued to bang into each other as they each continued to try to force the other off the road.

Savannah was having a hard time manhandling the heavy ambulance, but she mustered one last great effort and used the weight of the ambulance to force Dr. Hockman's car through a gap in the low divider and into the opposite lanes.

"Let me drive!" Hunter offered and grabbed the steering wheel as Savannah thankfully unfastened her seatbelt and slid out of her seat as Hunter slid over her and into the driving position. Dr. Hockman's car raced parallel to the ambulance down the oncoming lanes. Fortunately for him the ambulance's siren was making the oncoming cars pull over to the side of the road. At the next gap in the divider, Dr. Hockman jerked his car back into the lane beside the ambulance. The trees on each side of the road gave way to marsh grass as the road headed toward the high bridge over the intracoastal waterway.

As Dr. Hockman pulled his car up alongside the ambulance, Brill pulled out a handgun and took a shot. The bullet shattered the driver's side window, narrowly missing Hunter and exiting through the front windshield, leaving a bullet hole in the windshield.

"Damn, that was close," Hunter exclaimed over Savannah's shrieks. Hunter swerved over into the Mercedes, hitting the car so violently that it knocked the gun from Brill's hand and onto the pavement. Dr. Hockman fought to keep the Mercedes from flying off their side of the road and into the opposing lanes. Dr. Hockman regained control and pulled alongside the ambulance as both vehicles raced up the beginning of the sixty-five-foot-high span that stretches over the intracoastal waterway. The tall concrete bridge is divided into two separate spans with two lanes headed in each direction. A three-foot-high concrete wall lined both sides of the two lanes heading in each direction. The two vehicles rammed together several times as each tried to force the other into the opposing wall.

"Faster," implored Savannah.

"We can't outrun him in this," Hunter answered referring to the bulky ambulance as it made its way up the steep incline of the bridge.

"What are you going to do?" yelled Savannah.

"Hold on," said Hunter as Dr. Hockman jerked his car to the right to initiate another assault. The two vehicles had almost reached the peak of the bridge as Hunter slammed on the brakes of the ambulance just before Dr. Hockman's car was to ram into the ambulance's side. The left front bumper of the ambulance rammed into the right rear quarter panel of the Mercedes. Dr. Hockman and Brill had a startled look on their faces as the Mercedes spun in front of the ambulance. The ambulance hit the Mercedes again, broadside, causing it to go slightly airborne in the direction of the right retaining wall. The car hit the top of the concrete wall, which broke away, and the Mercedes disappeared over the side of the bridge.

The Mercedes fell toward the Amelia River below. Dr. Hockman and Brill might have survived the sixty-five-foot fall into the river except for the fact that a fuel barge happened to be passing under the bridge on its way up the intracoastal waterway. The explosion of the car hitting the exposed fuel barrels on the long, open barge was so great it sent fingers of flame high into the sky that reached above the side of the bridge.

Hunter and Savannah were surprised and confused about what had transpired, having seen the car disappear over the side of the bridge apparently to fall in the water only to be followed by the explosion and smoke all the way above the side of the bridge. Off in the distance, the young couple could see the flashes of lights from the sheriff's deputies' cars and state patrol cars headed their way since Betty had called 911 from the emergency room. Savannah and Hunter yelled in unison in relief as Hunter let the ambulance roll to a stop at the bottom right side of the bridge. Hunter and Savannah jumped out of the ambulance and exchanged a hug as they turned to watch the billowing smoke rising from the river. The young couple limped over to the railing with their arms around each other's waists where they realized what had happened when they spotted the burning barge. Just then the patrol cars pulled up and Hunter and Savannah wheeled to face them, realizing they had a lot of explaining to do.

Epilogue

After a thorough investigation by the state police, the city police chief, Jack Wheeler, and Bill Simpkins were arrested as accomplices to murder. The police chief wasn't directly involved with the act of murder but he was part of the conspiracy because Dr. Hockman had enlisted the chief as insurance in case there was an investigation. Dr. Hockman forced the police chief's cooperation by enlisting Lolita Gomez, the same woman Dr. Hockman was going to blackmail Hunter with, to have a brief, illicit affair with the married police chief. Dr. Hockman had taken pictures to prove the affair and was willing to use them to ruin the chief's marriage and career to force his participation. The investigation showed that Jack Wheeler, Bill Simpkins, and Dr. Hockman were splitting hundreds of thousands of dollars per year as their cut of the bonus for keeping costs down. Dr. Raja and several other doctors were also arrested as being accomplices in the scheme. The doctors didn't actually participate in committing the deed, which was left to Brill, but they did help identify the appropriate patients and, of course, helped cover up what was happening. Dr. Raja, it turned out, was lacking the necessary credentials from his native India to practice in the United States. Dr. Hockman was aware of this, but had helped Dr. Raja forge the necessary credentials and allowed Dr. Raja to practice as long as he went along with Dr. Hockman's plan. The other doctors were just greedy and needed the money that came from the bonus pool.

Dora Stimpson proved to be an unwilling participant in the scheme. Dr. Hockman had blackmailed Dora's participation by threatening to expose his brief affair with Dora to her husband. Dora was an old-fashioned woman living in a small town and didn't know if she could live with the humiliation of her husband leaving her. Dora also loved her husband very much despite his inattentiveness of late, and could not stand the thought of losing him entirely.

Once the scheme was exposed, however, Dora cooperated with the police entirely and also confided in her husband completely. Dora had kept meticulous notes on every patient in case she ever had to use the information against Dr. Hockman or any of his cronies and she knew who was involved and who was not. Due to her cooperation and testimony against the other remaining participants, Dora received a probationary sentence. Dora's husband also forgave her, even admonishing himself for being so inattentive as to drive her into Dr. Hockman's conniving ways. Dora's husband promised her that as soon as her probation was up, he would take early retirement from the mill so they could travel around the country together, which had always been their dream.

It was easy for Hunter to get out of his employment contract with Medi-Most due to the circumstances. Hunter decided to open a Norman Rockwell-type practice in Dr. Dickens' old office above the Island Art Association's gallery in the historic district in downtown Fernandina.

Everything about the practice location was wrong for a modern-day medical office. The office was located on the second floor, and there was limited parking outside the building. But Hunter had fond memories of being a patient there when he was a boy, and it was where he decided he wanted to become a doctor. Hunter decided he would just have a small practice limited to cash-paying and traditional insurance patients, and no HMO patients.

Savannah transferred over to Nassau General, the other hospital in the county, to run their emergency room and to support Hunter while he started his practice. Savannah hoped to eventually work with Hunter as soon as his practice became busy enough to accommodate her.

Hunter and Savannah were married on a glorious north Florida fall day in late October. Hunter chartered the Voyager, a wooden replica sailing ship, for the wedding. The young couple and their close friends and relatives set sail from the city marina and anchored the boat just off of the south tip of Cumberland

Island. A high-pressure area had blown in the previous day, leaving a perfectly clear, blue sky and pleasant temperatures instead of the hot, humid air of the Indian summer. A cool breeze whistled through the rigging as the couple was married around five-thirty in the afternoon, while the brilliant orange sun neared the horizon.

At the close of the wedding ceremony, Hunter and Savannah embraced in the traditional wedding kiss. As Hunter and Savannah's bodies molded together as one, the small replica cannon on board fired, and their friends and relatives cheered. As the young couple opened their eyes from the long embrace, then seeing their friends and relatives cheering them on with the tranquil background of the wild horses on the shore of Cumberland Island nibbling on the marsh grass, Hunter and Savannah realized they were in total bliss. Hunter gazed into Savannah's beautiful, yet tear-filled, green eyes and realized this union was forever.

Tony Stubits

Printed in the United States
1480700002B/76-93